Kingdom
of the
Gogs

By

R.K. DONNE

ISBN 978-1-0980-5132-7 (paperback)
ISBN 978-1-0980-5133-4 (digital)

Christian Faith Publishing, Inc.
832 Park Avenue
Meadville, PA 16335
www.christianfaithpublishing.com

Edited by John Matthew Fox of Box Fox

Illustrated by Keegan Blazey

Printed in the United States of America

CONTENTS

IF YOU HAVE SOMEBODY THAT HAS AUTIS
PLEASE HAVE PATIENCE, LOVE AND HOPE,
WE ARE ALL EVOLUTIONS OF OUR OWN,
THE EVOLOUTION THEORY IS MORE FREQUEN
THAN YOU KNOW, LOVE US AN ENCOURAGE US,
KNOW WE LOVE YOU
REGARDLESS IF WE CANT
ALWAYS SHOW YOO,
 YOU ARE DOING AN
AMASING JOB.

─BRODIE GITTINS

CHAPTER 1

Wales

"Brodie, Brodie—No!"

A sudden scream prevented him from taking another step.

There, in the distance in front of him, stood a figure in the darkness of the night. She held a bright light that revealed her black-and-white-checkered jacket. Her face was oval and extremely pale, framed with dark, wavy hair that draped across her shoulders and back. Her eyes appeared for a moment warm, loving, and familiar—eyes that had tenderly loved him from birth; then suddenly they changed and became cold, dark, and tormented in a very sinister way.

She stood glaring. The corners of her lips rose and twisted into a menacing smile.

"What's wrong?" Brodie asked. He was a stranger to this frightening expression.

"Come." She beckoned him into the darkness of the night; her voice was chilling and hollow.

Brodie attempted to walk towards her but could not seem to move. His legs felt weak and heavy. He tried to run, but the darkness around him did not move. He was out of breath and felt as though he had run a marathon, but even so he found himself permanently cemented to the cold blackness.

His mother's smile grew a little more twisted. The dimples in her cheeks were absent; the whites of her eyes grew black with dark intent. She began to walk towards him.

At first, a thrill of joy ran through his body like an electric current, but something was wrong. He tried to step back, but he could not move; he was without a doubt planted to the ground. He looked down to his runners, then quickly looked up at the approaching figure.

Her checkered jacket was slowly turning into green sand that disintegrated and fell from around her dark silhouette, leaving a void behind. Her expression was not welcoming; it had turned from menacing to enraged.

His heart began to pound; she was now merely two feet away. Brodie fell backward trying to escape. He quickly lifted himself up, looking into her face.

Suddenly, a large wolf-like creature pounced towards him. The woman had disappeared entirely. The wolf's pinkish raw gums were exposed, its mouth open wide to reveal saliva dripping down large yellowish canines. Its rumbling growl grew deeper as the animal attacked...

❦

For twelve years, Brodie had revisited that horrific scene—with the darkness, the woman, and the wolf—practically every night in the same dream.

Today, he woke up thrashing_his arms around in the small enclosed area. He looked about, having no idea where he was. Sweat beaded upon his forehead and the back of his neck.

His mother wrapped a comforting arm around him. Pulling him closer to her, she whispered, "It's okay, Brodie. It's all right," as she rubbed her hand against his arm.

Observing his surroundings, he recalled he was on the plane to Wales. He sat back in his seat, still a little dazed and confused, looking out the narrow oval window to his right to watch the green blanket far below pass by.

"Nightmare, Baba?" his mother asked as she watched him from the corner of her eye. She resumed reading her magazine—mindless rubbish, an invasion of the lives of celebrities and their families.

"Oh, I like those shoes, bit too retro for me, though," she said.

He glared at her. "Stop calling me 'Baba.' You make me sound like a sheep. I'm not an infant."

She smiled. "What do you want me to call you, then?" she said in a playfully demonic voice while dropping her magazine to tickle him.

He laughed.

The man in a flashy business suit on the opposite side of the aisle briefly raised his head to stare across at them, mildly interested, before focusing again on the laptop in front of him. He shook his head disapprovingly at the girl's idiocy.

"How much longer?" Brodie asked.

"Ahh, four days and seventy-eight minutes," his mum replied.

He rolled his eyes and continued to watch the land pass beneath them.

His mother, Katrin, was thirty-four. She was tall, slim, and very pretty. She had long, wavy, dark brown hair and a heart-shaped face with big brown eyes.

Besides the colour of his hair and eyes, Brodie resembled his mother, but he had inherited his blonde hair and his sapphire-blue eyes from his father.

She had been born in Wales and moved to Canada when she was eleven or so. Her parents had moved back to Wales when Brodie was about three months old. She had stayed in Canada—"chained by child," she would say if anybody asked.

They were on their way to Wales to visit his gumpy and Nei (traditional but awkward names for grandparents).

Finally, they landed. After collecting their suitcases from the luggage carousel, they headed towards the arrival gate. Brodie looked through the crowd for his grandparents. It was his first time meeting them in person. He had seen pictures and watched home videos of them. He was nervous.

"Oh my God." He stopped, and his mouth dropped at an unexpected sight.

Katrin turned. "What's wrong, slowpoke?" she asked.

He pointed. "Please say that's not them."

She looked at the spot where he was indicating. "Yup," she said, smiling as she redirected their roller suitcases towards them.

One was a tall, skinny man wearing a ball hat and holding a sign that read, "BRODIE AND DOPEY." Brodie began to laugh at the sight. Next to him stood a slim, shorter woman with long dark hair. She looked a lot like his mother in the face.

They approached the two.

"Hey, mun, give your gumps a hug," the old man said in a Welsh accent, arms stretched wide for Brodie.

Brodie didn't have a chance—the old man grabbed him before he could blink while Katrin was squeezed by her mother.

The drive home from Cardiff Airport was less than an hour. It was nothing like Canada; the Welsh drove on the wrong side of the road, and Wales was pretty much made up of farms and hills with the odd city in pockets of green.

Rhys removed the hat from his head, exposing short salt-and-pepper hair that stuck up in all directions. Brodie's grandpa had dark brown eyes like Brodie's mother. And after meeting the bean pole, Brodie understood where he got his height from. It was the first time he had seen his grandparents since he was maybe three months old. He was able to see where his mother got her playful personality from. During the whole ride back, his grandparents and mother reminisced over good old days filled with funny stories.

Brodie looked out the window, watching the early evening fields pass by as his gumpy explained the things he had planned for the two of them. "Guy time," the old man was calling it.

"Brodie," a voice snapped.

"What?" Brodie turned.

"I'm sitting right next to you, and I've called your name at least four times to get your attention. Thank you for finally leaving your bubble."

"You're welcome," he said in a sarcastic tone, looking out the window and refraining from turning his head to look at her.

"Well, do you blame him, Gormy? We've only been with you for an hour, and you're already boring us to death. He's been with you for twelve years. I would ignore you, too!" The old man chuckled.

"Give over and drive, old man," Katrin told her father in a playfully stern voice.

"What does 'gormy' mean?" Brodie asked, unsure if it was Welsh slang.

"Gormless means thick or stupid," Rhys replied.

Brodie smiled at his mother. Definitely gormless.

"Go back into your bubble," she said, ruffling his hair.

Finally, they arrived at the house, which was large and painted white. It stood two stories with three windows and a door on the front. They pulled into the driveway. Rhys jumped out to unlock the wooden gate on the side of the house. At the end of the driveway stood a brick garage. Centred above the door was a white plaque of a lion's head. To the side of the garage, a patio walkway led to the gardens. The walkway passed a medium-sized tree whose branches grew over a small pond. Miniature statues of Snow White and her seven dwarves surrounded the pond.

Brodie got out of the car, absorbing the garden his mother had played in. His mother gave him a quick tour of the garden before they entered the house. The garden itself was huge, including a wooden shed, a glass greenhouse, and a swing surrounded by large, multi-coloured foxgloves.

Although the inside of the house was very big, the kitchen they walked into was surprisingly cozy.

"It still looks the exact same, Mum," Katrin said nostalgically.

The kitchen led into the living room. It was large and sported a flashy green couch and matching chairs that flanked a peacock-tiled fireplace. The lounge had an entrance that led to the dining room, stairs to the second level, and the front door.

Brodie looked at the clock—11:33 p.m. He turned back to Katrin. "So, it's like six thirty-three in Canada, right?" he asked. He couldn't get over the time difference. Britain was five hours ahead of Canada.

"Yes, hun," she said, holding up a Welsh rugby shirt.

They hung out in the living room for a while, exchanging gifts and eating homecooked fish and chips sprinkled with sea salt and lashings of vinegar.

"Tired, cariad?" his Nei asked.

Brodie nodded. His mother escorted him to their room. The second floor was quite spacious: it had an office, his grandparents' bedroom, and a spare bedroom at the very end of the hall. This had been his mother's room for a few years when she was very young. The bathroom was opposite his grandparents' room. He washed up, cleaned his teeth, and headed for bed. He couldn't recall longing to go to bed more in his life.

Brodie and his mother's room were in the attic. A set of old ship stairs led to an open loft. It was awesome. His gumpy had built it all by himself back in '93. As he got around the railings, he saw two beds on opposite sides of the loft. The décor was plain cream and brown.

"That one was my bed," his mother said as a fond tear formed in the corner of her eye.

Katrin's uncle had taken over the property when her family had moved to Canada. A simple man, he kept the décor and most of the furniture they left behind the same. Unfortunately, he passed away a year after Brodie's grandparents moved back to Wales.

The contents of their suitcases were sprawled open across the floor. She tucked Brodie into her old bed with a big kiss and a cuddle. Before making her way back down, she promised to be up in a bit.

He lay in bed for some time. Although he was exhausted, he found he could not sleep. He went downstairs to see if his mother would be up soon. The second-floor front window caught his eye. Across the road in the distance of the dark field, a small flickering light caused him to stop in his tracks. As he watched the flickering light, he could overhear his family downstairs conversing.

"I didn't want to say anything in front of him, love, but how is he?" he heard his nei ask.

"You know what," he heard his mother reply, "he is doing so much better. But," she paused for a moment, forming her answer carefully, "he is the most intelligent child of his grade, even a year above. He's making a little more eye contact these past months, and the temper tantrums have cooled down a bit. But he still blacks out. He feels like an outcast and different from the other children. He has difficulties writing, and the school treats him like a baby. He has strengths in many subjects but has tantrums over his weak subjects, and he still wakes through the night."

The window had a built-in shelf seat. Brodie sat down, watching the light as he listened to his mother's report of his disability.

"The doctor says it's night terrors, but I don't know. He just shuts me out."

"But he's been doing that since he was little, hasn't he?" Rhys asked.

"Yes, and he's gone through numerous sleep EKGs and overnight studies at the hospitals, and he still wakes up. I feel helpless sometimes, as if I could do more for him if he would only let me into his bubble."

"You have done wonders for that child, and with the patience and love you have for him, you couldn't do anymore."

"Ta, Dad. He's amazing, though. He has been the best thing in my life, and I would never have changed a thing about him," Katrin said. "He has taught me so much. I've been utterly blessed. He's come a long way, and I'm so proud of him. He still drifts off into his little bubble where he blacks out now and then, but his social skills are getting so much better."

"With time, love. With time."

Brodie had heard enough, so he went back to bed. He would feel awkward going downstairs now.

Brodie had been referred to a specialist when he was thirteen months old. After a long period of waitlists to see the specialist, he was diagnosed with autism. He may have been a bit delayed in speech as a toddler and a bit ill-tempered at times, but then again, so was his mother. She once threw a pork chop at his dad when he complained about dinner. And, apparently, his mother's whole side of the family had atrocious tempers. He was smarter than the majority of kids his age. He knew he didn't fit in at times, but he just hated having a label.

He lay in bed thinking about it. He wasn't upset at their conversation, but he felt like people didn't really understand him. He saw things that others couldn't. He had heightened senses that others didn't. Well, that normal people didn't, he supposed. He didn't like making eye contact with people; it was scary sometimes. He could see the person's insecurities and weaknesses and horrible dominant traits; it was like he could see into their souls at times, so he avoided looking at people altogether. He could also feel people's energy, and he hated it.

His grades were not perfect. He was marked down in his strengths so the school could get extra funding. He was able to look at a mechanical or electrical gadget and take it apart, analyze it, and put it back together. He had photographic memory. His reading was university level, but he was sporting a needs improvement on his report cards.

Was he really that different that his abilities were classified as a disability? He turned over, and shortly after his anger dissipated, he fell asleep.

CHAPTER 2

A Walk with Gumpy

The old man took his small grandson's hand and led him up the path on the cliffs overlooking the sea.

"When your mother was a little girl, about the same age you are now, we used to walk up this very same path. I would run ahead and hide in the bushes, and then I would wait there and start to hiss as they approached. Your aunty was a lot older than your mom and would know better, but your mom would start looking around her, terrified of snakes. Then when she was close enough, I would jump out and scare her. It was funny," the old man chuckled to himself, reminiscing the past as he looked out in the direction of the sea.

He then looked down at the small boy and watched him as if he knew Brodie had eavesdropped the previous night. "I want you to know there is nothing wrong with you at all, boy. You are amazing. The only flaw with you is you are not living in Wales."

"The doctor told Mum and Dad that I am autistic but not as severe as I was when I was younger. I overheard them talking."

"You're very artistic, Brodes, just like Gumpy and your mum. When your mum was a teenager, she was very artistic, too. The rotten little toad-rag painted all over her bedroom walls."

Brodie laughed. "Autistic, not artistic."

"And your old Gumpy painted big black spiders over my door to keep Great-Granny out of my room. She didn't like that. She hates spiders." He sighed. "Nothing wrong with you, boy, to tell you the truth. I wish we never left Wales in the first place, but if we didn't, you wouldn't be here. As much as your dad can be a twerp at times, he did something right by you!"

"Gumpy, why didn't you come to visit us?" Brodie asked, not really sure he wanted the answer. "Did Mum make you mad or something?"

"Heavens no, boy. Don't be silly, and don't think such nonsense! Na, you're too young to understand, lad. One day."

"Try me, Gumps," Brodie retaliated.

"Your Nei and I—Well, we tried to make a go of it out there in Canada, but it was hard. Plus, the cold made my joints ache something terrible, and your Nei became homesick. It's an entirely different place compared to Wales. Canada is made up of different cultures and races. The land's secrets have been untold and forgotten, whereas Wales has preserved her past and secrets."

"What do you mean by secrets, Gumpy?"

"Wales is a land of beauty and mystery," the old man continued. "When I speak of secrets, I'm talking about folklore." Brodie's grandpa looked about and saw the day was racing away from them. "Come on, the tide will be coming in soon! Let's pick some cockles and head back in time for tea."

Brodie followed his grandfather down the path they had just come up, galloping along to try to keep up with the old man's long strides.

"It's all part of her secrets, yes. There are sharks and a few whales, but like I said, Wales has her secrets. There is what you would call magic in the land and the sea that surrounds her."

"Magic! Could you tell me what kind of magic, Gumpy? Please."

"Well, I suppose since you are half Welsh, it's your birthright!" He smiled. "There are creatures that live in the moor, the mountains, and on the land. Creatures that are not seen by the human eye very often anymore."

"Anymore… So people have seen these creatures?"

"Many people have, just a glimpse. Only some say naught, and some believe they imagined it. But then some are well tuned in to that world."

"What world, Gumpy?"

"A world that has been hidden and preserved from our kind for a long time. Only we Welsh descendants have lived on this land for thousands of years. We are strong in our beliefs and carry down the folklore. We don't always see creatures, but that doesn't mean we don't believe in them."

The old man paused, then exclaimed, "Come on, we should be getting back. Your mum will tan my hide if I have you back too late."

"Gumpy, can you tell me about the old stories, please?" pleaded Brodie.

"Will do—after tea. Now then, boi, tell Gumps how you are doing in school, then."

After half an hour of explaining his subjects in school, they arrived home. Brodie's grandfather parked the car and walked around the house a bit ahead of the small boy to reach over and open the large wooden gate to let Brodie through.

Brodie couldn't help but notice the white plaque of the lion's head. His mother had pointed it out the first time she had stepped through the gate, taking in all the detail she had missed and forgotten in the past twenty years.

When they walked through the door, his mother was sitting at the kitchen table, reading a magazine and munching on a chocolate bar. Beth, his Nei, was at the sink peeling new potatoes for the evening meal, but she quickly left the room to retrieve the furry little dog that seemed to run and hide every time she opened the oven door.

Katrin turned to the boy with a wide devilish smile on her face as she watched her son's eyes chase after his Nei. "When we brought you up to Peterborough in Canada to visit Nei and Gumpy, you were only a month old. Rohli, the dog, would not leave you alone. He would be all over you licking your face and hands. It was disgusting. So every time he would come near you, I would open the stove door, and he would soon shoot off like a bullet!"

"Katrin, that's bloody horrible. Poor thing's scared of the stove from your mum's cooking and all the bloody alarms going off," the old man said, shaking his head as he dumped his pale of cockles into the sink.

"I know. It did the trick, though! We should train kids like that, too." She winked at Brodie, who leaned over to take a bite of her half-eaten chocolate bar.

Soon, the room was filled with the smell of bacon; Brodie watched the old man frying the shellfish in the bacon fat. They looked like little clams sizzling in the heat.

Shortly after, the family sat around the wooden table, each with a plate full of cockles, bacon, and chips in front of them.

"You have been staring at your plate for five minutes now. Try it!" Katrin said.

"It's good for you. It will put hairs on your chest like Gumps," said the old man, smiling at his grandson as he pulled the collar of his shirt down to expose his hairy chest.

"I'm okay, Gumpy. I don't want to eat it," Brodie said, completely disgusted.

"Brodie, just try it. You will like it!" his mother said in between savoring sips of wine.

"Um, no, it looks gross. It looks like snot, Mum. You eat it." Brodie had always been a picky eater; the doctors said it came with the autism.

"I will give you ten pounds if you eat a couple," offered his mum.

"'S all right! Shoulda made something else for him to eat," said the old man disappointedly.

"It's good, Dad. we just don't eat a lot of shellfish at home," Katrin said as she looked at her father.

"Dad says shellfish are bottom-eaters, and they eat fish crap. Can I just have a ham sandwich please?"

"Brodie!" snapped his mother. Rhys burst into laughter at his grandson's cheeky comment.

CHAPTER 3

Welsh Folklore

After dinner, everyone helped clean up and resumed their seats at the kitchen table to hear what Rhys had to tell the small boy. Beth had finished her bath and soon came to join the family for the stories as she served treacle pudding.

"So, boy, you have heard of Merlyn, right?"

"Yes," answered Brodie, less than impressed so far.

"Well, Merlyn was born and lived here in Carmarthen. When he was about your age, the ruler of the land at that time left on missionary work. Merlyn foresaw two beasts fighting in the sky, two coloured flags, and the arrival of invaders.

"In no time, an evil man named Vortigen came to their small village, which was called Dinas Emrys. The king enslaved the villagers and had them build a grand castle. He ordered the people to build his castle on the highest mountain in the area so that he could see his enemies from afar. But the castle kept falling down. After the fourth attempt, he called for his advisors, who were apparently magicians, to explain the repeated incident.

"His advisors told him about a small child in the village who had the gift of sight, who would be able to explain the problem to the king, as they could not see the reason. The king sent for the child. Merlyn told the king that the reason his castle would not stand was because two eggs were nestled beneath the ground. These two eggs were near time to hatch. Every time the creatures inside the shells moved, it caused the earth to shake and tremble.

"Merlyn told the king his castle would not stand while the creatures lay beneath, and soon they would hatch and break through the ground to fight in the sky. The red dragon would defeat and kill the white dragon, then leave the country.

"The king was offended by the child's ranting. On his own banner was a symbol of a white dragon. He interpreted from Merlyn that he would be defeated. The king sent the child away and ordered the villagers back to work. After days of constant rebuilding of the castle, the ground suddenly ripped apart, sending shudders throughout the earth. The villagers began to flee down the hill from the tumbling stones of the castle. Suddenly, two beasts climbed into the air, tearing and biting at each other's throats, creating sounds of thunder every time they crashed into one another.

"The white and red scaly dragons soared through the sky circling each other and then attacked in full force. With a fierce blow to the neck, the red dragon defeated the white dragon. As the white dragon's limp, dead body plummeted to the earth, the red dragon flew off into the distance, never to be seen again.

"It was at that moment that the true ruler returned to the land, marching over the hills with his retinue, purpose and revenge in his strides. Amidst soldiers battling and fires smouldering, Vortigen and the king battled. The true ruler, the king, conquered the threat, freeing the villagers and sending old Vortigen packing."

"What happened to Merlyn, Gumpy?"

"Well, he grew up and apparently was an advisor to King Arthur and his Knights of the Round Table. I think he tried out for the NHL, too, at one point."

"Dad, don't tell him that," Katrin giggled.

With his autism, Brodie took his facts literally, which would sometimes result in vehement arguments down the road.

"So there were dragons in Wales! Nice story," said Brodie sarcastically.

"Too right, Brodie. Once upon a time, the skies were infested with dragons, but they went into hiding with the rest of the creatures of this land. The thing about dragons is that dragons are the most powerful creatures in this world," Rhys said.

"Do they breathe fire and eat damsels in distress, Gumpy?"

"I'm sure some of them breathe fire, and I don't know about them eating damsels in distress. If that bit was true, I would have taken your nei up the mountainside years ago."

"Dad!" snapped Katrin.

"Sorry, love, you're right. She's not much of a damsel."

Katrin shook her head.

"But I do know this—dragons have a method of preserving the present. They are full of magic. The old stories say the dragons are covered in scales, but of all of those scales, only the one not as bright and colourful as all the others contains true power. Now, child, I have no idea if that's true, but I wouldn't want to find out first-hand dragons are vicious, wild creatures that should never be crossed in any lifetime."

"What are the other creatures that live off the land and sea, Gumpy?" Brodie hung on every word from his granddad's mouth in anticipation.

"Well, there are creatures in the sea that, to the human eye, are camouflaged, but—"

"Like what?" Brodie gasped.

"Well, selkies are, for one."

"Selkies?"

"Yes, they are seals that shed their skins and turn into women, and they are mostly down the west and southwest shores of Wales and Ireland. Then, there are mermaids. Now, they are often spotted even today by the fishermen and people who walk along the coasts. The females are the most beautiful creatures in the world, but they are deadly. The males are a frightful sight, bloody hideous lot, real tummy-turners. They look a bit like your mum, Brodie."

Brodie burst into laughter "Ta, Dad, must get it from you."

Rhys puffed out his chest a bit, smiled at Brodie, then turned his head back towards his daughter and said, "Na, not me, handsome man I am. Must get it from your mother."

"Thank you, love. So you're not having a second helping of pudding." Beth frowned at her husband.

"All right, then, your grandmother on your mother's side." The old man chuckled. "There are loads of the old lot, like fairies, goblins, changelings, sprites, nymphs, elves, selkies. But there are also the dangerous kind—not saying that any of them are safe and trustworthy, mind you, but some are far more harmless than others."

"What are the bad ones, Gumpy, and what do they do? Are any around here?"

"Well, let's see. There are bogies." Rhys put his hand up to hide his other hand as he pointed to his wife. She quickly smacked his shoulder, and he started to chuckle again.

"Oh, Brodie, he's showing off now," Beth said as she rolled her eyes and turned her head away from the playful old man.

"Not true, woman. Hush now, I'm trying to talk to the boi. Where were we now? Right, bogies." The old man could not help himself and indicated once more to his wife, this time with his head. "Then there are dragons and mermaids, other goblins and fairies, sprites, some brownies, and the Phooka."

"What are they?" asked the weary little boy. The only thing keeping Brodie up was his piqued curiosity. "Are they around here?"

"No, boi, nothing will harm you here—nothing at all. Phooka are tall men with goats' heads. They live deep in the woods and avoid our kind. There are stories that have been told whose endings are not pleasant for our lot."

"Dad, no more. He will have nightmares," Katrin warned.

"No, I won't," Brodie protested firmly.

"Well, it's time for you to be getting off to bed after you have a cleanup," said Katrin.

"Gumpy," asked the curious boy, "how do you know they won't come here?"

"Well, that I can answer. There are humans, there are magical creatures, and then there are mediums, like Merlyn—humans born with special powers and gifts to foresee things the other humans can't," the old man explained.

"But Merlyn was a wizard," Brodie said with confusion.

"Yes, Merlyn was called a wizard, and women with the same abilities were called witches. They are all seers. It's just another name for them. These people were penalized back in the day."

"What does that mean?"

"It means, sweetheart, the people who were born with these talents were punished for being different," Beth answered.

"I know how that feels," Brodie quietly said to himself.

"Your Nei is a seer," the old man said.

The small boy quickly looked over to the lady across from him. He studied her face, trying to find a hint of something mystical about it. Her black hair hung long around her heart-shaped face; his mother looked a lot like the now-smiling lady. They both had the same lips and, maybe, the same eyes.

Wait a minute!

There was something...her eyes. Her eyes looked different. Brodie had never noticed that his nei's eyes were almost catlike. Actually, they were nearly identical to cat eyes, but the strange thing was that he had not noticed until now that they sparkled. They almost looked like they were lit up from the inside of the pupil as if reflecting light.

"Like real cat eyes," the small boy said loudly.

Brodie shot a look to his gumpy. He sat quietly filling his pipe. Brodie turned towards his mother to analyze her appearance. As if Katrin could read his mind, she shook her head.

"The only thing abnormal about your mum, boi, is her big gob," Rhys said.

Katrin smiled and rolled her eyes.

The amazed child turned back to Beth. "How come I've never noticed that before?"

Beth smiled warmly at her grandson and said, "Sometimes, seers are born with animal-like characteristics. Very few people have ever been able to notice my eyes that quickly! It took your gumpy fifteen years! When he finally realized, he said to me, 'You know, love, there is something a bit off about you. I've never been able to put my finger on it, but it doesn't make you ugly or anything, just a bit different, that's all.'"

"What happened then, Nei?"

"Well, I told your gumpy. He already had an inclination but loved me just the same."

"Are there any other seers in our family?" asked the small boy.

"The majority of the women of my mother's side of the family are witches. My mother had the eyes of a cat and temper of a shrew, as her mother before her, and so on."

Brodie turned to his mother. "But you don't have cat eyes?"

"No, honey, I don't."

"Naturally, your mother has inherited strong characteristics from us, your great-grandmother and I, but in a different way. Your mother has more compassion for people, animals, and above all nature than any other human I have ever known, an empath."

Brodie sat for a moment, trying to devour this wonderful bedtime story—because to him, that's all it was. Just a bedtime story.

Nevertheless, he continued. "So how do you know the creatures will not come here?"

Beth smiled once more. "I can't say we never get a visit from the other realm here or there. Often a pixie or a sprite will visit us and play a trick or two, harmless tricks, not ones that will hurt us."

"Like what, Nei?"

"Well, let's see. Their favorite tricks are to sour the milk and cream. They hide and move objects around the house. Just harmless little games that get very irritating at times. If you take a walk in my garden, I grow loads of different flowers to appease our little friends, but I also grow different herbs, too."

"So you cook for the fairies, Nei?"

"No, darling, though you're right in one way. Herbs are used for cooking, but in the old days, herbs were used to make medicines and to ward off unwanted spirits. I collect thyme, sage, and lemon balm. Once they are dried, I grind the leaves together, then sprinkle the remaining along the windowsills. The magic of the herbs keeps the mischief at bay. Every fortnight, I leave a bowl of fresh cream and a hefty piece of cheese from the local cows for our little friends as an offering."

Brodie looked around the room.

"When your mother was a little girl, she, your aunty, and I would hide behind the foxgloves at the top of the garden and watch quietly as the little ones would skip and dance about in the moonlight."

Brodie turned to his mum. "How come you never told me about any of this?" Hearing stories about his family's past made him feel more connected to them, less isolated, less…different.

"Brodes, it's not something you go around telling people, hun, especially back home. If I was to tell people in Canada, 'My mother's a witch, and I've seen fairies and little creatures,' they would have me committed in a heartbeat. If you say that to a Welsh person, the most you will get is a fellow encounter, or 'That's nice to hear.'"

Brodie looked at his grandfather, who raised his eyebrows and nodded silently. Brodie scowled, looked down to the floor, and said in a very disappointed tone, "You could have told me. I'm your son. I would have kept it a secret."

"Honey, you would have thought I was crazy!"

"No, I wouldn't. I would have believed you, Mum!" He tried to count the times he had thought he had seen something in the woods behind his house. He kept quiet. *This could all just be a joke*, he thought.

"Okay, Mr. I-would-have-believed-you, what about the time when your aunty told me she was at the bottom of the garden dancing in the rain when she met a friendly ghost, hmm?"

Brodie started to laugh. He stopped abruptly when he realized everybody's eyes were on him. Then he cleared his throat. "Well, Dad said, uh…"

"Yes, your father still makes fun of her to this day. But what was your reaction? What did you and your father call her for the longest time?"

A bit ashamed, Brodie muffled out quietly, "Aunt Looney."

Rhys began to laugh again.

"Right! Got my point? You would have been embarrassed to be my son. You and your father would not have respected me, and small padded rooms are not my cup of tea. It's a different world here."

"Can you tell me where these things came from and where they live, or is this a great big joke?"

"Well, the only way the boi will truly understand or believe is if he sees for himself!" the old man rumbled. "There are places across Wales that are home to many creatures. Some places are a bit more magical than others."

"Can we go to these places, Gumpy?"

"Well, there is one place close to here. It's called Llyn Celyn. It was a beautiful village that was home to many. People reared live-stock and grew vegetables and cereals to feed themselves and their animals. It was a happy and well-functioning little village. Until one day the villagers began to notice that the little brook which weaved its way through the village was slowly widening, and the water was beginning to flow faster and faster. Over time, the brook grew and grew until eventually the villagers had to abandon their much-loved little village, taking their animals and all they possessed and seeking homes elsewhere. A few stubborn old people chose to stay and face their fate, not wanting to leave the only home they had ever known.

"Then one day, a tremendous storm blew from the west. The storm did not relent. Three days later, the storm eased, but the town had disappeared—completely submerged under the cold, deep waters. It was said some time years and years later, an old man was walking his collie close to the banks of the lake when a strong mist crept down from the hills surrounding the area. To his astonishment, three beautiful, dark-haired maidens led three large white cattle into the lake.

"Time and time again, the old man would visit the same spot on the edge of the bank hoping to catch a glimpse of the beauty of the maidens, but never again did he see them. To this day, you can hear the bells toll from the submerged church. It is also said that grass and flowers still grow on the bed of the lake."

"That's not possible, Gumpy," Brodie said.

"Well, possible or not, it's bedtime!" the old man said contently.

Brodie yawned and said good night before making his way to bed. His attention was drawn to the distant light of the little church across the fields again. He couldn't understand why the isolated little church intrigued him. He imagined it was a safe place where the magical creatures could meet. He rubbed his eyes as he turned to proceed towards the attic.

CHAPTER 4

Raining Fireballs

The next morning, Brodie woke up with a million questions racing through his head, not sure if the stories from the previous night had been told to him just as bedtime stories or if they were actually true. He threw his shirt over his head and ran down the steep attic stairs, careful not to fall. Once again, his attention was caught by the little church off in the distance when he reached the window on the landing. It looked so old and deserted and kind of creepy, too. He couldn't understand his new fascination with the old church. *Oh, well,* he thought and made his way down the second set of stairs.

When he entered the kitchen, his mother was on the phone.

"Out of the question, and that is my final word on the matter," she said with a resolute look on her face. "I know you would take every care to make sure he stayed safe, but he is too young, and it's way too dangerous."

It was obvious whoever was on the phone had accepted defeat, as the conversation then turned to another subject before his mother said how much they were looking forward to seeing him and put the phone down.

"Who was that?" Brodie asked as he watched her pour a bowl of cereal then plunge a spoon into it.

"Your cousin Tom. He is coming to pick you up."

"Where are we going? Are you coming, too, Mum?"

"No, he wants quality time with you. He is taking you down to the beach. Then you are going to your great-gran's for tea. I will meet you there after. I am going into town with Nei."

⁂

An hour later, a tall boy in his early thirties was at the door. He had shaggy brown hair and was dressed for comfort. Brodie gave his mum a big hug and a kiss, then left with his shaggy-looking cousin.

"I still can't get over this," Brodie said.

"What?" Tom asked.

"How you guys drive on the other side of the road. Even your steering wheel is on the opposite side of the car," Brodie said as he climbed in.

"Well, I can't get over how big you are and that stupid accent of yours," Tom said, laughing. "But I guess you have an excuse. You were born there. Your mum was born here but still sounds like a Yank."

They were soon driving out of the small village.

"Are we really going to the beach?" Brodie asked.

"Hmm," Tom said, then he paused for a moment, wearing an inquisitive expression. "Good question!" he finally replied. "I was going to take you to the pub to throw darts and grab some lunch, but your mum was deadset against it, so were going with Plan B. We're gonna meet my mates down at the beach and do a little surfing before we go to Nan and Bamps."

Brodie became very excited. "I've never been surfboarding before!"

"Apparently, you might get eaten by sharks. Therefore, you're banned from it. But what your mam doesn't see nor hear won't kill her. I've got a smaller board for you, one my brother used around your age. I brought you his old wetsuit, too. Hope it fits you."

Brodie really adored his cousin Tom and viewed him as more of an uncle figure than an older cousin. He had traveled around the world backpacking and partying in the most exotic countries. Tom had visited Canada more times than Brodie could count. Above all,

Brodie loved being spoiled by his hip cousin. One year, Tom had visited and brought a real stuffed viper. His mum had almost had a heart attack. She'd sent Brodie outside to dispose of the disgusting thing. Brodie's dad had thought it looked really cool and had given him an old empty fish tank to keep it in.

Brodie was mesmerized as he got out of the car and followed Tom down the sand-covered wooden steps that led to the beach. The open water stretched as far as he could see, and the wind carried a salty tanginess and a smell he could not identify.

"What is that smell?" he asked Tom.

"That, mate, is a mixture of sea salt and seaweed," replied Tom.

When they reached the beach, they were approached by Tom's friends, who were already dressed with boards in their arms, ready to tackle the cold waves.

Tom's friends looked unusual. There were three tall guys: one was blonde and fit, and the other two were tall but gangly looking. The smallest of the two was dark-haired and looked like he had broken nose; and he looked a bit dopey.

There were two girls as well. One had dark hair with tacky blonde streaks. She wore far too much makeup that highlighted the spots all over her face. She was a bit dumpy around the middle. The second girl was a short brunette and very pretty.

After the introductions, Brodie followed them down to the beach and sat on the damp sand watching his cousin and friends laughing, chasing each other, and carrying on in the water like small kids. He was a bit nervous of the sea and the weather that was rolling in. The waves crashing onto the rocks and sand made him really uneasy. He decided to pass on the chance to surf, and spectate instead. Brodie couldn't help but laugh at his cousin and friends as they gracefully lost their balance from their boards and fell, crushed and momentarily hidden by the white caps each time.

As he continued watching the lively six, he suddenly became aware of a change in the atmosphere around him. Brodie felt a strange electrical surge under his skin that caused the hair on his arms to stand on end. Everything had become still, silent, and eerie. The cries of the gulls had disappeared. In the pit of his stomach, Brodie felt something was very wrong. The grey clouds rapidly advancing towards the shore blocked out the sunlight; the spray from the ocean made the air feel cold and damp. He dug his hands deep into his pockets in an attempt to keep them warm and wished he had worn a thicker sweatshirt. Even with the uncomfortably tight-fitting wetsuit underneath his clothes, he was cold to the marrow.

For a moment, the ocean became still, and in silence, Brodie looked up and down the shore. His uneasy feeling increased. The sky was growing darker. In the distance out to sea, large whitecaps advanced.

And then it poured; the rain pellets bounced of the water like paintballs. Everyone ran from the water, grabbing their belongings and running for the shelter of the parked cars. With as dark as the sky had grown, flashes of light could easily be seen dancing through the clouds; followed by loud crashes that sounded like large pieces of bark being ripped from tree trunks.

Tom, who had grabbed Brodie off the beach the moment he was out of the water, ran with the little boy towards the safety of his car. After thrusting his surfboard up onto the roof rack, he wrenched the back door of the car open.

Brodie hurled himself onto the seat before Tom slammed the door shut. He was drenched; water dripped from his hair. Outside, the weather was becoming steadily worse. The clouds were black. The wind was ferocious and caused the rain to come down in all directions.

Brodie opened the passenger door for Tom's friend Sarah to climb in beside him, but Sarah's large canvas bag had caught as she struggled to get in. Brodie jumped out to help her, and the driving rain hit him hard in the face.

Finally, she was in. As he turned to get back into the car, he spotted something along the raging waters hitting the shoreline.

"Tom, Tom, there's someone out there, quick!"

Without a second thought, Tom got out. Trying to see in the direction Brodie was pointing to, Tom cupped his hands over his eyebrows to get a clearer view, but it was no use.

"Brodes, there's no one there!" Tom shouted over the noise. "Everyone got into the cars. There wasn't anybody else on the beach. Just us."

Brodie hastily made his way towards the rail guard of the parking lot to get a better view, clutching the railing tightly and ready to sprint.

"Come on, quick. The storm's not going to give. It looks like it's getting worse." Tom ran over to him, reaching for his arm to get him back in the car.

"Don't touch me!" he screamed out loudly as he smacked his cousin's grip from him. He stood there looking out into the sea and shaking in anger. "I saw something. Someone is down there stranded."

A black shadow swept into the waves.

"Wow, Tom, what's wrong with him? Is he okay?" came a voice from the other car. "Do you need help?"

"Brodie, we have to go now," Tom said sternly.

After a few minutes of arguing back and forth, Tom was able to calm his little cousin down enough to take him back to the car. From visiting them in Canada, Tom had witnessed a few of Brodie's outbursts and remembered how Katrin had dealt with them. He remembered her grabbing him from behind and gently dropping to the ground in a secure bear hug whilst rocking back and forth. But the storm was not the time or the place for this.

Although the child's eyes remained fixated on the sea, Brodie had calmed and was more verbally approachable.

Once he was seated again, he strapped the seatbelt across his chest and looked out the window towards the sea, angry and almost in tears. Why would no one listen to him or believe that he saw someone? The sky was really dark but completely lit by the sporadically breathtaking lightning show.

Tom reversed the car and drove towards the main road, fishtailing as he drove off. The other car with his friends was close behind. The tires spun out at first, but finally, they were on the move.

"For a little guy, Brodes, you're as brave as lion," he said, trying to lighten the mood. "What would you have done if someone was really out there. The Mor [Welsh for *sea*] would have swallowed you, too! Your mam would 'ave killed me."

"Sorry," Brodie said after a few minutes. "I saw someone, or I thought I saw someone. I just—"

Brodie was interrupted mid-sentence by a bright crack of lightning and the rumbling thunder that followed.

Tom began to grow very vexed. He was getting jittery, grasping the steering wheel with locked knuckles.

"We 'ave to pull over till it clears up a bit," Tom said, concerned, looking at the road then back up to the sky.

Brodie looked out of the windshield up at the sky. The clouds were pitch black besides the purple-and-white flashes from the lightning. There were hints of orange and crimson throughout the angry clouds as well.

"Look, hey, look." He pointed up.

This time, everybody's eyes were glued in the direction that Brodie was frantically pointing to.

Fireballs spat from the aggressive storm in different directions. Brodie felt a jolt of excitement but also fear.

"What's happening?" one of the girls asked from the backseat.

As if reciting from a book, Brodie explained the scientific phenomenon that blazed through the sky. Everybody sat in silence, impressed by the child's advanced knowledge. *Who is this kid?* they asked themselves.

"It's an electrical storm. Usually, they are not as severe as this, though."

"Since we are closer to Bamps's, let's just go straight there."

"Holy—we never get storms like this in Canada." Brodie couldn't contain the excitement, and it became more present in his tone now. "I mean, I've never been in a storm as bad as this one, ever. I have only read about them in books."

"I can tell," Tom replied, trying to keep every ounce of concentration on the slippery road.

Brodie's surroundings suddenly became blurred as he looked out of the passenger's window up at the sky. He felt like he was sinking into water and hearing faint voices; everything grew hazy except

31

for the fire in the sky. For a moment, he was certain he caught a glimpse of an eye, then gradually made out the elongated face of a large lizard high above. The darkness swirled with a sudden disturbance. What appeared to be a tail sliced through the thick clouds, swirling the angry clouds so they spiraled in opposite directions.

In a blink of an eye, the lizard was gone. Brodie realized he was daydreaming again, but he kept his focus on the swirling clouds.

Then Tom was shaking him with a free hand.

"Oi, wake up, mate, Brodes. We're at Nan's now," he said, thinking the boy had dozed off.

Brodie's body gave a jolt of shock; he had not been asleep but had merely drifted into his own little bubble. When he looked out of the passenger window once more, he saw they had reached his great-grandmother's apartment.

Tom put his four ways [hazard lights] on in front of the apartment's main entrance so Brodie had less of a walk in the storm. He ran out, slamming the door behind him and making for the entrance. He waited there a few moments while the two cars parked. He was absolutely drenched from the beating rain; he stood there shivering amongst the other spectators who had come outside to watch the spectacular weather. He took a couple of steps towards the glass doorway, paused, then exhaled. It was picturesque. Every few seconds, lightning would light up the sky. Brodie had only read about weather like this in his science books, but it was amazing!

From around the corner, Tom quickly ran with a jacket over his head, followed by his friends. They came through the front door, trailing in puddles behind them. Brodie couldn't help but stare at the blonde girl whose makeup ran down her face. It looked very similar to Halloween makeup. He had made very little eye contact with them all day, but it was worse now that he felt they were judging him, as it was clear they had found his behaviour back at the beach very odd.

"Be down in a tick," Tom said to his shivering, huddled friends.

"It was nice meeting you, Brodie," the small group said with compassionate smiles.

"Yup," he replied while looking down to the floor. The carpet had been laid crooked.

Brodie and Tom headed towards the elevator but turned towards the staircase after the lights flickered a few times. Brodie squinted; the flicking and buzzing of the fluorescent lights drummed in his head. They headed to the last apartment down the corridor on the third floor. There waiting for them was a smiling, short little lady standing in her doorway, and as soon as Brodie was in arm's reach, she grabbed the small boy, who was almost the same height as her. She pulled him into her.

"Give Nan a squidge [Nan's famous hug]."

Brodie's great-grandmother was one of his favorite people in his life. He hugged her back with all his might.

She was so happy her eyes were light with tears of joy as she looked into the small face of the child in front of her. "Worried, Gramps and I was, worried sick. Your mam's been on the phone. She's on her way, she is. Now then, before the storm, did you 'ave fun, my cariad [Welsh for *love*]?"

"I've never seen a storm like this, Gran. It was cool. There were firebolts from the sky."

"But the main thing, my darling, are you all right?"

"Yeah, he's all right, Nan," said Tom after giving his grandmother a kiss and a squidge. "Seeing things and a bit wet, but all right."

"What's this now 'bout you seeing things?" she asked, smiling.

"Brodie thought he saw someone out in the sea," Tom said.

"I did see someone," retorted Brodie.

"Nan, I'm going to head out with my mates, back in a bit." He pulled Brodie in for a hug, and with that, the very tall, wet, shaggy Tom left the apartment, closing the door behind him.

Brodie hung his wet jacket and popped into the bathroom to get out of the suffocating wetsuit certain clothing drove him wild and this was one. When he returned, he looked around. His senses were overstimulated; he took in the fragrance of lavender and sight of hand-knitted dolls with plastic faces and white, braided wool hair sitting on the shelves of the old oak dresser. His great-grandparents also had a lot of brass hangings on the walls. He remembered the brass.horseshoe with the Welsh lady in the center that his mother kept in the kitchen window.

Brodie missed his mother thinking of the horseshoe and the crazy storm that continued outside; the weather was a wonderful sight, but it frightened Brodie a little.

He followed the corridor that led to the living room. In an armchair directly in front of the living room entrance was an old man sitting and reading the newspaper.

"Red sky at night, shepherd's delight, red sky in morning, shepherd's warning," he said in a thick Welsh accent. "The last time we had a storm as bad as this, it was 1994," the old man added, talking through his newspaper to the boy. "Aye, and what a storm it was. Your mam would remember."

"Really, Mum saw it?" Brodie asked.

"Saw it? She almost got blooming hit by a fireball."

"Really?" Brodie replied, picturing his mother getting smoked by a firebolt. His attention was focused on his great-granddad, who now lowered the newspaper.

He was a larger man with a full head of white hair. He wore glasses that made his blue eyes intensified in colour. Jim was his name. His appearance had a way of making you feel intimidated—he had been a bare knuckle boxer in his youth. But really, he was as soft as a teddy with the biggest heart.

"Now 'en, tell us what you did today," his nan asked while offering Brodie a plate of scones.

"Um, Tom took me down to the beach, and I watched them surf."

"Oh, now, that's lovely," she said, taking a bite of a scone slathered with strawberry jam and thick clotted Devon cream.

"But I didn't join them," Brodie said. "I was a bit scared. Then the storm came. We all ran to the cars. That's when I saw someone in the ocean, so I ran back to help, but nobody was there. Then we came here."

CHAPTER 5

Surprises

Brodie's great-grandmother Alice had returned to the kitchen to finish cooking dinner but was a little behind schedule due to the power outages that frequently happened. Brodie had given up on watching TV and turned to his great-granddad, who had resumed reading his newspaper.

"Bamps, what if someone had drowned today, and we just left them out there? I feel a bit guilty."

"You 'ave naught to feel sorry for. No one was harmed. Had you gone in the water, well then, that would be another story."

"I'm a strong swimmer, and the storm had just hit," Brodie said, looking in the direction of the window.

"I'm not on about the storm. I'm on about the mermaid you saw."

"The what?" Brodie asked in disbelief, turning his whole body towards his great-granddad.

"The mermaid that was trying to lure you down to your watery grave. Smart lad, you didn't go in."

"What?" He was in complete disbelief and couldn't comprehend what his great-granddad was saying. Did he have *gullible* written across his forehead?

"Well, I heard you and Tom say you thought you saw someone."

"But I didn't say it was a woman. Could have been a man," Brodie said.

"It's the storm that brings them to the surface. Many stormy nights had I crossed paths with them. Claim the lives of many and blame it on the storm, they do. As a young fisherman, I crossed paths with 'em, and those of voice who are just as deadly."

"Those of what, Bamps?" Brodie found the Welsh a bit difficult to understand.

"Water fairies, what do you call them in your tongue, um, sirens?"

"Gumpy was telling me about magical creatures the other day. I thought it was all just bedtime stories."

"What he say, 'en?"

"That they exist. I thought he was making it up, but Nei's eyes look like cat's eyes. That's one thing I never noticed before."

"Aye, and he's dead-on. Just mind your business, leave out the cream, and hang the horseshoe right-side-up, and naught will bother you," Jim said as he folded the newspaper. "Keep well clear of beautiful maidens. They'd be only trouble. Now as for your nei, there's a name for that lot. I won't go there."

"No, and don't," said the short, dark-haired women as she re-entered the room, this time carrying a tea tray.

Brodie got up to help his great-grandmother. He took the tray from her and set it down on the wooden coffee table.

"Your nei, love, is just really good with little home remedies. He's only having you on, love. Now then, let's talk about something else."

During the remaining time that Brodie spent with his great-grandparents, they shared stories of their past, including his gumpy's stories of putting rubber crocodiles between his great-grandmother's bed sheets with Tom's father to scare their mother. Alice pulled out pictures of Brodie as an infant and other family members to present.

"'Ere you go, lad, tell me what you see," said his great-grandfather as he handed Brodie an old photo. It was brown and white. The sides had chapped and stained over time.

When Brodie peered into the picture, he saw it was of a much younger couple. The lady was beautiful with dark hair that sat in

36

styled, pinned curls beneath a plastic rain cover. They both wore rain jackets. The man was taller, built and handsome. He wore a trilby and had his arm around his partner.

The picture looked like it had been taken on the beach. Half of the picture's background was the foot of the cliffs; the other half was the rocks and ocean behind them.

"Notice anything, Brodie?"

Brodie analyzed the picture. "You guys are very young! I am presuming it's you guys in the picture."

"Look past us a little farther into the picture."

Brodie looked past the focal point of his smiling great-grand-parents to scan the photo. There it was in the distance between Alice's and Jim's heads—perched on a rock near the foot of the cliffs where it looked like the waves crashed against a rock sat a now very noticeable figure. Brodie couldn't make out if the figure had a tail or not.

"Is that real or a statue, or did somebody play a trick on you?"

"Well, it was the year of 1948. Your great-nana and I were courting, um, dating at the time. We decided to take a drive down to mumbles and walk along the beach. Your great-nan's brother Ernie was told by their dad not to keep us out of sight. So the three of us set off for the beach with Ernie's camera. We all took turns taking pictures of each other that day, but nobody noticed anything or anyone in the sea. Ernie had the pictures developed a couple of years later."

Jim leaned over, looked at the picture in Brodie's hand, and gave a slight smile. "We had this picture framed for at least a couple of months before we noticed the silhouette in the background. When we realized what it was, we went back to mumbles many times to see if we could see the mermaid. But we never saw naught!"

"Bamps, you said you have crossed paths with mermaids before."

"Aye, Brodes, I 'ave, but not there, and we never saw anything on that rock for years. Now when I was fishing in my early years, the crew and I usually spotted a maiden in distress on the rocks of the stressed waters just before storms. But never did we try to rescue because we knew it would be the death of us."

The old man reached a hand out to receive the photograph; he looked at it and gave it a doting smile.

There was a knock at the door. When his great-grandmother opened it, in bounced his mother Katrin, shaking herself like a wet dog. Katrin handed her gran a bouquet of flowers and leaned in to kiss her cheek. She hung up her coat and told the three of her shopping adventures in town with her parents.

"Shumai, dew, dew, you're wet through and through, girl!" the old man said as he got up from his armchair to greet his granddaughter.

"Mum," Brodie got up to greet his mother and hugged her tightly, "I have loads to tell you."

They conversed over dinner. When the storm cleared up, the two said their farewells and left.

The roads were slippery. They twisted through the small villages; it had grown very dark with barely any light to guide them along the roads that were towered over by tall, dark bushes and trees on either side. The rain that fell against the roof of the car from the overhead trees sounded like the tapping of spider's footsteps on a drum.

Katrin clearly was not comfortable behind the wheel. She gripped it so tightly it looked like her skeleton was about to protrude from her skin. She leaned towards the steering wheel. She reminded Brodie of a blind, small old woman, the kind who perched themselves on thick books in order to see out of windows. It made him giggle.

It was close to 9:00 p.m. The clouds had not lifted nor looked as if they had shifted; they remained a large, thick, dark blanket that hid the moon and the sky above.

Brodie held back his protest about his mother's hidden secret. He knew better than to aggravate her when she was driving. She was concentrating so hard on the road that she looked cross between constipated and frustrated—perhaps frustrated she could not get any closer to the windshield.

Brodie let out a quiet giggle. He began to rock back and forth in the front seat and drifted into his bubble, trying to comprehend his sudden emotions and the uneasy feeling consuming him from within.

"Oh my God, Mum, can you get any closer? You look like the steering wheel's a book you're trying to read in the dark!"

"You try driving then," she snapped.

At that exact moment, Katrin turned her head from the road to her son, and—*bang!* The car suddenly hit something. The two jolted forwards. From the impact, the car swerved to the opposite side of the road. Katrin instinctively put one arm outstretched back towards Brodie, and the other hand clutched tightly onto the steering wheel trying to gain control.

It all happened in an instant. The high beams reflected off the trunks of the trees from the side of the road. The lights from the stereo and car displays flashed before their eyes. Brodie's heart pounded. He squinted his eyes tightly shut until the spinning stopped.

"Brodie!" Katrin yelled as she stiffly turned back to see if he was harmed. "Brodie!"

"I'm okay, Mum." He raised his hand to the back of his neck. With the palm of his hand, he tried to rub the tight ache from the muscle.

Katrin quickly unfastened her seat belt and climbed back, grabbing him and squeezing him tight. "I'm so sorry!" Katrin's voice trembled as she caressed the side of her son's face, checking for injuries.

"I'm okay, Mum. But I'm nominating you for worst driver!"

Even though her son was smiling and had used sarcasm in a playful way to lighten the moment, Katrin burst into tears as she gripped Brodie tighter to her.

"Mum, I'm okay. What did we hit? What if we hit a werewolf? What if it followed us from Canada! Oooh, what a great story that would be: 'Canadian Werewolves in London' or 'Canadian Roadkill in London!'"

"Brodie, we're not in London. Stay in the car," Katrin said, wiping her eyes and nose.

"Where are you going?" asked the wide-eyed child.

"Stay in the car," ordered his mother again. She leaned over him and reached into the glove box. She pulled out the large, black, police-grade-looking flashlight, opened the door, and then left.

Brodie watched the beam from the flashlight. He unbuckled himself and stretched up a bit to get a better view as she disappeared around the car.

The only view he managed to get was his mother zigzagging the flashlight back to the car. She opened the door and slammed it shut, hysterical with tears.

"What's out there?" Brodie asked in anticipation.

She stuck the key in the ignition and turned it to the left. She was trembling and breathing heavily. "I hit a kid!" stuttered Katrin.

Brodie gasped.

A small, partially clothed child lay face down on the ground. It was trying to get itself up from the roadside.

"Don't they keep a first aid kit in here?" Katrin asked herself as she frantically groped around the back seat before leaving the car once more.

Brodie followed her, and they ran to what looked like a child's body.

Katrin shook in fear and said aloud, "How could I have been so reckless!" She knelt down beside the body, crying and attempting to help the poor thing up to carry him into the car with the intention of heading to the nearest hospital.

"Pretty ugly kid," Brodie said, peering over his mother's shoulder.

It turned over. He was not a child at all.

"Mum, don't touch it."

Katrin jumped back.

"What is it?" Brodie quickly retreated to her side.

The thing turned over and got to all fours. He looked up at them both. He looked like a miniature human. He was hairy—really hairy.

From the beam of the flashlight, both Katrin and Brodie could make out his prominent features. He had a pudgy little face that was rapidly growing narrower. His hair looked like it was consuming him. Was it growing? What was this thing?

Whatever he was, he was crouching and held his little leg. A loud, horrible cracking and crunching sound came from the body that had positioned itself on all fours and now arched its back.

Brodie grabbed his mother's arm tightly and stuttered, "Werewolf."

A deep, raspy voice replied, "I am not a ruddy werewolf." In mid-sentence, his voice changed into barks. The small man before them had changed into a badger. He shook himself off and limped towards them, still barking as he looked around himself.

Katrin froze. Brodie now hid behind her. "Quick, get into the car. Stay away from it. It might have rabies," she ordered.

Once again, in a deep, raspy voice, the thing began to bark. He now looked like he was ready to attack Katrin. "I do not have rabies, you stupid woman." It was the most incredible sight—both mother and son would have agreed—the badger walking towards Katrin, barking as he did so. He had transformed into the small hairy man again and continued to limp towards her while pointing his finger up at her and looking around them.

"You can understand me? Are you hurt? Can I take you to a hospital or a vet or somewhere?" Katrin asked as she knelt back down and trembled with fear. She looked around her, probably to make sure there were no eye witnesses to the accident.

Brodie, who was still behind her, stared in disbelief at the unusual creature that was still looking frantically around them and sniffing the air.

"No, no hospital, no damn vet. I'm okay." He tapped his side, then in sudden hysterics, he turned his body around and quickly retrieved a tatty old bag that lay on the ground next to a small puddle of blood and collected rain.

"You're bleeding," Brodie quickly observed.

"Just a small scram on my arm, das all," the creature replied as he opened his ratty old bag and quickly threw it over his shoulder. He firmly gripped the bag under his arm and turned to Katrin. "It's not safe here for any of us. You and your kin must go now before it comes back."

"What before what comes back?"

The creature stood silent now, sniffing the damp night air around him and looking in every direction.

"Get in the car, Brodes, now."

The creature began to hobble away slowly. Brodie turned to his mother, who had jumped back into the car with what looked like relief.

"Mum, I think his leg may be broken. Can we take him with us?"

She hesitated, looked over, and said, "Fine, but put a dog towel down. There's one rolled up under the passenger's seat."

Brodie ignored his mother's second instruction and ran over to the creature to stop him from hobbling away. "Poor thing, you can barely walk. Are you going to hurt us?"

"No, boy, if you don't leave now, it won't be me that will hurt you!" the thing replied.

Brodie felt tremendous pity for the small creature that stood so much shorter than he did. "Come with us. We will take you anywhere you want to go. We can get away from whatever is after you," Brodie said as he looked around into the darkness.

"Diolch [Welsh for *thank you*]," the small creature replied after nervously stepping back a little from the child.

Brodie scooped him up, returned to the car, and gently set him on the back seat. He was a lot heavier than he looked.

A little afraid of what the thing was, he decided under no condition was he going to sit in the back seat and jumped into the front passenger seat. He buckled his seatbelt, and away they went.

Before any further questions were asked, the thing curled up, gripping his ratty old bag, and fell asleep.

CHAPTER 6

Imagination

The rain began to fall once more. On the whole ride home, Brodie did not take his eyes off the creature. They hadn't been able to ask him where his destination was, as he'd gone out like a light.

Brodie threw the towel over him to keep him warm. "Poor thing's wet and cold," he said as he kept his eyes on the immobile mound. "Where are we going to take him?" he asked his mother, whose eyes were fixed on the road ahead.

"I don't know, babes. Gumpy has an old wooden budgie shed up the top of the garden. I'm sure that will do for tonight."

They soon reached home. Brodie opened the car's back door.

"Hun, don't go near it, please. You don't know what it is or what it's capable of doing!" his mother insisted as she leaned in the back seat and scooped the thing up. She carried him round to the back and up to the top of the garden, where she placed him on the ground inside the shed.

Brodie popped inside the house to grab the cashmere throw from the couch and the dessert cream his grandmother kept in a navy-blue jug in the fridge. He wrapped the thing up and left the jug next to him. Brodie thought it was odd that throughout the trauma he had been through the whole night, he always clung to that old bag; and even in the dead of sleep, he refused to part with it. Afraid the thing would attack him, Brodie did not touch the bag.

They shut the door of the shed and made way towards the house.

"Don't say anything to Gumpy and Nei till we figure out what to do. Nei will freak out if we bring unwanted elves or whatever it is into the house," Katrin said as she tucked her son into bed and kissed him on the forehead.

She set up a bed on the floor so she could protect him from the potential danger the creature could pose and so she could sooth him after any nightmares he might have. More than those reasons, she slept beside him because she was in shock from the accident and at the thought that she could have killed him with her reckless driving. Brodie calmed her. He was her little angel. She wanted to be as close to him as possible tonight.

At the crack of dawn the next morning, after a restless night, Katrin headed up to the shed. To her surprise, she found nothing. There was no indication the shed had been inhabited the previous night. The car had a minor scratch and dent, but she could not recall if these had always been there. There was no evidence that the creature had even existed. She went back into the house, made herself half a cup of tea, and decided the phantom creature had only been a dream. She crept back to bed thoroughly exhausted from her wild imagination, the events of which had seemed so real.

Brodie rose early. He could hear the radio playing on the lower level. He got out of bed and tripped over his mother, who merely turned and pulled the blanket over her head. He rolled his eyes and went downstairs. When he walked into the kitchen, he found his gumpy sitting at the table reading a newspaper. Beth was at his side cutting into a grapefruit and placing the two halves onto a plate. Brodie did not want to say anything about the creature to his grandparents, but he wanted to take a slice or two of bread to the shed.

"You're up early, cariad," Beth stated.

Brodie quickly came up with an excuse. "Um, the sheep in the field woke me up. We don't have a lot of sheep in Canada, so I wanted to see them and feed them." With that, he grabbed a handful of bread and headed up the garden towards the budgie shed. He opened the wooden door and peered around cautiously.

The wooden shed was small. There were two large metal-wired cages on both sides of the door. The wall opposite the door was shelved and filled with garden tools. He looked behind the large empty plant pots, but there was nothing to be found. The creature had disappeared.

Not only the creature, but everything had gone—the blanket and the jug, too. Not even a hint of his presence had been left behind.

In one of the man-sized cages, flaps had been inserted for the birds to access the outer cage that surrounded two-thirds of the shed outside. Brodie couldn't really imagine the creature fitting though the flaps, but then again, he had never seen a creature like that ever.

"Was I dreaming?" Brodie asked himself as he returned to the house. He rushed up the attic stairs. "Mum, Mum, wake up! The thing disappeared!"

"What thing?" she asked.

"The creature from last night," Brodie replied.

"Honey, go back to bed. You were dreaming. You're having a nightmare." She was still half asleep. She turned over, pulling the blanket back over her head.

❧

A couple more days had passed by, and although Brodie checked the little shed four or five times a day, there was no sign of the little creature at all. The only thing that prevented Brodie from believing it had all been just a dream was his nei couldn't find the cream jug and began to blame it on the mischievous garden fairies. And his mother went a funny shade of red when anyone mentioned car accidents or driving the winding lanes.

One night, shortly after the creature's strange disappearance, the family was gathered around the table talking about the day's events. Large bowls of Beth's homemade Welsh beef cawl [thick stew with meat and vegetables in a thick, gravy-like broth] sat on the table in front of them. It was one of Katrin's favourite dishes from her childhood, and a visit home would not be complete without it. The plate in the middle of the table was piled high with large slices of crusty white bread, still warm from the oven. The two dogs that laid beneath the table raised their heads from time to time, smelling the scent that filled the cozy kitchen.

Brodie looked down to his bowl in front of him, stirring the contents, moving large pieces of vegetables around, and scooping up the broth to pour it back into the bowl. The consistency was wrong, the items in the bowl were not separated, everything was touching, and there was orange in the bowl. Orange made him upset; he especially did not like anything orange in his food. His hands felt clammy, and his throat felt constricted as he began to feel more upset.

After twenty minutes, and with a gentle coaxing from his mother, he scooped up the smallest piece of meat, cleaned it off with a napkin, and hesitantly put it in his mouth. He ate part of it but pulled a big portion out.

His grandmother smiled at him from across the table, then rose and returned with a plate of chicken nuggets, which had been cooling on the side. She placed the nuggets and ketchup in front of him, then took the bowl away as she congratulated him on his effort to try a new food.

His eyes lit up as he reached for the ketchup to pour on his plate.

"Confirmed Welshman you are now, boi" Rhys said proudly. "Cawl is traditional Welsh food."

Rohli rose under the table, stiffening, and was suddenly joined by Maggie; both barked at something that had caught their attention.

"Shut up, mun!" Rhys shouted down to the bothered dogs, but this did not stop the little Yorkie and Lhasa Poo from racing to the front door, barking as they went. Maggie had always been a bit of a yappy dog, but both dogs clearly sensed something was wrong.

Rhys rose from the table to quiet the racket they were making. He opened the front door. He was still holding onto his bowl of soup, refusing to part with it, and he continued to shovel what looked like ladlefuls into his mouth. He looked up and down the street. Nothing.

"You two, enough now," he said as he started to shut the door. Before he closed the thick door completely, he noticed a dark car. Its windows were tinted, and the chrome tire rims glistened from the streetlights—a very posh-looking car indeed.

It was parked on the opposite side of the street two houses down. It suddenly revved its engine. The lights came on, and it drove past ever so slowly at first, then gained speed. Rhys could see the ember of a lit cigarette through the tinted window as it passed; then it was gone.

Rhys called Rohli and Maggie back into the house. The little dog had mounted the front doorstep as a lion would to protect its territory, and Maggie was close behind. Rhys lowered a hand and stroked the dogs' heads, then closed the door behind them.

When Rhys returned to the table, he wore a puzzled expression.

"Who was at the door, love?" Beth asked.

"Ah, no one," he mumbled between spooning soup into his mouth again. His expression did not alter.

"What's wrong, then?" Katrin asked.

"Nothing," he said, looking at his family, who was observing him curiously. "There was a car on the street. I 'aven't seen that make in these parts of Wales before. Foreign car, perhaps imported, must have been visiting the good doctor."

"Maybe," Beth agreed. "The grandfather came to visit him last week and drove the old Rolls down, lovely old man."

Rhys turned to Brodie, put a hand on his shoulder, and said, "That's why Gumpy's ikle man is going to be a dentist or a doctor—so he can buy Gumps an old Land Rover. Never mind a bloody Rolls or whatever. That car was outside." The family started to laugh.

When dinner was finished, the family spent the rest of the evening catching up on favourite movies.

The next day, Katrin and her father were getting ready to visit Rhy's aunty Winifred, great-gran Alice's older sister. The family had stopped round for a quick cup of tea a few days before on the way back from lunch in town. Brodie was very fond of the lovely old lady whom he had just met and thought the two sisters were very alike in appearance.

Great Aunt Winni was lovely, but she continued to call Brodie *Rhys*. She enthusiastically gave Brodie a full detailed description of every single gnome in her garden, so enthralled with her "little friends," as she called them. She addressed them each as if they were something more than stone. It was time to leave when she had reached the fortieth gnome.

"Come on, Brode's, she loves you to bits," his mother said when he insisted, he didn't want to go visit today.

"I know, but there are a hundred more gnomes I didn't hear about last time before we came home."

Rhys looked over to Brodie. "If you come, I will buy you a sling shot on the way."

"Dad! That's bloody horrible. You can't go around encouraging that kind of behaviour."

"Yes, I can. He's gumpy's little man. Anyways, she has enough gnomes. She won't notice a few missing." He began to smile a devilish grin, the kind of expression that could only mean one thing—he was up to no good.

"Yeah, I wish you were this fun when I was a kid," Katrin said as she playfully punched her dad.

"Oh no, wouldn't promote such behaviour. Anyways, you can wind them up and send them home when they're not yours!" He began to laugh.

"Smart, cause he's only coming back to yours when he's finished smashing your aunt's gnomes," Katrin retorted as she gave him a smug look.

"That's okay. I will take a day off from rebelling. Anyways, Nei's going to take me for a walk to visit Aunty Ali and aunty mags today."

"See, smart boy, you give him options and freedom, and he will choose the right thing to do. It may be the more boring choice, but it's a great choice nonetheless. Gets it from me!"

"Give over, Dad. Are you sure you don't want to come?" Katrin asked, hoping Brodie would change his mind.

He walked his mother to the car and gave her a big kiss on the cheek as she pulled him close to her.

"I will see you later, baby. Behave for Nei."

"I will," he said. He looked at his gumpy, who was making faces from the window.

"Behave for Mum," Brodie said, smiling at the old man.

"No can do," the old man said.

A moment later, Beth came from around the corner. She held in her left hand a large box. "Brodie," she said, "do me a favor please, love! I don't have my glasses on. Can you tell me what colour this is?" She handed him the box. It was hair dye.

"Um, blonde bombshell," he answered.

"Oh, trust me to grab the wrong box. I'm supposed to dye Aunty Mags's hair today. I don't think she wants to look blonde. Right, I'm going to nip to the chemist to get the right dye. I will be back in a tic. Do you want to come? We could pop into the bakery. I will treat you to a cream cake or something!"

"Do you mind if I start walking towards Aunty Mags's house? I want to stop and look at the horses."

Being as Mags only lived a five-minute walk up the street and Beth would only be two minutes in the chemist that was just down the street, she did not object.

"Okay," she said. "I think Harry has the new foals out in the field this morning. They are really cute. I will see you in ten. Do you want an éclair?"

"Yes, please, Nei." He turned and began to walk away.

As he walked along what was supposed to be a sidewalk, he looked back towards the house. The one side of the road was lined with semi-detached houses. They had an old British charm to them. The row of houses stretched from the bottom of the hill to the very top of the hill and continued as far as he could see. On the other side of the road—the side he had just crossed—all the fields were divided by thick rows of trees. Standing desolated was the little chapel; it looked closer from the landing window than from the street.

The shrubs along the sidewalk merged into a four-foot stone wall; the stones looked ancient and faded. Each stone was different in shape and colour. Attached was an old rickety wooden gate.

When he arrived at it, Brodie stepped up and climbed onto the gate to get a better view of the horses. Thankfully, the gate was solid and bore Brodie's weight, but it was questionable how long the gate would hold. The scent of mud and manure was strong. The ground in front of him was covered in loose straw. Ahead was a large, beautiful copper-coloured horse; its crème-coloured tail swished to and fro, swatting the flies away.

The magnificent creature caught sight of Brodie and walked towards him. Brodie became very nervous. He had never been very close to any horses in his past. The large beast raised it neck over the gate. Its lips curled and twitched, showing off its yellowish-brown, elongated teeth that were in need of a good brushing. The horse lowered its head and nudged Brodie.

"He wants a carrot or an apple. Visitors usually bring them fruit," a white-haired man who had followed the horse up to the gate explained.

The old man was short. He wore a brown flat cap, a dark green vest over a brown jumper, and a pair of large rubber boots that came over his dirty corduroy pants. He had a wooden cane in his right hand and rested his left hand on the horse's back.

"Well you, my lad, must be Brodie Rhys. Your grandparents told me tons about you. You're the spitting image of your mum."

Brodie smiled slightly to be pleasant but did not look away from the horse.

"When she was about your size, maybe a little smaller, she would come to feed my horses. I could hear her call out to the fields from the kitchen window, 'Snowy, Shadow, cum 'ere,'" the old man recited with a chuckle. He pulled an old red handkerchief from his pocket, wiped his nose, then pushed it back into his pocket. "Back then, you sees, I had a white horse and a black horse. Your mam would always be at the gate or running through the field. The Sunday school is a couple of houses up. She would sneak out to visit my horses. Used to make me laugh, she did!"

"She hasn't changed," Brodie replied in a thoughtful tone, thinking of all the times she had stopped the car beside a field, then gotten out to see the horses.

"You are more than welcome to come visit my horses any time you want. Though you might be needing a pair of wellingtons, otherwise up to your neck you'll be in mud."

Brodie caught sight of a small black figure that was sniffing around the back of the chicken coop in the distance. "So you would not mind if I came to visit the farm? Do you have any chickens?" Brodie asked as he turned to look at the old man's vest, refraining from making eye contact.

"Tons, my lad, you can take some fresh eggs home with you for your grandmother. Speaking of your grandmother, here she comes."

Brodie turned and saw they were being approached by Beth, who was holding something in her hand.

"Hello, Harry. I see you have met my Canadian grandson."

"Shumai [Welsh for *hello*], Beth. Aye, strapping lad. Treny [Welsh for *pity*] he won't be here for long! Could use young muscle on the farm."

Brodie turned to give the old man a courteous smile, then quickly turned back to the beautiful, large creature in front of him.

"Well, hello, Copper," Beth said, holding out an apple for the horse to take. With no time wasted, Copper bit the apple from her hand and hung its head low. Like a scene from a movie, it nudged its head into her, and she gently stroked the exposed half of the beautiful and noble face. It was clear to see Beth was as passionate about horses as her daughter.

"Maybe next time I will bring you a nice big juicy carrot. Bye, Harry," she added whilst stroking Copper, as Harry had turned to walk away.

"Nice meeting you, lad. Come round anytime," Harry said as he nonchalantly lowered his head, trying to make eye contact with Brodie.

"Thank you," Brodie said as he focused once more on the chicken coop, acknowledging the farmer's courteous farewell.

"Right, change of plans. Mags and Alison are coming down to the house, your éclair is in the fridge. I forgot that I picked up two boxes of hair dye. James, the chemist, reminded me, god bless him. Must think I'm going senile."

"Nei, would you mind if I stayed here for a bit? I want to have a wander around here."

"Well, I don't mind as long as you keep close to the house. I will keep an eye on you from the landing window. Please stay where I can see you. But don't go past Harry's. Harry's house is as far as I can see from the window."

"Are there any wellingtons that will fit me?"

"Should be in the cupboard under the stairs. Have a look." She gave him a kiss.

❧

An hour and a half later, after rummaging through the shoe closet and finding old army hats of his gumpy's and other neat old objects, Brodie finally found a pair of green wellingtons that were close to his size. He left the house and headed back towards Harry's.

In the distance, Brodie spotted Harry on his tractor in the far field.

"I wouldn't mind a ride on that," he said out loud.

He then turned his thoughts to the black figure that he'd caught skulking about the chicken coops earlier on. Brodie climbed over the wooden gate carefully so as to not fall. He started to walk towards the chicken coop. Copper had joined him, nudging Brodie's side as if for a nibble from his pocket. A cockerel with the brightest emerald chest perched himself on the wired fence that divided the field from the sheds and house.

Brodie reached over to open the gate on the other side of the fence. He slipped through, closing it behind him and leaving a very disappointed Copper on the other side.

He could feel his heart begin to beat faster and faster as he approached the old hen coop. At the foot of the hen house was a door just large enough for the hens to wander freely in and out of.

Sliding back the bolt that kept the rickety old door closed, Brodie slowly opened it in order not to startle the hens inside. Then he had a little peek about.

Everything seemed calm and quiet within. Some of the hens were scratching around the ground, clucking as they did so, whilst several others sat serenely on their nests. One or two cocked their heads to one side, observing Brodie. As he quietly latched the door shut again, he came to the conclusion that if anything had startled the hens, old Harry would have heard the commotion and quickly come to investigate.

Looking around, Brodie could see a thin barbed-wire fence that separated the field he was in from a narrow gravel path. Taking great care not to get caught on the vicious-looking metal barbs, he lifted the wire and climbed through. The path took him right up to the old farmhouse. There stood a large open barn, which housed a big red tractor. Directly opposite was what appeared to be a very old stone building.

It looked enticing; Brodie decided it needed further investigation. Checking that the coast was clear, he scampered across the farm, slipping and sliding a few times in the muddy puddles. He was glad he had decided to wear the wellingtons.

He crept silently around the side of the old building and found to his relief that the heavy stable door was partly ajar, enabling him to squeeze through without much difficulty. He found himself in what was obviously the old stable block. Harnesses and old tack hung on the white-washed stone walls, and the ground was strewn with loose straw. Sunlight streamed in through the dirty panes of the stable windows; tiny fragments of dust seemed to dance and twirl in the bright beams. An aroma of hay, wood, and animal pervaded the air, and Brodie decided he quite liked it!

In the corner to the right was a flight of wooden steps leading up to the hayloft above, but immediately to his left was a row of stalls for the horses. Brodie, after checking that no one was about, began his search there. There was no trace of the little black-and-white figure anywhere. He began to make his way to the hayloft steps when something heavy dropped against the floor above him. A soft shower of sawdust and hay drifted down from between the wooden floorboards.

Feeling decidedly nervous and holding his breath, he quietly made his way up the old worn steps. Once he was on the top step, he slowly raised his head so his eyes were level with the floorboards. He cautiously looked around. Bales of hay were piled up everywhere, and farming tools and many other pieces of unidentifiable farming equipment rested against the bales. Brodie's heart pace increased. His hands grew sweaty as he looked over to the corner of the other wall. Crates had been roughly stacked into the corner; the area was used for extra storage and covered in a blanket of dust.

The creature was hanging upside-down by one leg from the large central beam in the hayloft. The black-and-white badger was barking, spitting, growling, and clawing at the air around his stout, round little body.

Brodie held his breath; he couldn't move. He was sure it was the same badger his mother had hit, the same badger that had disappeared the next morning from the budgie shed. The same badger he had been looking for.

"I'm not going to hurt you," he said nervously. "I want to help you!"

The badger continued to bark and hiss. Brodie looked around him for an object to help free the angry little creature without touching him. His eyes fell on the tattered little carry bag the creature had had in his possession the last time Brodie had seen him. The bag now lay on the floor underneath the hanging badger.

He looked at the creature and said in a tone filled with excitement, "It is you. I thought so." He reached down to pick the bag up, and the creature began to bark and claw into the air. As he barked, he started transforming into his little elf form.

"Don't touch it, or I will—" The creature stopped when Brodie returned his belongings, dodging the angry little claws that tore through the air.

The halfling looked at him; his rage had ebbed away.

"Thank you," he said, still trying to free himself while clinging on to the bag.

"If I help you get down, are you going to hurt me?"

The thing shook his head. Brodie looked around him, his eyes fell on a crate that had been knocked over; its contents had spilled onto the floor. He used it to climb up to release the creature from the suspended trap.

It took a couple minutes, and once the creature was free, both Brodie and the creature dropped to the floor with a thud.

The halfling quickly got up and made a sprint towards the staircase, then stopped. He turned to Brodie and asked, "How did you know it was me? Why are you following me, boy?"

"I wanted to see you, to see if you were real and not a figment of my imagination. Sometimes, I see things that others can't. I'm not going to hurt you," Brodie replied. "What are you? And what was chasing you that night? You disappeared the next morning. I wanted to see if you were okay, not suffering any injuries from my mum's terrible driving, but you had gone." Brodie paused a moment. "Then today, I thought it might be you I saw around the chicken coop!"

The small creature—now almost man like—looked rough. He was covered in dirt. His eyes were black as midnight. They were missing the white part of the eyes and looked like two large, shiny, black buttons.

"What are you, if you don't mind me asking?"

"I'm a changeling, part elf, part animal," the creature replied.

"Can you do magic?" Brodie asked.

"Tricks that deceive the eye!"

"Do you have a name?"

"What's it to you?" the thing asked obnoxiously.

"Curiosity, I suppose. I'm not going to hurt you! You're not very polite, are you?"

"And your name?"

"What's it to you?" Brodie asked in the same sharp tone the creature had used.

"Well, I suppose gratitude is in order for saving my life and the lives of others!"

"Brodie."

"Well, Brodie, only name I 'ave been referred to is Grub, but answers to anything, I do. Not like other humans, are you? The last human who laid eyes on me tried to beat me with a broom handle, found me in the cellar's pantry, she did," Grub said as he scratched the inside of his ear and smelt the air; this seemed to be a habit—one of his animal traits.

"You should have left me. If they catch your scent, you will be in grave danger!" He walked slowly and very wearily towards Brodie; he was still hobbling from the accident.

"Who?" Brodie asked in alarm.

"Seen them, the others have, around these parts. They searched around your home, too, the night you and your mother brought me here. Hoping I remained in the area, they have searched all around these parts."

Brodie looked confused as he asked, "Why do they want you? Will they hurt you?"

"To them, I'm disposable. They will stop at nothing to get what they want. They will kill whoever stands in their way."

"What are they, and what do they want?"

Out of nowhere, a grasshopper landed on the floorboard in front of Grub. Its armour made the sound of an eggshell cracking as the insect split in half. Its limbs split from its body as if it was emerging from a cocoon. A second later, it stood upright in front of Grub. Its wings slowly dropped from its armor.

Its voice was musical, but Brodie couldn't understand its language. He rubbed his eyes in disbelief.

"A fairy."

Grubb looked like he understood every word. He started to shake; whether this was due to fear or fleas, it was hard for Brodie to be sure.

A moment later, the fairy jumped into the air, and in the blink of an eye, it resumed its former grasshopper form.

"Wow, that was amazing, what was that?" Brodie said.

"We have to go. We have to get out of here now. They're here. They will have picked up your scent!" implored Grubb, tugging at

Brodie's sleeve. "They're on the street around your home," he said frantically.

"What? What do we do? How do we get out of here? What about my mom and my family?" asked the frightened boy.

"Brodie, I promise I will explain everything, but you can't go back there! Not right now! I need your help. You are not safe. We both need to get far away from here. Then I will explain everything, please."

Brodie sensed the extreme urgency in Grub's voice. "I don't have a choice, do I?" he asked, looking into the nervous black pools of Grub's eyes.

"No. I need you to listen and listen carefully," Grub demanded. "I'm going to give you something to help us get away from here. Listen, Brodie, when I give it to you, you must think hard and concentrate your mind on getting out of here. Think of an animal, one that would fit in around here, like a cat. Ask your body to change to a cat or a wild duck or something, then leave. But most importantly, do not let them see the thing I'm going to give you. Hide it from them somehow. Then follow the grasshopper and the dragonfly. They will take you to safety for the time being.

"Wait there for me. Do not leave, and do not touch the object after you have reached the safe place! You won't know how to, but I will change you back when I come to you or until another of my kind comes. I understand this is scary. I am sorry, child, I promise I will explain everything to you, but please do not get caught."

Before Brodie could ask questions, Grub pulled out what appeared to be a small metallic plate from his bag. It glistened and shimmered a burnt copper with flecks of tarnished gold.

Grub placed it in Brodie's clammy hands and ordered him to concentrate. It was warm and hard like metal.

The boy had an animal in mind. As Brodie was about to object that nothing was happening, a magnificent, remarkable, astonishing thing happened. He felt pins sprouting from his entire body and a strong cramping sensation in his muscles and bones followed by tremendous pressure.

The plate fell to the ground. It wobbled.

In a matter of seconds, he had transformed.

Grub smiled, then placed the object back into its scruffy bag and hung it around Brodie's neck. "Go now," Grub said. "Follow the grasshopper, but try not to look conspicuous."

Brodie ran down the stairs with the bag hanging from around his neck. The smell of the barn had intensified. Halfway down the stairs, he paused, then quickly ran down the remaining steps. He kept close to the old walls of the stable. The ground felt different under his new feet.

My boots, he thought, *I'm not wearing any!* He had a perfect ground view and spotted a little grey mouse running along the base of the stalls. He reached the entrance of the barn and looked once more around him. Grub had taken his badger form once more; he hobbled into the shadows just behind Brodie. The grasshopper jumped in front of Brodie, taking long sprints towards the fields.

Brodie followed, squeezing his body flat to the ground to crawl under the wire fence he had entered through earlier. The bag caught on a loose wire; he turned to free it, then trotted away towards the field, keeping close to the long grasses that grew along the fence.

In the short distance in front of him, Harry was returning in his tractor. Trailing behind proudly was a small white Jack Russell with brown and black patches. Back near the wooden gate, Copper nibbled on the scattered hay from the bale. As Brodie continued on, he noticed a few more horses and their foals in the distance.

He couldn't help but think of his mum and what was going to happen to his family. Were they in danger? He didn't even know what the people that he was supposed to be avoiding looked like.

He then caught scent of a strange aroma. It smelled of after-shave mixed with tobacco and another scent he could not put his finger on. The only thing he did know was that it smelled like trouble.

His whiskers tickled against the grass; he wanted to scratch his face but resisted the urge. He lowered his body close to the ground and peeked up through the tall grasses along the fence. He felt his ears lower, and his head sunk slowly to the ground again.

There, about fifty feet away and standing behind the wooden gate observing Copper, was a tall figure dressed in a dark grey business suit. He looked like a man from some large firm, a Londoner perhaps, but at the same time, there was something intimidating about the stranger. His dark hair was styled and sleek.

The grasshopper landed next to Brodie. "Don't move. Try to stay calm. They can smell the fear," it said in a musical whisper.

From the tall grass, Brodie could see the man scanning the field. After a second or two, he slowly walked away. Brodie's paws were cemented to the ground. He had held his breath for a minute or so, then slowly exhaled. A beautiful sapphire-and-black dragonfly swooped low over his head. It made the familiar musical noise.

"Run," demanded the grasshopper.

Without a second thought, Brodie sprinted into action. He followed the dragonfly to the back fields. He could feel the bag pounding against his side as he ran away from the farm, his family, and the potential danger. Was it the bag or his heart that was pounding harder?

CHAPTER 7

By Moonlight

Adrenaline raced through his veins as he ran through the fields. He could feel the wind through his fur, and all the different smells that surrounded him pounded against his face. Above weaved the dragonfly through the air, directing Brodie to his destination. The grasshopper was close by. It, too, was flying at a speed that was consistent with Brodie and the other insect.

Brodie felt like he had been running for a long time. He was out of breath, and his paws began to ache. Soon, he would wake from this exhausting dream. Brodie was not used to the sharp rocks and twigs that cut into his new padded feet; he had to stop. They had entered a wooded area some time ago. He had no idea where he was. They had taken a quick break for Brodie to have a drink from a nearby stream. Then they had resumed their traveling.

When they finally arrived at the insect's destination, he had no idea what time it was. Brodie followed the insects through a small entrance between a tight group of old trees submerged deep in the woods. Hidden from the shadows of the setting sun, the path was narrow and grew deeper into the ground. The earth slowly rose into walls, and roots sprouted from the base of the trees hanging down the sides of the walls. In the distance, an archway made of various stones led to an open area. The archway was ancient-looking and covered in a thick, lush blanket of green moss, as if it had stood for thousands of years.

As Brodie walked underneath it, he was amazed at the carvings and symbols cut into the stone. He wondered if it was the same language the insects spoke. Brodie felt an overwhelming feeling of peace and tranquility wash over him as he walked through the archway that opened up to a green pocket hidden deep in the woods. It had a feeling of secrecy, a place where old Celtic rituals were preformed, perhaps. It was towered over by old trees covered in moss; he looked up and around the trees and felt alive here. A small waterfall trickled over a muddy, washed-out hill, creating a little brook that wove out of sight between the trees.

He had never encountered anything as serene as this and strongly wished with all his heart that his mother could see this amazing place. She would have gone crazy with the camera.

The trees that secured this secret little area were large. The trunks were split from years of growing. Birds and insects high in the treetops were the only things Brodie could hear apart from the small waterfall. Ferns and wildflowers occupied the spaces between the trees.

As he continued to observe his surroundings, he noticed that every single tree that surrounded him housed wild fungus and thick moss, which looked like green velvet blankets. Brodie strained to see if all trees were covered in elm oyster mushrooms—they were!

An irritating itch behind his ear caused him to scratch quickly without deliberation with his hind leg. He paused; the long travel, his nerves, and the beauty of this new discovered place had caused him to forget what he had become and how the magic had really existed. He trotted vigilantly over to the bank of the little stream and timidly peered into the clear water; he gazed into a new reflection.

"And wake up, Brodie," he told himself.

He focused on the face that stared up from the water. A small, handsome, red fox mimicked every movement that the stunned boy made; he reached one paw over the reflection and brushed the surface of the water softly. The image broke into shattered ripples but soon resumed mirroring the image of the little fox.

"Wow," he gasped loudly as he caught sight of his tail.

❦

Time passed. Brodie waited patiently for Grub, but the small halfling had not come. The dragonfly and grasshopper where nowhere to be seen or heard. They had disappeared, leaving Brodie all alone in the unfamiliar woods that grew darker and darker.

Every noise made him jump. He turned at every sound. His new body provided Brodie with a set of highly amplified ears that he was not grateful for.

The cold night air bit at his nose, and the frightening noises scared him tremendously. He curled up underneath a nearby bush that provided a sheltering awning of leaves, a small nook for Brodie to crawl under and hide from any danger that the dark woods threatened.

He tucked his nose under his thick bushy red tail. He was extremely grateful for his thick new snug coat. Brodie closed his eyes, praying that his exhausting day had been a dream and soon he would wake to his mother sleeping on the ground next to him in his gumpy's safe, warm attic. His fur was thick and toasty warm. He lifted his head once more to listen to his surroundings before curling the tattered old bag and burying his face into his tail, effortlessly drifting to sleep.

❦

Brodie's furry new ears stood on end and twitched at any slight noise. At first, he would raise his head to investigate. Not only had his hearing intensified, but his vision had become sharper. It was amazing. It felt like he was wearing a pair of night-vision glasses, the kind soldiers wear in the army. He could see his surroundings as clearly as he did in the day. He would often spot a small field mouse scattering about or insects emerging from the ground and basking in the small light patches from the moon. After some time, he did not respond to the noises around him but merely lifted one ear out of habit.

A whimsical giggle interrupted the quiet; the soft laughter caused Brodie to freeze. Finally, he had woken up to the sound of his mother laughing at his sleep talking. He felt a deep viscous growl escape from his chest; he knew then it had not been a dream.

He had no control over his animal instincts.

"I won't hurt you, dear child," came a silvery, silky voice.

Brodie raised his head from underneath his tail and slowly looked up. Kneeling in front of the bush was a beautiful lady. Her face was young, her hair sparkled a silvery white and draped long over her body. Her eyes appeared as if they were diamonds fit into her eye cavities, with large black pupils centered in them; they looked friendly. Her skin was milky white and glistened slightly in the moonlight.

But wait—she was not in the moonlight.

Brodie had never seen anybody as beautiful and yet so abnormal in his life. Her dress was the most unique feature she obtained. It gripped his attention. It looked as though her dress was made of melted white gold or silver that had been poured over her body and remained liquid-like, though it also danced in the breeze. It looked both as if it was made from precious metals yet at the same time as if it was as flexible as fabric.

She held out a milky white hand. "Do not fear me, little friend, for I do not possess a reason to harm you, for you are so far from your home. I can hear your heart's plea for your loved ones."

Brodie slowly stepped out from his little protection and kept his eyes on the breathtaking figure kneeling at his level in front of him.

"I only wish to ease your heart's pain, my little friend, and to shed a little of my warmth and glow on your soul to protect you from the dangers that seek you tonight."

"How did you know—"

Before Brodie could finish his sentence, the angelic sight before him spoke again. "You must be careful, child. You are soon to enter a world that is different from the world you know. Trust nobody."

His whiskers swayed slightly in the night breeze; it tickled.

"Who are you?" he asked in an irresolute tone.

The silhouette illuminated a glow like an aura—a warm but familiar glow. A dragonfly suddenly flew around the lady and soon was joined by others; their wings glistened like thin sheets of silk. This made the large insects look like fireflies in the dark.

The grasshopper perched itself on a branch that hung low just beside the lady. Once more, its armor made the sound of an eggshell cracking as the large grasshopper split in half. Brodie watched with amazement. He now focused on the miniature human that a second ago had been the large grasshopper.

His focus was interrupted by the soft voice of the lady before him.

"My name is Mairwen. I am a child of the mirrored star [the moon]," she said.

"Do you live here in this forest?" Brodie asked, looking around for a house or some sort of living accommodations.

"I live on the moon, in the sky far above this place with my siblings," she said.

"The moon! Do they live on the moon with you?" Brodie asked as he looked up.

"No, my brother is a blacksmith on the sun. My other siblings live on other moons and stars that orbit the earth."

"Aren't you lonely on the moon all alone? Don't you get bored? There is nothing up there!"

"Oh, on the contrary, my little friend, I have my gardens to maintain."

Brodie was absolutely puzzled now. "Excuse me for sounding rude, but it has been proven there's no life on the planets above. The Luna landed on the moon in 1959. There was no life on the moon then. Plus, NASA is constantly sending satellites up to gather information and explore. They haven't found any gardens." Brodie huffed. *What crock,* he thought. *People living on the planets? Baloney.*

"My darling, naturally, they see the things we want them to see. When they enter our planet's atmosphere, the gasses and magic blind them, preventing them from seeing the true planet's beauty."

"You cast spells so people can't see the moon?" Brodie asked sarcastically.

"Not quite. They see what I allow them to see—a magic vapor we created in our atmosphere that psychologically alters the human's five senses, a safety mechanism," she said.

64

"How does that protect humans? Are there dangerous aliens that would kill them or would invade earth? Does the magic do that to the aliens, too?" Brodie was beginning to get restless.

"Aliens? What are they? There are no aliens. The magic vapor is there to protect us. Each planet contains a little bit of the old magic—a magic that was from a time of our mother. My moon is home to great waterfalls, rivers, and gardens. My gardens are different from the gardens of earth. They are my pride, my love, and my companions. If mankind were to see the delights and beauty of our planets, they would once more claim them for themselves, and once more, we would be outcasted and killed off from the human's greed. We were ignorant to the human's ever-advancing technologies; we thought we were safe on the stars and moon, a place they would never find us."

Brodie sat silently for a moment, trying to make sense of everything. "So really humans could breathe on the moon, Mairwen?" Brodie finally asked, not sure if this was one big dream he was playing along in.

She smiled. "My name has never been addressed by a human before. Shuttles are magnetized to our planet's deserts, a space we have recently created for those occasions, so humans believe they are orbiting my moon by foot, but they are simply orbiting a portion of my desert. There is a strong magnetic and magical force that prevents them from crossing the desert's boundaries and entering my gardens. Had they accidently entered my gardens, the psychological alterations from the magic would cause them not to see hear, touch, taste, nor smell anything. If they were to collect samples of my moon, the samples would turn to rock or disintegrate to sand once they exited the moon's atmosphere."

Brodie said nothing; he was unconvinced, but he adored the idea and wished his bedroom held the same characteristics; then he would never be told to clean his room again by his nosey mother.

"Mairwen, what do you mean 'outcasted and killed once more,' or 'claimed for themselves'?"

She took a deep breath and quickly spoke as if she could sense something. "You have been entrusted with great power that you must—"

Both Brodie and Mairwen turned to the sound of twigs breaking. The quietness of the night had quickly changed. A noise made from high above in the treetops sent shivers along Brodie's spine. The sound was identical to that of live electrical wires.

"Brodie," Mairwen called. She looked concerned. The small fox turned his head from the direction of the forest and looked at her diamond eyes. She held her arms open and smiled. "You are safe. Do not worry." Her voice was as soft as music and very calm.

Dragonflies suddenly circled the lady and Brodie, seemingly coming from nowhere and creating a barrier around the two. Brodie shook with fear as he spotted a black shadow slowly shifting amongst the trees.

Brodie sneezed as a familiar scent tickled his nose—strong aftershave. He backed himself towards Mairwen; he had kept his distance from her up to now.

Something vibrant caught his attention. His jaw dropped as the white fungus that grew on the sides of the trees turned a luminous blue. Then the dark figure walked between the trunks. Brodie bit the tattered bag tightly in his mouth and backed farther into Mairwen.

The dark figure crouched his torso towards the ground, holding outstretched a pair of black-leather-gloved hands as he walked towards Brodie. Brodie's heart pounded so hard he thought it would break through his chest; he wished for his dad. It would have taken one hit from his dad, and the stranger would have been down; he missed him so much he could feel the tears growing in his eyes. He wanted his mom to hold him safe in her arms as his dad protected them.

"Cum 'ere, 'as a nice boy. Then cum 'ere, you little…," a deep raspy voice ordered.

Brodie thought of his father once more running through the woods, spearing this threatening stranger to the ground, protecting him.

"Cum 'ere, you…"

It was the man from Harry's farm, but how had he found Brodie here?

"Brodie, relax," Mairwen ordered. Brodie felt his body thud against Mairwen's legs as he backed even more into her, but she did not move. She lowered herself to pick Brodie up. He still bit the tattered bag tightly. He could feel and hear her heart; it was steady, with not a hint of fear.

He quickly turned his head towards the right. A deep growl came from the tall fern between the trees. It caused him to curl with fear in Mairwen's arms. The grasshopper had joined the dragonflies; they continued to circle the two in their fairy forms.

From the tall ferns, two large eyes reflected the light.

"What's that?" Brodie asked out loud. His fur stood on end, his ears pressed flat to his skull, and his eyes jumped from the danger that waited patiently in the fern to the man that stood erect, slowly approaching Brodie and Mairwen.

"Be gone with you. We possess nothing of interest here," Mairwen ordered.

"But I fink you does, love, bof of youz."

Brodie could not keep from staring at the silver set of reflected eyes. He wanted to be with his family, kept safe by those herbs his Nei hung.

"Brodie." Mairwen lowered her head so the top of Brodie's furry head touched her chin and lips. "Please refrain from thinking of your family. Hold tight to that bag, and do not wriggle so." Mairwen began to step backwards.

The man walked forwards. Every step she took, he mimicked. His smile grew; his eyes were ablaze like fire.

"Nowhere to go now, luv. Gives us the dawg. Wev' got you surrounded."

Mairwen continued to step backwards. She stumbled slightly as she came to the water's edge, but she remained poised and calm.

"You're wasting time," the man said impatiently. The anger grew in his voice. "Cum on, hand him over, and you won't get hurt." The man's shadowed face gave a grimacing smile.

As those last words came from the man's mouth, a wolf stepped out from between the ferns. Its mouth snarled, its lips curled, and it slowly loomed towards Mairwen and Brodie.

A great belt of laughter came from the man. Before the large, disfigured mongrel could reach the two, Mairwen flung herself backwards into the pond. She grasped tightly to the frightened little fox. The insects that swarmed around them in circles followed her to the water like darts against a board.

As he tried to free himself, the last thing Brodie remembered was Mairwen's soft musical laughter from above, a stream of inappropriate words from the man, barks and pained howls from the hound, and an overwhelming feeling of warmth.

Brodie thought perhaps the dog had grabbed him; maybe the thing had bitten into a nerve, and the warmth he could feel was his own blood. It was exactly the same feeling as getting into a warm bath. He could feel the warm water consume his tiny little body, but to his bewilderment, he did not feel wet. He tightened his eyes shut and clenched his teeth into the bag as he held his breath.

"Welcome, my little friend."

Brodie opened his eyes as they walked through a shimmery glass wall. He quickly closed his eyes once more to protect them from the shards of glass they were about to penetrate. It was the most unrealistic feeling in the world; once more, Brodie felt the warm waters trickle over and consume his entire body, but he remained dry.

"It's all right, my friend. Open your eyes and breathe. You are safe!"

He opened his eyes; the bag had dropped from his mouth when he relaxed his jaw in astonishment. He dived from Mairwen's arms to retrieve the bag. He put his head through the arm strap and looked around him. His paws were now wet. He lifted each one, disliking the wetness, he looked up to Mairwen.

"Here, let me help you," she said. As she picked him up, his back arched. He leapt into her arms, fully trusting her. He looked around them, taking in the mesmerizing beauty of this foreign place.

"Where are we?" he asked.

Mairwen smiled but did not answer.

He inhaled and exhaled large lungfuls of air as he looked up into the sky. Beautifully lit stars shone high above them in the sky. They were brighter and magnetized. *This must be her home,* he thought.

Brodie continued to look around him. Mairwen had not exaggerated about her home. It was beautiful. Everything was silver; the stars that surrounded them in the sky glistened, as did the leaves on the trees and the petals of the flowers and the surface of the still pond. Everything looked as if it was made of platinum, white gold, or pure silver. The grass under his paws was soft as moss. The willow trees that grew from the ground on tilted angles were motionless. The leaves from all the trees merely hung and glistened. There was no breeze in this strange place, unlike on earth where the trees and leaves danced from the breeze that swayed them to and fro. Large silver lilies grew tall amongst other amazing flowers. It was an incredible sight.

Mairwen placed Brodie on the ground next to the pond and sat next to him. His body temperature was neither hot nor cold but remained balanced. Right in front of them was a large pond. Dragonflies swooped low, kissing the surface of the water as they transformed into their miniature human forms. The starlight bounced from their wings.

"How did we escape? What happened to that man and the dog?"

Mairwen crouched over the side of the riverbank and peered down. "Look," she said softly.

Brodie got up and trotted a couple of steps to the river's edge and lowered his head. The water's surface contained clear faces and figures like a flat-screen TV with HD. Brodie had a bird's-eye view of the scene he had just left.

There were now two men arguing. They were both dressed in grey business attire; they looked a bit like gangsters that had escaped from the 1930s. They both spoke with weird Cockney accents.

"Where the—Where did they go?" the one said angrily, looking around them.

"Well, I don't naw, do I? Haw the ruddy hell am I supposed to naw?"

"I knew it was that nosey kid," the taller of the two exclaimed. "I fought I saw him snooping around that minging farm," he added.

"Now that badger's given us the slip—"

"Don't matter 'bout the badger no more. Didn't you see the fox had somefin' on him? It's the kid he'll want now. I told you the bad-

69

ger did a switcharoo, didn't I? Good thing I caught the kid's scent. Oferwise, we wouldn't haved known it was him in disguise, eh."

"Well, aren't you employee of the week?" the other said in an agitated growl. "We would have had him if it weren't for that bloody woman. We should stay 'round here 'case he comes back."

"Good idea, Garret. Now you're using your loaf."

Brodie turned to the lady who sat next to him. She had been watching him, reading his reaction.

"Excuse me, but you seem to know more about what's going on. Could you please tell me why they are after me, where we are, and how we got away so fast?"

"Those men seek something in your possession, something the badger gave to you. All you need to know for now is that you are safe here."

"Are we on the moon? How come I am not suffocating? This does not look like the moon," Brodie said in a confused manner.

Mairwen remained smiling.

"What was that strange wall we came through? And why is it so beautiful here but yet you won't share this beauty with the humans?"

"The best way to answer all of your questions, my little friend, is to start from the beginning."

Brodie nodded with agreement and sat down.

"That was a brave thing you did helping the changeling escape. Your friend has entrusted and endangered you with the object in your possession—an object which, in the wrong hands, could endanger the dragons. I cannot tell you why, as it is not my secret to share, but you have to believe me."

Brodie sighed. He just wanted answers and to go home.

CHAPTER 8

Myth or Reality

"In the beginning, there were two powerful immortal spirits that shared an empty space. These two spirits were lovers and could not be parted. They balanced each other. The male was strong and all powerful. He created the planets, the sun, and the mountains.

"The female had the power of creation. She gave birth to the elements. Her partner created the stars and the moon in the sky as a gift for his beautiful love. They were beautiful. They twinkled and lit up the darkness of the sky.

"They lived on earth and shared the beauty of their surroundings and creations. They produced many offspring—animals, plants, and so forth. They lived happily for thousands and thousands of years. Mother of Nature, as she was called, gave birth to animals and insects and other species that were part animal and insect and part image of their father. They became the keepers of nature. They cared for the animals, plants, trees, and elements of the earth. They lived for thousands of years in peace and harmony.

"Soon, Father of the Universe created man in his image. It was one of his greatest creations ever, but he could not bear the thought of creating man without a partner, for he loved his wife and could not fathom an existence without her. So man's heart would not want for anything, he would be given the greatest gift of all—love.

"He tried to create woman in Mother of Nature's image. Although he could not replicate her beauty and perfection, his creation of woman was sufficient. Over many years, Father of the Universe watched his own creation grow with pride. And through the years, his creation grew in numbers.

"Mother of Nature was upset with his creation. The humans, as Father proudly named them, were greedy and selfish. They killed and bickered amongst each other for power and territory. As his creation grew in numbers, they named their Father God and sacrificed offerings of his own kin. Not only had his creation grown out of control, but many were wicked and cruel. Man killed the halflings and the magical creatures out of jealousy. They feared their differences and forced them into hiding.

"Mother of Nature was upset and could not bear to watch her children be destroyed and slaughtered. She begged her love to control his creation, but it was too late. He had very little power over the humans. He could only influence a few. As he stood back unable to intervene, he watched the destruction grow.

"Mankind diseased the land, causing corruption wherever they settled. Father, who had grown remorseful, pleaded for his love's forgiveness and begged her to follow him to a new destination to start over. But she could not abandon her children. She stayed to aid them. She used the very little power she had left to give her children gifts of camouflage and magic to protect themselves.

"Father left. To where he went, that is unknown to this day. Mother could not stand her children suffering. She lay on a bed of peat moss and closed her eyes, becoming one with the nature she created. Her tears turned into the babbling brooks. She still lives but within earth and its elements. She created safe passageways for many of her children—the last of their species, children who could not camouflage themselves or possessed little magic."

Brodie was suddenly aware that he was being watched intensely. A peacock as white as snow cried as it fanned its tail and walked a little closer. Silver-and-white koi swam in large schools in the pond, surfacing to glimpse at the stranger that a moment ago had peered into their waters.

"It has only been the last couple of decades that the humans have accepted us."

"Then why haven't you taken the animals back to earth?"

"They will never be free or safe from the humans," she said compassionately.

Brodie thought about zoos and museums and understood.

"These are not ordinary animals, my child. They have adapted to the non-human environment once again and prefer the peace and seclusion."

He looked around, taking in the amity of this dreamlike place; he understood completely as he watched the animals.

Mairwen reached a hand out for the peacock; it came without any hesitation, and she stroked the breathtaking bird.

"I can visit earth one night a month when my moon is full and reflected on the surface water of earth, creating a doorway so I may enter and then thankfully leave," she said.

"Can others cross through? What happens if you're not near water, or the clouds hide the moon?"

She paused and leaned over the small pond to pick a white water lily that sparkled as if someone had sprinkled a container of glitter over its beautiful petals. She swept her hair to the side of her face with her other hand and gave Brodie a warm smile.

"Unless I tightly hold or embrace you in a hug, nobody can enter my passageway. If the clouds conceal my moon and no reflection is cast upon the waters of earth, then I am stranded. My brothers and sisters hide me on earth until an opportunity arises for me to leave. But only twice in a thousand years has that happened."

Brodie was shocked that she was older than a thousand years. She looked so young. Twenty-three at most.

"Sunrise soon approaches. You will have to flee, or for thirty days, you will remain my guest."

Brodie did not want to leave this harmonious place. He watched as the peacock was joined by another, then as both disappeared into the grass. Some of the other animals had transformed to their elfish or goblin forms, and others merely continued with their business.

73

He suddenly remembered his family.

"Mairwen, can I see my family from the waters?" he asked with a hint of hope.

"No, I'm sorry, Brodie. It's odd I cannot see them."

"What about Grub? I don't know how he would have managed to get away from those men if they followed and found me that fast."

Mairwen whispered something as Brodie quietly waited. "Here you can see him."

Brodie peered over the river's edge and looked once more into a dark image Mairwen pointed to. He spotted Grub hobbling; he was in his badger form. Without the tattered bag around his shoulder, he looked a part of the forest. The only giveaway that he was not a true badger was he was walking on his hind legs. He looked in pain.

Something caught Brodie's eye that caused him to jump in fear—Grub was in a part of the woods that looked familiar.

"He's heading towards them, and he doesn't even know it! Can you see the men?"

The image changed back to the scene that Brodie had stepped away from roughly twenty minutes ago.

Two men paced back and forth around the open area while another man lay on the ground resting against the tree with his hat placed over his face. The fungus on the tree was still a vibrant blue above. The wolfish hound had disappeared. *Perhaps he caught the scent of Grub,* Brodie thought.

"Grub is heading towards them. He will walk right into their trap," Brodie frantically explained. "Can you please take me back? I have to warn him."

She picked him up in one big scoop. This time, the small red fox was ready as she stepped back into the pond and said, "You are always welcome to visit me. Just call my name into the reflection of the moon." She scooped another lily from the water and placed it in his bag. "When you have resumed your human form, place a petal on your friend's injured leg, then bind it to him."

With that, she stepped farther into the pond. Her dress trailed on the star-kissed surface of the water; then she was submerged.

They resurfaced in a brook deep in the woods. Brodie looked around himself. The place and smell were familiar. He was a little ways behind Grub but could easily catch up to him.

"Thank you for everything," he said as Mairwen placed him on the ground. She smiled, then disappeared.

He bit tightly down on the bag and ran in the direction that smelled of hay and Grub. His heart pounded. Brodie had no idea exactly how close they were to the gangsters or where that dog had disappeared to. He ran and ran till he finally caught up with the badger.

"Grub," he whispered loudly when he was in close enough range for the badger to hear him.

Grub turned in Brodie's direction and hobbled to him.

"Brodie," the badger said loudly in ecstatic surprise. "That can't be anyone but you. Not often do I run into talking foxes in this realm. We are close to where we have to go. It's just a little further ahead, boy. Then I will explain everything."

"Grub, we can't go ahead. They are waiting for me. It's a trap! There are three of them and a scary-looking wolf. I followed the dragonfly there, but they somehow found me."

Grub gasped in horror. "How did you get away?" he asked the fox, who was now slightly out of breath and panting hard.

"A lady named Mairwen rescued me. She took me to her home through a reflection in the water. If it wasn't for her, they would have caught me. But they are there now, waiting. Except the wolf has gone. He could be close to us now."

"How many men were there when they came after you?" Grub asked in a serious tone.

"Two, I think, and a large wolf."

"And you say three are there now? Then, no, they are all there waiting. We will have to get to the other realm another way. We will have to go back the direction you just came from and follow the brook to lose our scents."

It was the funniest sight indeed—a fox and badger walking side by side. As the sun rose, they did not stop, but watched the clouds change different colours in the horizon. Brodie insisted they should take a break; Grub's hobble looked like it was getting worse. Grub refused, ordering them to carry on.

After some time, they left that dreaded woods following the brook that twisted and cut through fields. The brook joined to a river. They continued to follow it until they reached a small village. Cars passed on the roads, and people went about their morning routines. The air was filled with fresh baked goods. It made Brodie's mouth water. He was so hungry that the smell of the breads from the bakers made his stomach twist in pain. The roads were lined with bricks. Flower baskets hung from the awnings of the buildings and window-sills. Houses and shops were attached to one another and well-kept; it was a pretty little village. The river ran alongside the cobbled road. Short black poles with linked chains were placed as barriers to prevent people from falling into the canal. Often, an old man here or there along the riverside would make a double take at the odd sight of the two walking side by side before continuing fishing.

"Grub, I can't go on. I'm starving. And I want to go home," Brodie said in an exhausted tone. He sat himself down next to a well-maintained shrub, then collapsed to the ground.

"All right, all right, I know, I'm sorry, boy," Grub said as he left Brodie's side, following the scent of baked goods cooling on the windowsill of a baker's shop.

Grub had resumed to all fours once they'd come into the vicinity of humans. Once he was near the window, he stood on his hind legs and grabbed two loafs from the windowsill. Then he quickly returned to Brodie's side, handing the poor boy the warm, soft bread. It was so fresh Brodie devoured it within minutes. Grub finished half, then placed the other half in the tattered old bag that remained around Brodie's neck.

"What's this, Brodie?" Grub asked. His black eyes widened as he pulled from the bag the glittering white lily.

"Oh, I forgot, Mairwen gave it to me. She said to pick a petal off the flower and put it on the area that hurts you, then bandage it."

Grub reached behind him, tore leaves from a tulip patch, then placed the petal over his leg, tying grass around it to keep the petal in place. Within a matter of minutes, the badger made a face that looked as if he was about to attack; his jagged teeth showed, which made Brodie uncomfortable.

In a humorous tone, he said, "It works. It bloody works," and gave a barky laugh. It was the first time Brodie heard the old badger laugh, and he mistook the happiness for some type of cough.

Then Brodie realized it was laughter, and he began to laugh with his companion. "Here, you can have your bag back," Brodie said.

"No, it's better off with you. You're younger and faster than me."

They had to be careful not to talk and be caught by the humans around them; they had hardly been noticed.

"Grub, what's going on? Is my family safe? Who is after us and why?" Brodie asked under his breath.

"In time, in time, I owe you an explanation, but not here!" he answered.

As they reached the end of the little village, Grub grabbed two bottles of milk that the milk man had just left on the doorstep of one of the houses. He placed them into the bag, which was a little heavy around Brodie's neck. Then they continued to follow the river.

They did not stop; they had to continue their mysterious journey. Along the river, strange-looking boats were docked and tied parallel to the walls of the river. The boats were made of wood and painted in different colours with decorated trimmings. They reminded Brodie of smaller and more colourful versions of Noah's ark. There were no boats like this in Canada.

A sudden loud noise caught both fox and badger off guard. It came from twenty feet away. On the very last boat, a pudgy little man with jet-black hair looked like he was yelling to himself.

The yelling intensified.

"It sounds like he's being robbed," Brodie said.

Brodie then spotted the frightful-looking wolf, who had seemingly come from nowhere, jumping into the canal boat. Grub grabbed the strap of the bag and pulled Brodie to the nearest boat. The boat was long and occupied a small deck on which Brodie could see was a small space for a stairway down into the cabin. On the deck tucked into the corner was a barrel, coiled ropes, and folded blue tarps. The lodge stretched from one side of boat to the other and had many small round windows. The roof was flat and occupied with flowerpots.

They boarded the boat, careful not to be seen or heard. Brodie was more afraid of the dog catching their scent. They hid underneath a tarp that had been tucked between the cabin and the barrel. It was a small space, but they had to hide.

The motor started on the boat. Brodie was fearful that the loud pounding of his heart would give them away.

The captain, or the owner of the barge, surfaced to the small deck to untie the ropes of the barge from the wall of the canal. He coiled the ropes before throwing them on top of the tarp, which caused Brodie to jump. As they slowly chugged from the docked barges, they could hear men's voices quarrelling. Grub held a paw to Brodie's muzzle to keep him silent.

"Well, he's not going to be happy, is he? How many times has the blasted thing slipped from us? And naw you say the kid has disappeared. Gawd knows were eel be."

"She's probably hidden him somewhere. I told you we should have attacked the three when we had the chance 'stead of hiding in the bushes waiting for that idiot and her brat to leave."

"Where are the others?"

"Still waiting at covert court for the kid to reappear," the other voice replied.

Realizing a barge was approaching, the men paused so their conversation could not be overheard by any other human. It would not sound right for any person to converse about a lost child like this. It would set off alarms.

The boat passed. They continued to quarrel, but their conversation was now muffled from the distance.

"Oh, that was close," Grub gasped in relief.

"What were the chances of that? They could have gotten us there. But there was no way they could have passed us. I saw them. They were waiting where Mairwen and I left them."

"They're not normal humans. We'd better get some shut-eye while it's available," Grub advised, trying to change the subject so as not to scare the poor boy. "They think you're still with Mairwen, so they won't be on our trail for a while."

"Grub, when can we change back?" Brodie's skin felt irritated; he felt like bugs were festering in his fur. He scratched himself. He was not used to this new body and longed to be human again.

"Not yet. We are safer in animal form for now."

"How did they know about Mairwen?" the boy asked himself aloud.

"The only people that can disappear through the elements are the old lot." Grub scratched his plump, balding, pink tummy. "And those idiots are familiar with the old magic." Grub paused. He reached into the bag and pulled out the bottle of milk. Peeling back the tin foil cap, he drank deep. He wiped his muzzle of the creamy residue and looked at Brodie. "Now get some shut-eye. We might not get a chance later."

Brodie closed his eyes once more. It was an effortless sleep the exhausted boy fell into.

The old wooden barge followed the zigzag river through the quiet countryside. The sun had hidden behind heavy clouds, leaving the cooler winds below. Autumn was slowly approaching, bringing with her the crisp chills and the changes in the vegetation colour. The surrounding trees on both sides of the riverbanks swayed peacefully. Their branches hung low, shedding their leaves of gold, orange, and brown on the water's surface. The colours were not significantly bright, but they were pretty. While conkers, acorns, and other nuts rained from their worn-out structures, animals scattered back and forth on the grounds below to collect them.

The breezy, dull autumn day passed by as the two drifted peacefully along the quiet waters. Both were sound asleep under the old folded tarp. The sound of the chugging engine and the water slapping softly against the boat's sides were the only sounds to be heard besides the birds in the distance, but a new sound was growing close. At first it sounded like an animal sniffing, but it quickly changed to a clawing and rustling of the tarp.

Brodie woke in a panic. He nudged Grub, who woke with a grumble.

"The wolf, it's found us," Brodie whispered in horror.

The animal began to whine as its paws grew closer to the two.

"Not wolf! It's the captain's mangy mongrel," Grub said as he reached into the bag that had been tucked between them. He pulled out a bottle and sprinkled out a paw full of dust, then he leaned forwards to where the intruder was trying to dig its way through. As soon as the thing's nose was in sight, Grub told Brodie to cover his nose and close his eyes; he then blew into his hand.

The mutt began to sneeze and yup and quickly ran away from the two into the barge.

Brodie began to cough. "Oh, what is that stuff?" he said, choking in disgust, pulling back the tarp a little to air out their small area.

"Troll's breath, it's the foulest stench on the earth," Grub said as he wiped his paw against his fur. "He won't be back." He turned away from Brodie to resume his previous sleeping position. "It's all right. We stink. Nothing's gonna come near us now. That's for sure."

Brodie lay back down. He gave a yawn and asked, "How could breath turn into powder? That's not possible." The stench lingered and made Brodie feel nauseous.

"The breath is collected in bottles and stored for years. Eventually, it turns to powder. Now try to get some sleep."

Brodie had trouble sleeping. Not only did it stink, but he was restless. He was cramped in the tiny corner. Grub lay on his back beside him in deep sleep, snoring once more. When Brodie finally did manage to get a little sleep, visions of wolves, trolls, and demons taunted him in his dreams.

When he woke again, he lay curled up on the wooden floor hidden under the plastic tarp. Missing his family, he wondered what state his mother would be in. He thought about how his mother was overprotective. Sometimes, she was a bit embarrassing around his friends or strangers. But now, he would have given anything to listen to her silly made-up songs or bad punchlines to jokes that always ended with "Do you get it?".

Above all, he thought of how he'd felt safe in her warm loving arms; she was the only person who understood him. Brodie had been diagnosed with autism at the age of two. She was his best friend, treating and loving him as a normal child. He missed her so much.

Tears began to shed a little at the thought of his family. His father was so far away working on the oil rigs and would have no idea what was going on unless Mum told him.

Brodie poked his nose through a crack in the tarp. It was getting dark now; even though there was a trace of the troll's breath, the fresh air smelled sweet and damp. It was carried by a cool breeze. He felt a small droplet of rain on the end of his blackberry-shaped nose. He poked his entire head through the space and took long breaths of the night air.

Then he turned his head quickly. He thought he saw a shadow pass by him. He became nervous and hid under the tarp.

Bang, bang, bang!

The frightening loud noise came from the deck of the barge.

Brodie began to panic. He wondered if they had been caught by the owner, led to their hiding place by the dog. His jaw dropped, his eyes widened, and he quickly turned to check on Grub. The badger quickly got up and poked his head out to investigate the commotion from beyond the tarp. Brodie exhaled in relief but quickly focused again on the strange scene that was taking place two feet away from the barrel and tarp. He didn't dare move.

"Heavens forbid, don't make me shoot again," a man's voice called out in anger; it sounded like the same man who owned the canal barge.

"Come an' get me then, stupid taffy," a second eerie voice said.

"I'm counting to tree. Then I'm shooting. I'm not going to be robbed by a bloody goblin, not tonight, not ever!" With that, the first man cocked his shotgun and shot in the direction of the small person on the rooftop overlooking them. The shot missed the goblin and smashed one of the flowerpots.

The sound of the gun being fired was loud and left not only an echo but a smell of burnt gunpowder and smoke. It made Brodie jump and quiver with fear. He had never been in the presence of ammunition before. It happened so fast, Brodie didn't know what was going on. He only caught fragments of the conversation—something about goblins and a robbery. He quietly watched from a crack in the tarp.

When the owner of the barge had shot the gun, the force of impact caused the barrel to point in the air. At that precise moment, the strange little creature jumped down from the rooftop and pushed the man off the barge. It was like a scene from a horror movie. It was hard to tell whether it had been the impact from gun that had sent him over the side or the shove the goblin had given him.

The creature clapped his hands in satisfaction and laughed. Running up the stairs from the cabin came the dog. It barked and charged for the goblin. The goblin was too quick and caught the mutt mid-pounce. The poor thing was chucked over the edge into the riverbank with a howl and a whine. Once more, the goblin clapped and whipped his hands together in delight.

"Right-o, to work I go," the creature said in a hymn. As the thing turned, he looked down, noticing movement and the noise of plastic.

The tarp was pulled aside slightly. Brodie froze in place.

"Wello, wello, what 'ave we 'ere, 'en? A stole away," the goblin said loudly.

The sound of the man splashing in the water and trying to catch up to the boat was noticeable and interspersed with frequent swears as the goblin walked towards Brodie with his hands still clutched together. Brodie lowered his body in a stance, ready to attack.

The goblin reached up beside him for the life preserver that hung on the wall and turned, chucking the flotation device into the dark waters.

"'Ere you go, 'en," he said, followed by a chuckle. He turned back to Brodie, tilting his head as he analyzed the little bushy fox; Brodie growled.

"Do you want me to chuck you over 'en all?" he asked Brodie as he wiped his hands once more.

"No need for that," the raspy voice of the badger came as he crawled out from beneath the tarp.

"Ah, a changeling," the goblin said as his beady little eyes widened.

"We pose no threat. We hitched a ride, das all," replied Grub.

"Any more on 'ere?"

"No, there was only the one human that we heard and the dog, but there could be more down below," Grub answered.

The goblin walked past Brodie and headed down the stairway. Grub followed, as did Brodie after a second or so. The three cautiously walked into the cabin below. The goblin took off searching each of the rooms.

"Quick, before he comes back. Put your paws into the bag, hold the plate, and think about your human body. Wish your body to change back, and only think of that. Now."

Brodie reached into the bag that hung around his neck. He pressed his paw tightly to the smooth disk, which felt warm, and concentrated hard.

Instantly, the hairs shrunk back into his body. It was painful. The outrageous pressure returned; he could feel his body transform—break, almost. He lay curled on the ground from the pain.

"Wow," Brodie said as he looked at his hands.

Grub began to look around for the goblin.

The goblin returned and gave a look of sheer disgust. "Ach avi, another one," he said.

Under the lighting, Brodie examined his hands, patted down his body, and looked up at the grubby thing standing before him. The goblin was not very tall, maybe a few inches taller than a three-year-old. It wore an old leather hat on its hairy little head—it looked like an old aviator hat. Its clothes looked old and dirty and very moth eaten. They had clearly been handmade. His brown, torn pants were held up by a belt that had a pickaxe tucked into it, and an old oil miner's lamp that hung from an iron ring weighed his belt down slightly.

His face appeared old, his nose was long and crooked, and his eyes were small, black, and beady. His face was dirty and wrinkled, and his teeth looked all decayed; a few were missing. The only thing he had in common with Grub in appearance were his long, elfish ears that sprouted out from his head in opposite directions.

The goblin smiled and looked at Grub. There was a gruesome, menacing way in which the thing smiled. It caused a shiver to run up and down Brodie's spine. He looked like trouble.

"My name is Grub, and this, this is Brodie. And you, my friend?"

Brodie took a seat at a table nearby. He sat away from the thing, not trusting him and keeping an eye on him.

The goblin outstretched an arm to the side of his body and gave a bow. "My name to friends is Kol. To foe, I am known as the Coblyanu. And where might you be going, 'en?" Kol demanded, politely looking at both Grub and Brodie; his stare seemed to linger on Brodie more.

Brodie tried to avoid making eye contact with Kol; from a young age, he had always been able to look into a person's soul through their eyes. It made him uncomfortable, but he couldn't see anything in Kol's eyes—just cold emptiness, which made him even more uncomfortable.

"We are heading to the Threshold Rock," Grub replied politely but briefly so as not to give this curious stranger too much information.

"Well 'en, heading back that ways myself," Kol belted out with joy as he slapped his knee. "I'm heading to a mine just by there. Had to get my barge back. Bloody humans nicked it."

"You mean you nicked it from the human," Brodie retorted, then quickly lowered his eyes to the wooden floor.

Kol sat silent, which caused a moment of awkwardness in the cabin, then he gave another belt of laughter. He sat directly across from Brodie and said, "Don't fear me, child. My bark is worse than my bite. I'm a mining goblin. I've worked with humans before. Often a group of human miners will be in the mines with us. I don't mind them. I like their hymns and jokes. Well, some of 'em at least."

Brodie looked at Kol with curiosity and asked, "Why did you heave that guy over the boat and leave him to drown, then throw the dog overboard to join him?"

Kol pointed up to the wooden support beams on the ceiling. A tarnished brass plaque was bound into the wood. Grub and Brodie lowered their eyes back to the goblin, who tapped his long, curvy, dirty fingers on the wooden table almost impatiently. He turned in his seat and lifted his shirt to reveal a scar on his back. Brodie glanced back up to the plaque.

"Aye," Kol said with a mischievous grin. "There was a time when the humans killed our lot. Rewarded they were for delivering our heads to their kings. We fled to the mountains, forests, and underground. My kind began to dig passageways in the earth to get around secretly. When I was younger, not so long ago, we came into contact with the humans. We were digging passageways through the mountains while they were digging to collect the rocks. Strange things, the humans. They were in our domain now. The first lot that came into contact with our kind hardly any made it out alive, but they kept coming back, intended on collecting the rocks of the earth, you see. They respected our space, and over time, we respected theirs. Always stayed close to the surface, they did.

"One day, not so long ago, a boy bit older than you, bys the look of you, wandered down into the mines, didn't 'ave a clue there was underground rapids close by. The boy slipped. A rock caught his shirt." Kol paused; an expression of dissatisfaction crossed his dirty, crinkled face.

"What happened then?" Brodie asked.

"Well, one of the miners heard the screams of the boy and raced to save him. He was the closest human to the boy. I heard the child, too, and came to help. It was just me and the human at first. The miner couldn't reach the child, so I stretched out my axe so's that the boy could grabs on, but he was gone. The waters ate him up before I could pull him out. As for the miner, he slipped, broke his leg, an 'ad a concussion from whacking his head against the rocks. The rest of the humans that followed the screams found me with my axe reached out for the boy as he disappeared and the human bleeding unconscious on the ground. They thoughts I tried to kill 'em both. The boy was found days later washed up and lifeless on the other side of the mountain.

"His father punished me, chained me, and branded me with an iron horse stamp. He worked me as a slave to pay for the crimes I didn't commit. My prison was the barge at night. Back then, the canal barges were used to ship coal along the river. They kept me in here. They didn't feed me for days at a time. They would beat me and throw chunks of coal at me. That's how I got my name, you see. My

85

arms and legs bled from the rough iron shackles that peeled the flesh from my bones. The humans killed any goblin in sight from then on. All on my lonesome, I was for naught."

"How did you ever escape?" Brodie asked. He felt sorry for Kol as he gazed down at the scars that covered the goblin's wrists.

Kol rubbed his wrist. He could feel Brodie's stare. "The goblins turned against the humans. They thought I was dead, mun. My cousin caught sight of me shackled and kicked around, enslaved by the humans. The night before they planned an ambush, the miner woke out of his concussion. Once he was told what had happened, he got up from his bed in a strange dress and traveled in the pitch of night to the barge. He freed me, shooing me off with a loaf of bara [Welsh for *bread*]. But I liked it on the barge, didn't want to go. He told the rest of the miners the truth that I had tried to save the child and thats he had slipped."

Brodie gave Grub a puzzled look.

"Bread," the badger answered.

"Isn't it your tongue, too? Don't you speak Welsh?" Kol asked.

"My mum's Welsh, but I was born in another country," the boy replied. "What happened then?" Brodie was caught up in the story and wanted to hear the rest of Kol's tale.

"Well, I went back to the mines to my kind. The miners apologized. We wanted the barge, and gave it to us, they did. They moved away, no longer safe nor welcomed in the dark tunnels of our earth. It was great, mun. For years, we used it to hide animals and churns. We nicked at night from the nearby humans. Cause we live in the mines, any humans passing the barge in the day would often make off with it thinking it was abandoned or sell it to some stranger for an easy penny."

"Why did you keep the brass?"

"To remind us not to trust humans. They are a bloody savage and cruel lot."

The three continued to talk for hours, mostly listening to stories Kol told. When Kol asked about their journey, Brodie and Grub remained quiet. They gave very little information to the tricky, untrustworthy stranger.

"Threshold Rock, 'en, ah," Kol repeated a few times, watching for a reaction from the two. A sly smile slithered across his face.

"I know parts of this area, but I'm hoping the water nymphs will guide us," answered Grub.

Brodie shot Grub a puzzled look. Grub had no idea where or what they were searching for.

"I can do better than that," Kol said, the intensity of his stare increasing. He reached into a pouch that was tied to his belt, pulling a hideous face as he groped around for whatever it was he needed. One eye squinted closed, the brown tip of his tongue suspended out of the corner of his mouth, and his head tilted sideways. A moment later, he straightened up, producing a large brass coin.

He held it up to show the badger and the child; the coin was tarnished and very old. It was scratched and slightly bent. No profiles of any queen's, animals, plants, or any other symbols were visible on either side.

Both Brodie and Grub exchanged a look of bewilderment.

Kol flicked the coin into the air and said loud and clear, "Threshold Rock."

The three watched the coin spin and turn in the air as it went up, then as it came down. It rolled a little as it hit the surface of the table. Brodie gasped with delight.

The clear surface of the coin now revealed a defined and protruding image of a goblin's profile. The goblin's head looked wicked and evil; it wore a similar hat to Kol's, although its ears were larger and far more crooked than Kol's. Its beady, evil little eyes looked forwards in the same direction that its long, crooked, hooklike nose pointed.

"Wow," Brodie said, astonished. Even Grub leaned across the table to study the coin.

"Which ever way its nose is pointing, that's the way to the Threshold Rock. The coins are magic and guide us home when we are lost, which hardly ever happens." Kol got up and quickly disappeared.

"Where did he go?"

"Probably to navigate the barge," Grub said to Brodie as they both studied the hideous goblin head.

CHAPTER 9

The Barge, the Mines, and the Mystery

Grub stood up to stretch; his pink-and-white balding stomach expanded. He turned and walked on his hind legs towards the cupboards. As he walked, he transformed into his miniature human elfish figure.

Brodie stared at the black carpet that grew on his back. He giggled to himself, thinking the hair that grew on his dad's back was not bad compared to this.

Once he got himself up on the counter, Grub began rummaging through the cupboards for something to eat. Brodie could hear his tummy growl.

After feasting on a tin of baked beans, Brodie washed himself up and fell asleep on the double bed that looked and smelt fairly new.

Grub transformed back into the badger and curled up on the ground beside the bed. He clung more tightly to the bag now than ever, not trusting Kol. And as for Kol, well, they didn't know what he did the remainder of the night—probably got into some mischief or other.

Dark shadows raced across Brodie's closed eyelids early the next morning. The disturbing pattern woke him.

He opened his eyes and looked around him after a stretch and a long, tiresome yawn. The shadows across the small boy's face had been shadows between rays of sun beaming through the trees. He got himself up and knelt on the pillows to look out the window.

It became dark in a matter of seconds as the boat chugged on. He quickly threw a door open, hoping it was a closet door—it was—and grabbed the thickest wool jumper he could find. He threw the cream shirt over his head and made his way to the kitchen.

Grub and Kol were not in the kitchen; he made his way up the steps to the deck where he found the two standing stiller than dead air. Grub and Kol watched the trees as they passed by. Both their expressions were uneasy; it caused Brodie's skin to break out in large goose bumps.

"What's wrong?" he asked quietly to whomever would answer him.

"Ssshhh," replied Kol. "Fairies of these woods, they be neither friend to you nor me. If they catch you, don't you cry. You won't have time before you die," the goblin recited, still staring out into the trees.

Brodie's eyes opened wide in fear as he looked up at the tree-tops; he was relieved when Grub barked in his raspy badger voice for them to retreat into the barge.

Brodie quickly followed; the ratty old bag remained secured around his neck. When they entered the kitchen, Brodie was very surprised; he had not seen the two fairies on the kitchen table when he'd passed through before.

The dragonfly and grasshopper were in their fairy forms working together to remove the lid from a jar of honey that had not been on the table a few moments ago. Grub reached over, unscrewed the cap, and placed both lid and jar on the table, then licked the sticky honey off his furry little paws.

Both fairies reached into the jar scooping out handfuls of the sweet golden syrup. Their wings reflected the hanging light above the table, revealing the metallic blues and purples within them.

Brodie slid into the seat across from Grub. Grub's paw rested underneath his bristled chin. He looked out of the small window centered above the table and looked lost in deep thought.

Brodie, finished observing Grub, lowered his eyes back down to the fairies; he was absolutely fascinated with their tremendously large appetites for their size. *I wonder if Mum has ever been this close to a fairy?* he asked himself.

A hefty nudge was given by Kol as means for Brodie to move down. He sat down and glanced at the fairies. "Starved they look, eh?" Kol said as he elbowed Brodie in a playful manner.

Brodie smiled and rubbed his arm where the goblin had elbowed him. It had felt similar to being quickly jabbed by a big rock. His thoughts were interrupted by Grub.

"We'll have to go through. That's the only option we 'ave. It won't be long before they find out that the boy's not with Mairwen anymore."

"I'll come, too, then," Kol said, smiling a few yellowish teeth that were ground down to expose the brownish dentin. "These woods belong to the Tylwyth Teg and other types of nasty fairies and beasties. Been up along this bank night and day, I 'ave. Still gives me the willies." Kol paused as he stuck a finger in his ear, wiggling it frantically. He pulled it out to view his fingertip. "Could 'ave sworn sumthin crawled down my lughole then." He continued as he wiped the glob of dark brown wax on his pant leg.

Brodie slid over discretely, putting a little more space between him and the foul goblin.

"I know my way around, you see. There's a mine just up the river a bit. We could leave the barge. Then I could show you a shortcut."

"Perfect," Grub said as he dipped his paw into the jar of honey, interrupting the fairies' feast.

They both looked up in dislike but continued eating. In a matter of seconds, the dragonfly circled Grub. It was faster than anything Brodie had ever seen.

"All right, all right, just the one, all right," Grub blurted out. Brodie did not understand what it was the thing wanted. The soft musical chime was all Brodie could hear.

"How come I can't hear them? Sometimes I can, but other times not so much," Brodie said.

"Why do you want to hear them? Not missing much. Less annoying when you can't hear them," Kol said, giving a chuckle.

The dragonfly darted out of the window, which was ajar, and disappeared into the gloomy-looking woods. Grub looked out the window, then shook his head.

"You're gonna 'ave to change back, you knows! What dwells in these woods, they're not fond of the humans," Kol said to Brodie as he gave him a serious look.

Brodie gave Grub a concerned look back. The question in his mind was answered by the discrete shaking of Grub's head in disapproval. They spent the rest of the canal trip around the old wooden table strategizing over routes and old worn maps from Kol that looked centuries old. They ate whatever food was in the small fridge and cupboards. Then they packed a few perishable items in a backpack Brodie found in the closet. Kol found a bottle of brandy in one of the top cupboards and helped himself.

Whilst Kol was distracted by filling the brandy cap full of the golden-brown liquid for the fairies, he did not see Grub and Brodie slip out of the room. Grub closed the door behind him.

"I told you I would explain things, Brodes, but not here not with him around. I don't trust him, and once he finds out what we have in our possession…" Grub shook his head in detest. "Don't worry, your mother and family are fine. The fairies go back to check on them. That's where they have been disappearing to. I promise, Brodie, I will explain everything soon, but I warn you now, be on guard with Kol. He's a goblin, a breed of trickery and disseverance. We have to pass through the forest to get to Threshold Rock. Once we are in the fairy realm, we will be safer. Then I will explain everything."

Brodie nodded. He understood. Grub handed back the tatty old bag and asked Brodie to keep it around his neck and under his jumper, away from the goblin's greedy roaming eyes.

"Brodie," Grub called, wanting the boy's full attention, "I'm sorry I have put you in danger. There is danger following us and danger ahead of us. I'm sorry that you have been dragged into this and away from your family."

Brodie smiled. "Let's just say you have made my visit to Wales more exciting now. Anyways, I wouldn't leave a friend stranded."

Grub smiled. His smile gave Brodie the creeps even though he knew it was harmless. "If we get into any situations, you have to change back to the fox and keep running," Grub said in an almost whisper.

"I don't remember how I did it in the first place," Brodie exclaimed.

"Reach into the bag and grab the scale, wish for your body to turn into the fox and nothing else. You have to want it above anything else in the world."

Brodie gave a nod as he pulled the jumper off to put the bag around his head and shoulder.

"But, Brodie, one other thing. Whenever you put your hand in the bag, you have to clear your mind. Don't let any thought enter your head., I don't know how it works with humans. You're the first. It's a miracle it worked for you to get you out of that barn unnoticed."

"But I was noticed, Grub."

Knock, knock. They both jumped at the pounding knocks on the small bedroom door.

"You two coming out? We're almost there!" Kol yelled.

Brodie threw the backpack over his shoulders and followed the two to the deck. "Where are we?" he asked as he looked up around him.

"We're near the mines now!" Kol answered.

The sun, still behind large trees, exposed rays of light; the shade left the cold wind feeling colder and eerie. Dark clouds were rolling in, soon to hide the little light the sun provided.

The river turned into a small lake within large rocky dugouts. They had come to the end of their water travels. Kol grabbed the ropes of the barge, hopped over the side into the cold water, and dragged the boat to a large iron ring that was embedded into the side of the boulder.

"Follow me just up here," Kol said, pointing to a shallow area of the lake.

Brodie was not impressed that he had to walk through the water. The shallow waters washed up to a dirt path that split into two directions; one way led along the lake, and its trail disappeared from view. It was probably a way to the top of the hill. The other path led the way to a large aperture on the base of the rocky hill. Wooden beams supported the entrance of the mine. The darkness was fearsome, and it startled Brodie.

Grub shook his fur, disliking the water as much as Brodie did, then peered into the black opening, sniffing the air for danger.

Abandoned in the entrance of the mine, old wooden ladders lay against the walls of the tunnel, and there were coils of wet rope on the ground. Two small freights filled with coal were left on the tracks that led into the darkness. Kol scraped a piece of flint against the rocky wall of the entrance, trying to light a loose bit of rag on fire. To Brodie's surprise, it worked.

Kol opened the little door of his iron oil lamp and immediately set fire to the rope, discarding the rag into a shallow puddle. He shut the lamp's door and guided the way. He really didn't need the lamp. His vision had adapted to the darkness, but he thought it would comfort the small boy.

It was dark but dry for the first couple of feet. The tunnel grew narrower and damper. The light of the lamp reflected on the beads of water that trickled down the rocky black walls. It was cold, and the air was stale in area's. The echoes of the drafts passing through the tunnels scared Brodie. To him, they were cries of ghosts and wicked demons gallivanting in the tunnels ahead and below. The noise seemed to surround them.

Grub sensed the boy's discomfort. The lamp illuminated the wet slippery path a little in front of them, but black shadows protruded from the rocks of the walls. The bodies of the three were outlined by the light only if they were close to the lamp. Otherwise, they blended into the darkness of the mine. Grub grabbed Brodie's arm to comfort the boy and to avoid slipping. The pads of his trainers did not grip the wet stone of the ground very well down here.

They ventured deeper and deeper into the mine. Brodie was able to distinguish between the goblin miners and the human miners when they entered different mining pits. It appeared that the goblins would leave tools and ropes in dugouts in the walls; the only things the humans left behind were empty cages.

Curious about the things he observed as they passed through, Brodie caught up to Kol. He was taking large steps.

Concentrating on the steps he was taking, and the path underneath him, Brodie asked Kol, "Why don't the humans leave their things in the mines, too?"

Kol turned his torso to Brodie. The light from lamp created ghastly shadows across Kol's face and intensified his ugliness. It made Brodie jump.

Brodie stuttered the words out as Kol slowed his strides to maintain speed with the smaller boy. "W-Why don't the humans leave their equipment in the mines, too?" he asked again in a nervous tone.

"They don't leave their belongings behinds cause we nicks them. We lives here so we can do what we wants and keeps what we find."

"But why do you steal their tools? That must get frustrating," Brodie said. Grub gave him a nudge.

"The only other creatures who have got tools like the humans and better ones at that are the dwarfs, but our kinds don't see eye to eye," Kol explained.

"Why are there empty cages?"

"The humans 'ave weak lungs. Clearly, they're not meant to be down here. They cage the birds 'case there's toxic gasses in the tunnels they dig in. And they call us the cruel lot."

"What happens to the birds if there are toxic gasses?"

"They die," Kol replied, giving a menacing smile.

Brodie was a little disturbed by his answer and gruesome smile; he slowed his pace to walk with Grub, leaving Kol to lead once more.

The tunnels took them on long, twisted routes. Often, Kol would pull out an old worn map. Kol looked like he had trouble with reading.

Do goblins know how to read? Brodie wondered as they continued.

They stopped for a few moments or so, then carried on. The trickling and dripping of the water made him want to pee. Countless times, Brodie had little spasms from walking through large spider webs. He often felt the thin sticky threads cling to his face. He hated it.

"Should be just 'round this next turning," Kol whispered loudly.

A draft of cooler air sent a shiver down Brodie's spine. As the three walked slowly and quietly around the corner, lights bounced off the rocky walls. Both Grub and Kol turned to Brodie and ordered him to remain silent and close.

After they crept out from the darkness of the hole in the rocky wall, they entered a large dug-out tunnel. It was much larger than the miner's tunnel and more like a large hall. It was magnificent. The floor was laid with cobbled slate. Miniature streams and puddles inhabited its grooves. The three inched along the right side of the cold wall a few feet until they reached the opening of the hollow part of a cave.

Kol grew more nervous, sensing something was wrong. The slate-covered ground grew into a platform. A few feet ahead was a large underground river that looked a little rapid. A little stream branched from the river along the left side of them and exited the cave through an opening in the wall smaller than the one the three had just come from.

A cold, bony hand pushed Brodie tight against the walls and into the little shadow that was provided. Kol wore a serious expression as he pointed straight ahead across the river.

A little wooden raft bobbed on the water's surface. Behind the raft at the base of the cave's wall was a staircase that had been carved into the rock. The staircase detached halfway up into two separate staircases that joined on either side of a large rock balcony.

From the distance and in the dim light, at first Brodie could not see them, but then…

Brodie gasped in horror. "What are they?" He clapped his mouth, afraid his question would echo in the cave.

"Silver caps," Kol whispered back, not taking his eyes off them, "and just as vicious as they look!" he added.

Kol wasn't kidding. Two figures paced back and forth on the rock balcony in front of a large, oddly shaped wooden door. From a long distance away, they appeared almost human, but the harder Brodie focused on them in the dim-lit cave, the clearer they became. Their clothes looked like old stained potato sacks with holes torn for their arms and heads and a belt made of rope. Their bodies were thin and sickly looking, and both looked as though they had neglected personal hygiene centuries ago.

Brodie could not make out their faces clearly but thought their features resembled an angler fish. Their teeth curved inwards. They were hideous. Their hair was white and thin as a ninety-year old's; it hung across their shoulders like wet, greasy blankets. Brodie noticed both silver caps wore a piece of tarnished armor. One wore part of a mesh medieval-style shoulder-and-arm sleeve. The other wore a tarnished helmet. Its cage was bent outwards as if ripped from its placement, and it was dented on one side. The poor bugger that previously owned it must have taken a terrible blow to the head.

Both silver caps carried long axes and lite torches. They were obviously guarding the door. Brodie wondered if they were guards on duty protecting a kingdom of these ugly fishy-faced demons. His imagination grew wild with the thought of the society that lived beyond that wooden door.

Brodie looked around to observe his surroundings once more, this time trying to take in the detail. Above, the ceiling of the cave had been carved like detailed tiles. It looked like one of the large, decorated cathedrals from Rome.

Kol backed up ever so slightly, then turned, advising the other two that they should all leave. The cave was dimly lit by torches that were scattered along the walls in iron placements. They had to sneak along the cold shadowed stone walls, and one by one, they slipped back into the darkness without being seen. Slowly and quietly, they backed themselves along the walls, careful so as not to trip or be detected. Kol kept his eyes on the monsters as they left. Once they retrieved to the safety of the darkness, Kol paused for a moment.

They did not return to the tunnel. Instead, they decided to exit the cave through the smaller hole.

"We're gonna have to lower ourselves into the stream through the railings without getting caught," Kol instructed.

Grub decided to go first in order to direct Brodie through safely, leaving Kol to help the frightened boy from behind. They each climbed through the space, taking turns to go when the silver caps briefly turned their backs to them.

The drop was short, but it made a splash. Thankfully, the waters of the river behind them drowned out the noise they created. But they remained careful nevertheless and ducked after the drop.

Then they slipped through the narrow crack in the wall where the stream disappeared. When they were a bit of a distance away from the silver caps, Kol sighed in relief.

"Phew, had they got hold of us, they would 'ave ripped us apart on the spot!" Kol said.

"You say that like it's a good thing," Brodie said, slightly shaking, disturbed by Kol's statement and the images of the silver caps that lingered fresh in his mind.

"Well, let's put it this way, 'en those goblins are the worst kind there is. Doesn't matter if you're human or fairy or even another silver cap. If you cross them, they will tear you apart like a piece of bread wiffout a second thought."

"Why are they there? Do they live down here?"

"No, they don't. These caves are the mining goblin's territory, but funny thing is, there's no sign of another goblin. Somfins not right," suggested Kol.

Feeling a little out of breath, Brodie paused a moment, his hands upon his knees. "But what were they doing on that balcony?"

"They're guarding the door to the other realm. We will 'ave to use the Threshold Rock above ground," Kol said.

Brodie's feet were like icicles. They had been wet and cold for well over a couple of hours. He just wanted to go home; he wanted his mom more than anything. Well, actually, that bit was a lie. He really wanted a warm, dry pair of socks and shoes more than anything. His hands were icy and felt frostbitten, and he had trouble breathing in the confined space of the new tunnel.

"I thought this was that trash rock?" he asked as his teeth chattered together.

"There are three doors. One on the actual Threshold Rock above ground, and one underneath it, deep in the earth and an entrance in the lake!" Grub answered. Grub was now on all fours for better balance on the slippery rocks in the stream. His snout was held high in the air in case the depth plummeted.

The deeper into the narrow tunnel they went, the wider the tunnel became. The only light down here came from Kol's oil lamp. The angler fish features of the silver caps bothered Brodie in the darkness. Kol, too, was thinking about the silver caps. *They had no business down in that cave,* he thought.

He turned to Grub, holding the lantern in front of his face. "What do you think they are doing in there, and why do you think they're guarding the door?"

"Don't know! But there was two of 'em. I smell trouble. The quicker we get to the other entrance, the quicker we will find out," Grub said.

It was the first time the two conversed like they had a mutual understanding.

"Why is it bad there was two of them?" Brodie asked, not understanding the despair in both voices. "And why did they only have one item of armor on? That was a bit weird."

"The silver caps are singletons, which means they stick to themselves. Even when they partner up, after the female conceives, the male abandons the family shortly after the goblin child is of age. It, too, is abandoned by its mother. They are evil, evil creatures, finding joy in bloodshed and misery of others. It is extremely rare to see two males together without violence," Grub said, pausing in between sentences as he tried to avoid deep spots in the stream. "They usually wear the armor as trophies of the victims they have slaughtered. They only wear the armor of the strongest and fittest opponents they defeated."

Brodie thought about the helmet he had seen. The cage had been ripped out. The metal was jagged, sharp, and crushed and protruded outward in all directions. The side of the helmet had been completely dented in from a strong blow to the head so much that it did not fit right on the silver caps ugly head. He imagined the violent scene and the poor soldier that had suffered a barbaric death.

"Now that helmet is worn with the utmost savage pride," Grub said.

"Exactly," Kol added.

They followed the stream to a brightly lit opening. Grub and Kol were on guard; they cautiously popped their heads from the shadows of the cave. Brodie was happy. They were finally out. He could feel the rays of heat warming the icy-cold blood that ran through his veins. He tried to take in his surroundings, but the brightness of the sun pierced his eyes. He rubbed them as they burned in pain. Soon his eyes adjusted to the light and opened from their tight squint.

They came out the other side of the mountain, the stream run off down the hill side, connecting to a lake nestled in a hidden valley. "It's over there," he said loudly. "Follow me."

The three walked down the steep, grassy hillside. Grub, who remained in his badger form, was quickly at the bottom and sat patiently waiting for Kol and Brodie to join him on the ground. Brodie, on the other hand, tapped the bag that rested against his waist, making sure Kol hadn't stolen its contents in the dark mine below. Brodie had slipped onto his backside once or twice, and once they had reached near the bottom, he had lost his balance completely, causing him to roll down the remaining distance.

"Wow, up," Kol had called after the tumbling boy, who passed him with rolling giggles. It was the first time he had laughed in days. He got himself up, brushing the dirt and loose grass from his clothes.

Once they were joined by Kol, the three sat down to eat and rest amongst the tall grasses. Brodie pulled out jam sandwiches from the bag that he had made back in the barge. They were a bit squished but yummy.

The sun sparkled on the surface of the lake, and the wind shifted the clouds over them.

"Where are we?" Brodie asked.

"Um, Llyn Celyn," Kol belched out.

Why does that name sound so familiar? Brodie thought. He pondered on it for a few moments while eating his sandwich, then became distracted by Grub's voice.

"We only have a couple of hours of daylight left to find the door. We better get a move on."

The beautiful dragonfly darted around Kol and Brodie, then landed on Grub. It remained in its insect form, slowly moving its wings while it spoke in its musical chime, but there was something different about its behavior.

"No, how long?" Grub asked. He quickly turned, looking past Brodie and Kol to the hills behind them; both paid attention to his every move.

"What?"

Grub gave Brodie a very intense look. "They picked up our scent in the village. They know you're not with Mairwen anymore. A forest fairy directed them on our trail after spotting us on the barge." Grub looked up at the now clouded sky. "We still have a couple of hours to go."

"I'm going back into the mines. Not a single miner did we pass! Strange, I say. That's not a good sign. Be back in a bit." Kol got up, climbed the hill in large steps, then was gone.

"What time is it?" Brodie asked. He looked at the hills covered in long green-and-yellow grasses. The wind was beginning to pick up, and the clouds hid the sun, leaving the boy to shiver in his wet trainers that he had found in the closet of the barge they fit a little larger and he wished he had kept his wellies on.

"I think I saw a foxhole hidden in the grasses on the way down. We should rest in there till night fall. Change back," Grub ordered.

Remembering the warm, thick fur and the blanket-like tail, Brodie did not object. He removed the bag, replacing it over his sweater, then reached into the bag to grab onto the warm disk, wishing for his body to turn back into the fox. Soon enough, the boy felt the pins sprouting from his entire body and a cramping sensation in his muscles. It was not as bad as the first time but still very painful. In a matter of seconds, he transformed back into the handsome little red fox.

He felt much better already. Grub turned to the dragonfly, who had perched itself on a long grass.

"When and if Kol returns, tell him to wait by the water here for us and wake me if I am not already awake." He turned to the fox. "Come, let's wait for night fall."

Brodie bounced around after him, finding the hill no obstacle at all now.

CHAPTER 10

Midnight Passages

As Brodie followed Grub into an abandoned fox or badger hole, he reminded Grub that he was entitled to an explanation. Once snug in the den, Grub began, "I saved an injured draigate—"

"What's a draigate?" Brodie interrupted.

"If you stop interrupting me, you will find out," Grub said sternly. "A draigate is a baby dragon. They are a lot smaller than adult dragons but very strong. Back in the old days, any magical creatures had an instant death penalty. In order for the extinction of all our kind, the human kings demanded creatures were slayed on the castle grounds for rewards. The highest rewards went for dragon eggs and sprits that looked like human women. These rewards were large, usually a title to land and a fair bit of gold.

"My kind and the kind of many at the time found refuge in the hills and deep in the forests. I came across a group of villagers years back. They were beating something with clubs and their farming instruments. The thing they were beating gave loud painful cries. From the short ways away, I could see blood. The humans laughed. Evil things, they were, brutal back then, you see. About five of them joined in on the wickedness."

"What did you do?" the bothered boy asked, completely absorbed in Grub's story.

"Had to intervene, didn't I? Had to help the poor thing. No living creature in the worlds deserves that. So stepped in, I dids, use a little magic, scared away all the humans. One tried to grab the thing as they ran away, but it dropped. It must have been too heavy. But when I got there, it was a draigate, still in its egg."

"Oh, that's sad! Was it dead?" Brodie asked.

"Close to, barely alive. They smashed part of the shell. It was not even near ready to hatch either, so I took him home with me. My wife and I took care of it. I cleaned it up 'en left it in its remaining eggshell for days, I did, wrapped it up in a blanket and put it in a pot high over the fire and fed it hot, fermented honeydew and elderflower wine."

"What happened to it? Did it die?"

"No, it survived. It had been battered by the humans so bad though, it was missing an eye. Funny little thing almost destroyed my den. It was the most colourful I'd seen in a thousand years, burgundy. Because its growth cycle had been disturbed by those monsters, its one wing hadn't developed properly. I'd searched the hillside for its kind so I could take it back, but I fink the humans made off with the rest of the eggs."

"That's so sad. What happened to it?"

"In a village nearby where the mongrels lived, a great fire broke out one night. It consumed and destroyed the whole village. Our kind went to watch and celebrate. Mind you, many wanted to see the humans suffer and die. We stood in the thicket watching. Two large dragons swooped through the sky, streams of blue-green fire forced from their mouths incinerating the straw rooftops off the cottages below. And there he was…" Grub paused a moment as if reliving the moment in his head.

"Who was there, Grub?" Brodie said, a little agitated from the slight delay.

Grub yawned.

"Who?" Brodie demanded.

"Mabon Haul," he answered.

"What's that, or who is Mabon Hail?"

Grub gave a raspy laugh once more, displaying his little yellowish-mayonnaise-coloured teeth. It was a frightful sight, but Brodie was now very assured that the badger was not going to attack every time he saw this jagged sharp sight; Grub was merely smiling.

"Mabon Haul is the name for one of the old kind. The name means 'sun child.' You have already met his twin."   "Oh,   he's Mairwen's twin. She kind of told me about him. Are they identical?" Brodie asked.

"Very masculine, he looked like a god," Grub said as he tried to get comfy. "He approached me. He told me that the humans had slayed the majority of the dragons in the land, he said. The dragon that I had saved from death was one of its last kind, and he hid it in the hills. He had returned to collect his creature and punish the humans for their crimes, which was fine by me. Blasted thing drank its weight of my fire whisky and my spiced mead and set fire to my den many times. In exchange for my help with the draigate, he gave me a rare gift. A gift, he said, that would cause trouble if used for wrong reasons or met the wrong hands, he gave me a dragon scale. It holds such incredible power."

"What happened then?"

"He walked into the flames and was never seen again, not by me at least. The creatures of the forest sometimes spot him here or there, in meetings with his siblings or rescuing species. It is said they have to return to the forests and the deserts from time to time to recharge their energy. Some time later, those of us that possessed these rare gifts were approached by a group. The leader was a very polite man at first, very persuasive and cunning. He offered us wealth and power, but there was something about his energy, something evil. The way he spoke down to us, but also the greed he possessed, greed that was strong enough to reveal an aggressive and intimidating side to this demon. There weren't many of us. A few were charmed. Driven by hatred for the humans, with the thought of such power they would posses, they could rid the land of the parasites for good as the humans had done to our kind for thousands of years. They were the weak ones."

Grub was trying to get comfortable but became very cautious after smelling the stale air of the tunnelled den. He quickly crawled over to where Brodie was and reached into the bag. His whiskers twitched. He made a funny face, which made him look like he was constipated. His tongue curled up over his top lip as his eyes looked up in concentration. His paw searched fanatically through the bag; the straps pulled tight against Brodie's neck.

What was he looking for? the little fox wondered. *He finished all the milk.*

After obtaining the object, Grub was in a sudden rush. He disappeared out of the entrance they had just come through, both paws clutching a bottle.

"Where the hell has he gone now?" Brodie placed his furry head back onto the dirt ground.

A few moments later, he returned wearing a proud smile—again, a frightful sight.

"Where did you go?" Brodie asked.

"Giving hopper a quick task!" Grub answered as he circled a patch of gathered moss and loose grass. He lay down, closing his eyes and licking his nose in content.

"Who was the guy after you, Grub? What happened to you guys? Did you receive more power from him?"

"No. The foolish and weak few that gave into that villain were killed. After refusing and seeing the slaughter of the others, many fled into to the hills from fear. Dayton and his group began to kill for the items they were denied, power-hungry like you wouldn't believe."

"But doesn't your kind have magic? Couldn't they use their magic to protect themselves?" Brodie asked.

"The man behind the trouble was said to be Merlyn's older cousin from Merlyn's father's side. Both boys grew up without a father. In those days, to be fatherless was bad news. You and your family carried a horrible reputation. Sometimes, the king's soldiers took advantage of their authority and left the maidens of these villages behind with offspring. These women were single mothers left as common filth to others. In most cases, a couple eloped secretly to avoid punishment or taxes from the king or lord of that land.

Peasants often lost their secret husbands from being drafted to war or illness. The widows, therefore, left with their young and their reputations, grieving for their secret partners.

"Ahem," Grub cleared his throat. "The village women were terribly nasty to each other," he continued. "In order to scare and keep the husbands' wandering eyes from the newly single maidens, the town's wives would convict these poor women of treason and witchcraft and devilry.

"Once in a blue moon, a fairy or sprite would fall in love with a human. These children, they were unlike any other human child. They were mediums—humans with the power of our kind. Merlyn and his cousin were mediums."

"But I thought Merlyn was a wizard," Brodie said. Then he remembered the conversation his family had had the day that his gumpy first told him about magic.

"What do you think witches and wizards are, boy? Well, it was said that Merlyn's cousin, whose name was Dayton, possessed a different type of magic from Merlyn and not nearly as powerful as his famous cousin. They say Merlyn's magic was natural and very powerful. Whereas Dayton, he could only skip back and forth through time. He was said to be one of the most evil wizards ever. Through the ages, he has carried different names, Rasputin and so forth. He learnt a way to drain magic from others to help his power grow. It was a combination of people—Merlyn, Aanieda (Merlyn's younger sister), and another wizard—that stripped him of his powers and kept him prisoner inside a tree. Even today, you can sometimes see faces in the trees. They call them the green men, the faces of trapped prisoners.

"Merlyn put a spell on the old tree that if ever the tree was cut, releasing Dayton, the village would fall soon after. When Merlyn's tree is cut down, so shall tumble Carmarthen town. Long years passed by. Locked in the tree, Dayton watched the others wither and die with age. Then one day, the tree was cut down, releasing its prisoner. Shortly after, the town flooded.

"Dayton tried to take the power from our kind, and don't ask me how he did it either. It's much too nasty to think about," Grub said, shaking his head low and disapprovingly. "But a little bit of brownie or pixie magic here or there were mere buttons to what he had possessed previously. He craved more power it was rumoured he traveled to different countries, studying the dark arts of different cultures. When he returned, he brought back a group. They looked as if they were straight from the dirty thirties—they became his henchmen. They had a unique power of their own. Each country has their own different elves and fairy folk closely related to those here but different in appearance and magic. Like us, his henchmen could transform. They were humans that could change in an instant to pumas; some were racoons, some coyotes, and his personal bodyguards are wolves."

"So he has werewolves as bodyguards?" Brodie paused for a second. His ears lowered as he retraced something in his thoughts. "How ironic. The night we hit you, I made a joke that we hit a werewolf."

"Maybe you have a little magic to you because you almost did," Grub said in a playful, sarcastic tone. "Not as werewolves you think, or as the kind the humans have created in fantasies. These beasts as we know them don't burst into wolves from full moons or infect humans with their bites. His henchmen are worse. They instantly turn at will as you turned into a fox, but they don't need a dragon scale to help them. Dayton would send his men after us, and they would scent us out to our deaths. I'm good as gone, but if they catch you, he will kill you just for getting involved."

"What about my family?" Brodie asked.

"Safe for now. As I said, Hopper's been keeping an eye on them. They're being guarded," Grub said. As he finished his sentence, the large beige grasshopper crawled through the entrance; she spoke in her musical language.

As Grub and the grasshopper conversed, a strange noise caught Brodie's ear: heavy breathing and heavy footsteps. It came from behind them in one of the tunnels of the foxhole.

The small fox got up to see what was causing the noise. At first, a light bobbed back and forth and up and down, growing slowly brighter. Brodie's heart grew to a rapid beat but tamed when he heard Kol's cursing.

The tunnel was large enough for Kol to crouch through. "Bloody tiny thing. Whoever made this tunnel needs to stop shaming its species and leave the digging to the miners," Kol grumbled.

He entered the area where the fox and badger watched him. Brodie had walked over to greet him, and Grub resumed his conversation with Hopper, but all eyes were still on the goblin.

"Any luck?" Brodie asked.

"Not a single one left! Equipment all over the place, but not a single goblin! Gone, disappeared, no trace!" Kol said as he scratched his face with his rag.

"Where do you think they have gone? Do you think they have gone to a different mine?" Brodie asked.

"No, I don't know why they would leave the hill. It has the most gold and this is home. The only ones left in the mines are the silver caps, a big scruffy dog, one funny-looking human, and a woman, beautiful she was. She said she was looking for her baby, probably taken by the Twyleth Teg, poor sods!"

Brodie shot a sharp glance to Grub, who met his stare.

Grub got up on his hind legs and wobbled quickly over to Kol; one paw grabbed Kol's vest. "What?" he demanded, snarling. "Repeat what you just said."

Brodie's ears stood on end. He began to quiver as he rocked back and forth.

"All right, no need to get pushy, blimey." Kol wiped off his vest and explained. "Well, I fought it was odd not one bloody goblin in the tunnels, but equipment and lamps left on the ground. So, I know my ways around, you see, so figures I would just check to see if the silver caps had a hand in their disappearance. It was an odd sight, seeing those two working next to each other, no bloodshed or nought. So, I crept back through the tunnels till I reached them. Only when I gets there, they weren't there alone, you see." Kol paused to wipe the sweat from his bony forehead.

"Go on," Grub demanded.

"All right," Kol said as he shoved the rag back into his sleeve. "A human couple and their dog said they were looking for their child. Odd thing was the silver caps didn't attack them. I was waiting for the kill, but nothing. It felt wrong. It's not their ways, you see, especially humans. Hates them, they do!"

"What did they look like?" Grub asked, looking at the fox, who sat rocking back and forth.

"The woman was beautiful—for a human at least. Long, dark hair didn't see to much of her face but one time she turned, she was really pretty like and had on a black and white coat. Oh yeah, she had a gold and—um, what was it now? Right, a gold frog that moved about on her coat."

Brodie stood and paced to and fro. "Maybe it's Gumpy and my mum." He became excited of the idea, but he felt awkward. "My mum, she's come to find me."

Grub ignored Brodie and insisted that Kol continue.

"The husband was all in black. He was a strange one, and his dog a big furry thing. Haven't seen dogs like that in Wales since long times ago. Kept looking at the river while the humans talked, kept looking where we was against the rocks earlier. Think the man was a bit bonkers, caught him having a full-blown conversation wiff his mut. Not like the conversations the human miners have wiff their dogs. No, looked liked he thought the beasty could talk back."

"Where did they go, Kol? Did they see you?" Grub asked anxiously. Hopper took off through the entrance of the den.

"I fought the dog saw me or heard me, but it got distracted when the silver caps pulled a bit of commotion. So, I came straight here before the Threshold Rock closes, and I missed you two."

"We have to go now. How far are we from the rock?" Grub asked.

"Not far at all," the goblin replied.

"You lead the way," Grub ordered.

Kol quickly shuffled his way through the tight tunnel. He had to put down his lamp to squeeze through and grab onto the long grasses to pull himself free from the tight entrance. He froze for a moment and looked around on the deserted hill into the lonely, dark, cold night. The coast was clear, so he got to his feet and carefully climbed down the steep hill.

Then out popped Grub's head. He smelled the air and started to follow Kol but paused to wait for Brodie. Brodie came out of the den; the tattered old bag was still in his possession. He raced out into the open thicket of the hill blanketed by the darkness of the night. Grub pulled his bushy little tail back and whispered, "Be quiet, follow me, and stay low." The two followed the goblin to the waterfront.

Dong, dong, dong. A distant sound froze the little fox in mid-step. His ears perked up as he concentrated on the sound.

"It's the tolls of the bell from the chapel," Grub said, noticing the fox had paused.

"I can hear it," Brodie said as they swiftly reached the water's edge. They continued forwards, following the goblin. *It's the most beautiful sound,* Brodie thought.

"Where is the chapel?" he asked Grub, looking around behind them to the hills.

"Down in the blackest depth of the waters," Grub replied, pointing to the lake.

The dragonfly soared over their heads, her wings gently clapping together.

Kol yelled back, "Hurry up. It'll be gone soon."

They raced around the lake, keeping to the water's edge, until they were on the opposite side from where they had started. The hills were bare; the long grasses swayed in the midnight wind; and the smell of grasses, earth, and the fermenting debris that had washed up on the shore of the lake was overpowering. The only sounds Brodie could hear were the deep breathing of his two companions, the grasses and reeds rustling in the wind, the water kissing the shore, and the tolling of the bells from deep below the lake.

In the close distance, Kol had stopped at a large rock that sat upright. It was placed directly on the water's edge. A strange light emanated from the rock. It was a bright light shaped like a pinstripe that shone out of a rectangle-shaped dark spot centered on the rock. As he approached closer, he was able to make out more details of the strange sight. The light from behind the rectangular darkness was shining from behind an old wooden door. The door had a rustic, circular door knocker that was centered, its hinges were fastened into place by rustic iron ivy that spread along the door from its hinges.

Everything emanated a slight green light. From the base of the rock grew patches of daffodils that appeared to sparkle slightly in the darkness. Kol opened the heavy-looking wooden door and word-lessly walked through. Grub put a paw against the door, holding it open for Brodie.

"Brodie, Brodie, no!"

The sudden scream prevented the fox from taking another step. He turned his head in the opposite direction. His ears stood upright as he moved towards the noise. Grub transformed quickly to restrain him.

There on the hill across from where the rock was positioned stood a figure. In one hand she held up a little light that revealed her dark checkered jacket. But not enough light was provided to detail her appearance. It did not matter. Brodie could tell by her voice it was his mother, Katrin.

"Mum," he yelled out.

"Come to me, baby," she beckoned into the darkness of the night.

Brodie struggled, trying to free himself of Grub's tight grip around his body. "Let go," he barked. "It's my mum. She needs me. She's found me." He tried to nip at the hands that held him tight.

"No!" Grub replied. He struggled to control the wild kit in his arms. "It's a trick. It's not her, Brodie. Please trust me on this. Look past her, Brodie!"

Brodie could not see past his now sobbing mother. She held a lamp in one hand. it looked like she was holding something else against her side in her other hand.

"Brodie, please, Daddy and I, we miss you. Please come, baby. Mummy will take you home back to Granddad's away from all this nonsense."

Wait a minute! Brodie thought. Never once in his life had he ever heard his mother refer to her father as *Granddad*. Everything felt so familiar; he had been here before. He felt an icy shiver run under-neath his fur along his spine as he relived this déjà vu. He had been here before, but in his darkest dreams, he was always alone when he faced this demonic woman who posed as his mother. He began to shake as he revisited the memory of his nightmares. He stopped wriggling and hung limp in Grub's arms in shock. He wanted to get away from this scene. There was no waking up now, and he knew what was to come.

Despite what he knew, his heart felt otherwise. He longed for his mother. The rise and fall of her tone of voice was unbearably similar, even the way she sobbed.

Grub raised a pointed finger to where the woman stood. From the middle of the hill, she stood pleading for her son to return to her, but on the hilltop where Grub pointed, two large animals stood patiently waiting.

Brodie let out a small gasp as both beasts disappeared. The pleas grew impatient, and the sobs grew to demands. "Baby, come here this instant, right now! I have been worried sick. Get over here now or—" She began to walk towards them slowly.

Brodie gave a little whimper as he said, "That's not my mum. Go, now," recalling what was to come next. Had it really been his mum, he would have been suffocating in her arms by now. She would have run over to him. He exhaled.

With that, Grub turned and walked towards the door, patting Brodie on the back empathetically with one hand. Brodie, who was still in Grub's arms, rested his head against his friend's shoulder and took one last look at the impostor who looked and sounded identical to his mother.

He whimpered slightly as he suddenly caught sight of three large dark beasts racing towards them. Their claws gripped into the earth as the vicious shadow's got closer and closer; they caused the little fox to jump in fear. But it was too late. The door had closed. By the time they would reach the rock, the passageway would be gone entirely, leaving the impostor and the beasts locked out on the other side.

Back in the human realm, days before these events, a very bored Rhys walked around his auntie's garden, looking at the creepy little porcelain dwarves that inhabited the little garden. He walked over to the pond, where the large goldfish sucked the surface of the water in hopes of being fed.

Rhys could hear his daughter a short distance away with his aunty Winifred talking about the secret lives of the gnomes, how really, they came to life when nobody was watching and how Pipper the cat had caught and almost eaten one the other day.

Rhys rolled his eyes and chuckled. He had so much love for the old lady. He lowered himself to the ponds edge the grout between the stone tiles needed fixing.

CHAPTER 11

Another Realm Entirely

When the three walked through the portal, they stepped from a bare and lifeless scene. Lonely hills rolled for as far as the eye could see, hills that were the only companions to the isolated lake.

Brodie could not recall being lowered to the ground, but felt his mouth fall open in awe as they stepped through a door and he absorbed his new surprising surroundings. The door with the rustic ivy hinges had disappeared completely, leaving the rock rough, gritty, and bare.

The sight that had captured Brodie's breath and caused his adrenaline to pump through his arteries with pure excitement was the lake was now surrounded by lit trees. The trees were mixed species, they grew across the hills like a patched blanket lain across a bed. Their leaves were full and bushed out. From the sporadic light patches in the trees, Brodie could see hints of colours.

The beautiful golds, oranges, reds, yellows, and browns of the leaves were lit with warm glowing lights similar to twinkle lights on a Christmas tree. The lights floated aloft in the trees like thistledown seeds in the breeze. The once-dark waters now revealed a blue light that shadowed shapes of old buildings from its secret depths below. Everything felt magical, from the twinkling trees to the lights in the deep waters of the lake to the smell of harvest, cinnamon, nutmeg, baked goods, and many other gathered spices that were enticing, deliciously rich, and intoxicating.

"Welcome to our realm," Kol said with his arms outstretched, smiling. Kol pointed to the trees "Fairy's" he told the little fox.

Excitedly, Brodie continued to look around him. The ground was completely covered in leaves. The only part of the ground that was free from the debris was the lake and a narrow path that had been cleared.

"Come on, let's get a move on. We are much safer for now, but there are creatures here that we should avoid," said the short, dumpy, hairy little man who walked towards the path, seeming to know exactly where he was going.

Grub's new figure would need a little getting used to. Brodie was so used to his animal form and a little embarrassed to inform the changeling that his hairy butt crack was exposed.

Grub had no idea what time it was. All he knew was it had to be around midnight for the door to open to this realm. Grub led the way while frequently assuring the two that followed their destination was just up ahead.

The twinkling lights in the trees and the illuminated lake were soon out of sight and replaced by darkness. It was dark and chilly, but Brodie's thick red coat kept him warm. The rich aromas that occupied the air made his mouth salivate. Not only did the scent make his mouth water, but it prompted what felt like painful jabs in his stomach—jabs of hunger.

They continued on the path for some time. Grub would smell the air, making sure they were going the right way and not being followed. Or maybe it was just an animal trait that was very dominant in grub.

"We should be there soon."

Wherever we are going, it feels like we have been walking for days, Brodie thought he felt whiney and exhausted.

The path was leading them into a darker, thicker part of the forest. Without fairies to brighten up the trees or light up the way, it was dark and spooky. Kol, who was walking close to Brodie, let out an irritated sigh as he reached for his lamp and noticed it was not there.

"My lamp! Where's my lamp?" Kol asked aloud.

Grub looked directly at Brodie and shook his head.

Brodie noted this action, then turned to where Kol had stopped. "Where did you have it last?" the little fox asked.

"Bugger, thoughts I 'ads it down in the mines! Wait, I did," the goblin said.

"Maybe you dropped it in the portal when we crossed through," Brodie said.

"Yeah, maybe. It was my favorite lamp. Crafted by the mountain elves, I won it, on a bet! That's a'right. Sad thing that. Just have to find another elf to make another, that's all," Kol said disappointedly.

The two continued to walk, catching up to Grub. Kol was taller than Brodie when the child was in his animal form. He had grown accustomed and very fond of the new fox body. He felt swift and powerful. He had been just a regular little boy before now. *Well, as regular as a child with autism could be,* he thought, and then he sighed.

"I'm sorry about that woman," Kol said, deeply apologetic. "It must have been really hard for you there."

The reminder was unbearable and felt like a burn in the pit of his inner core. He missed his mum so much. To Kol, he compared the disappointment of the impostor to a handsome and enticing gift that once opened turned out to be a pair of mouldy old socks.

"I don't mind old socks, never was one for cleaning too often, have all the ladies after me then, wont I?" the goblin explained.

"I can tell. I can smell you a mile away, your doing a great job of keeping the girls back," Brodie giggled.

"Why you cheeky bloody bugger…," Kol replied with a smile, reaching over to swat the swift, dodging fox.

Both Kol and Brodie thought this journey would never end. But then the three stopped in a small break in the forest; the path had led to a wooden gate. Although Brodie's new foxy eyes had night vision, the house behind the gate looked nothing more than a tree stump covered with reeds and a mound of earth packed around it. The fallen tree limb was still attached and housed with large white fungi. Two round holes brightly lit from within suggested that this earthy mound was in fact somebody's home.

Grub turned to look at the two with his hands upon his knees, trying to catch his breath from the never-ending walk. He was not as young as the others; it was easy to see Grub was used to his animal form.

"Right 'en, we'll stay here for a few days till we figure out what our options are and how close in pursuit our friends are of us."

"Where are we? Whose home is this?" Kol asked before suggesting they take shelter in the coal mines.

"My cousin Llyr. His hospitality will be a comfort after this night's commotion," Grub said.

Brodie looked down, remembering the imposter and the sneakily approaching beasts.

A wooden door opened. Out popped the head of a pudgy little weasel. Both Grub and the weasel walked towards each other with their arms outstretched and embraced in a bear hug.

"Did you get my message?" Grub asked as he transformed back into the badger to get through the door.

"Yes, she arrived yesterday. She was very much afraid. She was being followed, so she went with her intuition and passed the message along, which obviously I received. Food is ready, welcome to my home," the weasel announced as he urged the three to enter the warmth of his little hut with a courteous bow. He turned from Grub to face the others. Both Brodie and Grub thanked Llyr.

Llyr's furry little smiling expression and tone of voice drastically changed as he latched eyes on the mining goblin. His tone was low as he leaned towards Grub. "Urgh, a goblin. Really, cousin? Vile, filthy creatures."

Both Brodie and Kol overheard the distasteful comment. Brodie looked up to Kol. He pitied the goblin and was worried about how Kol might react. Nobody liked to be talked about and made unwelcome.

But Llyr's attitude did not seem to bother the soot-covered goblin, who was now wearing a huge smile as if he were faced with a challenge.

Brodie did not know what to make of this strange reaction and continued to walk inside the hut.

"Ah, yes, Llyr, this is Kol, our friend we made on the run," Grub replied, ignoring the comment.

Kol walked through the archway of the door and shone a yellow-stained smile at the little weasel.

Once Kol passed, Grub promised Llyr he would explain at a more convenient and private time.

Kol turned with a rather concentrated stare. "What the 'ell is that smell?" His face scrunched in dislike. He smelt around him and looked at the pudgy little weasel. "Oh, that's gonna take getting use to, that is," he said as he turned his nose up at Llyr.

Llyr started to open his mouth, but Grub held a paw up and shook his head. "Not now. We have loads to discuss. We need him close by," Grub said as he made himself comfortable on a large wooden chair covered with hay.

Llyr shut the door, urging everybody to the fire to warm themselves with a glass of dandelion wine. The wine definitely had a peculiar taste and a rather bitter aftertaste, but Brodie threw it down his throat. It had a rather warm sensation.

The hut wasn't much to the eye from the outside, but within it was warm and cozy, very inviting. A fire cracked and climbed into the contained area of the stone fireplace. All of the furniture had been handcrafted from wood. Celtic knots were finely carved and detailed into the legs of the tables and chairs. Little tin and brass spoons hung above the mantel piece. Long wooden chairs filled with fresh hay and covered with thick wool throws were positioned around the fire. The walls were bare of colour; it looked as though dry mud had been used to cover the interior. On the other side of the den, a second fireplace was maintained in what looked like Llyr's kitchen. It was a smaller fireplace but large enough to fit the large pot that hung from a hook. Brass pots of all sizes hung across the far wall. The kitchen tabletop was thick and resembled an old wooden cutting board; it was covered with dim candlelight and the bottle of dandelion wine.

Llyr disappeared to a corner where his bed was boxed in by a wooden frame with doors. A moment later, he approached the three with an armful of thick wool blankets. He distributed a blanket to everyone except for Kol; he merely dumped Kol's blanket over his head.

Kol, who found the situation amusing, smiled, wrapped himself up, and walked over to the kitchen table to retrieve the dandelion wine bottle.

Llyr then handed out hot bowls of cabbage and leek soup. Llyr sat down to join his company and eagerly listened to the adventures the three had faced.

Brodie laughed as Kol downed the bottle of wine, trying to quench his thirst without any luck. "You remind me of my gumpy," the fox said to the goblin as he moved the larger vegetables around with his spoon.

"I likes," the dozy and inebriated goblin hiccupped he was about to say something but continued to drink. Shortly after, Kol had consumed the remains of the bottle, nothing but deep loud snores were to be heard from him.

"Well, now he's asleep. I should bring out the good stuff." Llyr reached into a cupboard and retrieved a dark bottle of cedar cherry ale. Brodie was denied a glass of this sweet-smelling ale by Grub, as it was made by the fairies.

Llyr had not thought about the consequences of feeding a human fairy foods and wines. Grub explained to the small fox, "If a single drop of that touches your lips, you will never be able to leave this realm unless you have permission from the fairy queen! And nobody knows where she has gone. Been gone a long time. Rumours have it, she was kidnapped!"

"What news, cousin?" Llyr asked. He was a lot more chipper from the sight of the sleeping goblin on the soft dirt ground.

Brodie was thankful that Grub had entered his life. Yes, he wouldn't have been parted from his family had the changeling not crossed their path, but because he had, Brodie had been introduced to a whole new, exciting, magical world, a world he felt deep down he belonged to. Plus, Grub was very protective of him. He wondered if Kol, trickster that he was, would have said anything about the fairy-made whine.

He smiled. He watched the flames of the fire dance to a rhythm of their own. From drinking close to his weight in dandelion whine, his eyes grew heavy, and soon his surroundings grew dark. Brodie joined Kol in a peaceful sleep, leaving Grub and Llyr to a private discussion.

❧

Though Grub had sent Llyr short messages through the fairies, for the remainder of the night, he recited their nerve-racking adventures and their many close encounters with their foes.

Grub looked over to the chair where the bushy little red fox had curled up in a peaceful slumber in front of the fire, still wearing the tattered old bag.

He gave a quiet chuckle; he was just as thankful for Brodie as Brodie was for him.

"There's something almost magical about that boy," Grub told Llyr.

Brodie opened his eyes. He was still exhausted but had been awoken by the irritatingly loud rumbles of the goblin. Brodie looked over to find that Kol was spread across the floor with his mouth wide open; drool ran down the side of his face, glistening in the light of the fire.

He looked up at the mantle for some sort of indication as to what time it was. He gave up and rested his head down on the chair again. Grub and Llyr were still in conversation. He tried not to eavesdrop, but it was hard not to.

"Well, I used the last of my troll's breath, gonna need a refill along with a few other things."

"You can get that at the boot market tomorrow," Brodie heard Llyr reply.

"Good! We will have to be careful. He has spies all over the place I'm told, if it weren't for that poor lad, they'd have 'ad me."

"Oh, it's horrible. He's not been seen here, but rumours have it that he's united with the Gragged Anywn."

"No! Get, that can't be! I don't believe that for a second," Grub replied in horror.

"Yes, that's the rumour, and what's more, he has united with Teagan. It hasn't been safe, cousin. That's for sure. Large wolf-like wolves have been spotted around our parts! Folk have gone missing. Even the banshees have disowned the roads at night. Everyone keeps to themselves now. It's almost like the calm before the storm," Brodie heard Llyr say.

"Llyr, I can believe Teagan would get caught up with him. She always had an evil, wicked streak about her, and she is a witch just like him. Whatever that nerdwaiden is up to, I bet it's no good. We are all in trouble. It's a treny. I've dragged that lad into this."

"What's a naiden?" a small voice asked from the chair across the room. He could not pronounce the word that had been used.

Llyr coughed on a mouthful of ale. After almost choking, he composed himself, holding his paw over his mouth.

"Achem, nosey, what are you doing up?" Grub's voice came from across the room of the den where he was sitting at the table.

"You try sleeping next to that." Brodie looked down to the sprawled-out goblin.

"He has a point, cuz. If the noise doesn't get you, the smell sure will," Llyr replied.

"I had a nightmare, and I have to use the little fox's room."

"Right, it's outside, 'round the back." Llyr got up to lead the way. He lit a small lamp similar to Kol's and left the hut with the fox. It was a clear enough night that Brodie did not need the lamp, but it was a comfort. They walked along a path that branched off behind the fallen part of the tree where a little wooden shed stood in the cold dark night. Brodie found it much easier to cock his leg against one of the nearby trees than to squat on his hind legs in the enclosed dark shed.

Once back in the warmth of Llyr's den, he fell back to sleep. Witches and demons and wolves weaved through his dreams for the remainder of the morning. Meanwhile, Grub felt responsible and very guilty that the small boy had overheard their conversation and was concerned of the fears he might have accidently planted in Brodie. He was a very unusual little human.

It was quiet, dark, and peaceful. But the stillness was suddenly broken by a loud distraction. Brodie turned to it.

"Brodie, Brodie, no!" The sudden scream stopped the boy mid-step.

In the distance in front of him stood a figure in the black of the night; a bright light in her hand was held high. Her face was oval and extremely pale, framed with dark, wavy hair that swept across her back in the breeze. Her eyes appeared for a split second warm, loving, and familiar. Then they turned cold, dark, and tormented in an evil way. She stood glaring at the small boy. The corner of her lips raised into a twisted, menacing smile.

"Mum, what's wrong?" Brodie asked. He was a stranger to this demonic-looking woman.

"Come to me," she beckoned into the darkness of the night. Her voice was cool and hollow. Brodie tried to run from her but could not seem to move. The muscles in his legs felt weak and heavy. As he tried to run, the darkness around him did not move.

Her loose, wavy hair had turned into matted dreadlocks. The dreads appeared snake-like as they quickly slithered themselves into a messy bun that sat at the back of her head. Her beautiful oval face was no longer, her button nose grew crooked and hook-like, and her thick pouty lips shrivelled up, leaving a wrinkled paper-slice of a mouth in its place.

The black-and-white jacket disappeared. A stained and ripped brown dress covered the hag that now stood before him. His eyes fell upon the emerald-and-gold frog pin. Its limbs twitched. The emblem vibrated, then cracked open. From within the emerald shell emerged a fenland green frog. Its slimy skin contained black markings. The thing croaked as it climbed from the hag's chest to her shoulder. Its eyes were golden and fixated on the boy.

The lamp that had been held high in her hand had disappeared and been replaced with a branch-like, rickety, old, tethered broom; its bristles were made of thin twigs.

Brodie gasped in fear. He tried to step back but could not move. He was planted to the ground. He looked down to his runners then quickly looked up to the approaching figure. She reached a bony hand towards the boy, gripping the air, trying to get the child.

Brodie gasped again. Gasping for air; he took deep lungsful. His little fox body quivered with fear, rapidly moving from his panting.

"Yes, I had that same reaction, too, when I saw him this morning. I would much prefer a brownie," Llyr said, gesturing to show his comment had been directed towards Kol.

Kol, who had duly noted this, smiled and chuckled to himself, probably plotting some horrendous trick to play on the cheeky weasel at a later time.

"It was a nightmare but different from the ones I've had before." All eyes rested on the fox.

Grub carried a large wooden pail to the kitchen table. He darted over to the side of the chair, concerned for the quivering little fox.

"Are you okay?" he asked.

"Yeah, just a bad dream," Brodie replied.

They all sat at the table for breakfast—a hot serving of cow's cream—which Brodie was not allowed to have because the cattle had been born from an elf cow. The food it produced was fairy food. Brodie dined on freshly baked bread and water.

Llyr apologized to Brodie for the lack of breakfast. The bread was warm and crusty on the outside, when pulled apart, it was soft on the inside. Butter would have been welcomed, but even the butter came from the cow.

Llyr began talking about forbidden foods again, but Brodie tuned him out as he drifted off into his bubble.

He stared at the dirt ground, trying to make sense of the nightmare. The woman's appearance had drastically changed. It had not been the usual nightmare he'd had a hundred times before.

"Mmm." The smell of the rich cream was deliciously inviting. He raised his nose to the air, taking it in.

Kol, who sat opposite from Brodie at the table, observed this and teased the poor kit with the forbidden food as a child torments another child with a desired toy. Of course, he was only playing, and

Brodie could see that. Llyr declared Kol a complete moron when Kol continued teasing Brodie by licking the bowl and savouring every drop.

"Did-Did you just call me a carrot, stinky? Well, now you're confusing me. Animal, vegetable, or mineral, what am I?" Kol smirked as he questioned Llyr.

"That's enough, you two," Grub said.

"But he's calling me a carrot, a bloody carrot of all things," Kol playfully argued back in a thick Welsh accent.

"We all have to get along. We have rough roads ahead of us, no time for immature differences."

Kol looked at Llyr, raising his eyebrows, and gave him a stern look as if Grub's message was for Llyr only. The weasel merely rolled his eyes and shook his head. Brodie giggled.

After breakfast, Grub, Brodie, and Llyr knelt on the ground in front of the fireplace. Kol stood up from the table where he had been carving a piece of wood with an old, rusty, and dirty-looking knife. He walked to the front door, announced he would be back in a tic, and then left, shutting the door behind him.

Grub asked for the bag, and Brodie passed it to him. Grub nonchalantly turned to the wall where the door stood sandwiched between two windows to make sure Kol had gone and not peeking through the thin glass. He then emptied the contents of the bag onto the woven rug in front of the cooling embers.

Llyr's little black eyes opened wide as he looked down at the dragon scale. The scale was as large as a tea saucer. Brodie had faintly remembered it being a copper, but next to the fire, it appeared to be rose gold with small green and bronze flecks. It was amazing. It was beautiful. It was the first time Brodie had properly set his eyes upon this magical object. He tried to imagine the beast that had shed this scale but could only think of the red dragon on the Welsh flag.

As he stared at it, something caught his attention. He looked down into the scale and watched fire dance in its shimmering beauty, but the fire had long gone out in the fireplace. He could have sworn he saw the shimmer gather and form faint images across the face of the plate.

His focus was broken when the tattered bag was thrown over the scale by Grub. Brodie looked up.

"We have to be careful. It's a rare treasure that has to be protected at all times."

Llyr got up and rummaged in his cupboard. A moment later, he returned with a folded cheese cloth. Grub quickly and delicately wrapped the scale, then placed it back into the bag.

Slam. "It's bloody cold out there. We're due for snow shortly," Kol said, rubbing his hand along his arms.

"Thought goblins can't feel the cold?" Llyr asked suspiciously.

"Well, not really, but I was thinking about the lad. He's human, in' he?"

"Well, we should go to the boot market soon. When Dayton's lot cross over, that will be the first place they look for us," Grub said as he rummaged through the contents of the bag that lay across the floor. Kol nosily peered over his shoulder to catch a glimpse of the guarded treasures. Grub picked up oddly shaped bottles and frantically shook them, listening to the remaining contents.

"Oh, please don't open that in here. It will take days to remove that smell. It's bad enough a goblin's here. It's going to take just as long to rid his stench," Llyr said, eyeing the bottle of troll's breath.

"Hmm, definitely need s'more troll's breath," he said, placing the empty bottle back into the bag.

"Oh, too bad Stinky doesn't have his own line. His stench is far more offensive," Kol said, chuckling as he resumed his seat at the wooden table, ignoring Llyr's previous remark.

"Ha, ha, funny, aren't you, Goblin?" said Llyr.

"Can be," the goblin replied as he smiled and continued to carve, refusing to look away from the piece of wood in his hand.

After sifting through what was needed from the boot market and what was garbage, like the empty milk bottles, they got ready to head out. After a strange look from Grub, Llyr asked Kol to help him bring in a heap of coal for the night since the weather was soon to change. Kol, who was the master of coal, jumped at the chance to impress the little weasel with his diverse knowledge of the rock. They left, leaving Grub and Brodie to pick up the fragments of litter.

"Okay, we haven't got much time. He will be back in a sec," Grub explained as he transformed to his elfish self. "If Dayton's lot have crossed over, they will be looking for a badger and a fox. You are going to have to change back," he said.

Brodie reached into the bag, shuffling his way through an open crease of the cheese cloth. He clutched onto the warm scale and instantly transformed back into his twelve-year-old self.

"Wow, that was quick," the newly human boy said, looking at the fingers of his hands.

"Yes, that was," Grub said in an awkward tone.

Outside, it was a brisk, cool morning; the overcast sky hung heavily. They began to walk. Grub passed Brodie back the bag, urging him to keep it around his shoulder under his wool sweater. When Grub had left the den, he'd grabbed a cloak. He called out to Llyr and Kol to leave the coal and join them to the market. Llyr raced to Grub's side, complaining of the vile goblin and inquiring the length of his stay in a rather fed-up and worried manner.

"Well, you do start it," Grub responded, laughing.

Llyr, who was about to retaliate, stopped as he caught sight of the human child. Llyr quickly ran back to the den, having forgotten his money, and soon returned with a small pouch.

Brodie smiled, then turned to see what was taking Kol so long. He was dawdling behind with a mixture of boredom and sadness overshadowing his behavior. After spotting this behavior, Brodie stopped to wait for phim. Upon seeing this, the goblin's walk became a little more chipper. The four followed the path of the fallen coloured leaves through the forest until it disappeared.

CHAPTER 12

The Boot Market

The air was crisp and fresh; a slight wind blew from the east, causing a never-ending shower of the yellow, red, orange, and brown leaves. Brodie was in awe of the vibrant colours; he recited many facts about trees and the many other plant specimens that interested the other three.

They continued to walk. He felt a breeze along his back and wished he was in his fox coat again. The thick fur had kept him snug as a bug in a rug. Grub and Llyr walked side by side, leaving a peppier Kol as company for Brodie. The goblin was whistling away, quiet and content.

Often, Llyr turned to glare at the irritating sound, but Kol continued.

"Why does he dislike you so much? You haven't done anything to him. It's a bit rude, really," Brodie said.

"Well, he doesn't like me because I'm drop-dead gorgeous." The boy giggled at the goblin's remark. "No, he doesn't like me because he thinks I nicked his fuwch a few years back!"

"What's a fu—" The boy could not pronounce it right. It came out as a rather obscene word.

The goblin laughed. "A fuwch is the Welsh word for cow, but the Welsh cow in this realm are elfin animals and very sacred."

"Ah." The boy nodded, understanding. "Did you nick his cow?"

Kol smiled a large toothy grin, then said, "Who, me? Never, never nicked a thing in my life." He quickly raised and lowered his coarse black eyebrows.

"I think he's really rude to you and he's judging you for wrong reason" he said to the goblin compassionately.

Thing is nobody like goblins, not really fare but there we are en" Kol responded a hint of sadness to his tone.

"I know how you feel, I used to freak out a lot I had to wear a specialty helmet so I wouldn't smash my skull, people would look at me like I didn't belong that my mother should have disciplined me I couldn't help it, lots of things set me off like sounds, people staring, smells my clothes not feeling right. So I know how you feel and for what it's worth I really like goblins, just not those silver caps." Kol smiled at the boy.

Brodie laughed as the goblin began to sing. Brodie liked the playful trickster. He reminded the boy of his gumpy. He even looked a bit like his gumpy, too.

"My gumpy was a miner when he was younger."

"I like him already," the smiling goblin said.

"I think he was a rope spicer."

The goblin laughed at the enthusiasm for conversation the boy had. It had been ages since another person or fairy besides the other mining goblins had ever given him so much attention. "You mean splicer?" he corrected.

"That's what I said, splicer," Brodie said, smiling back. "You worked in the mines? What did you do?"

Kol reached deep into his pocket pouch and pulled out a handful of shiny rocks. The rocks were rich gold with a hint of rose.

"Is that—? Are they real gold?" Brodie was amazed by the treasure. He had seen similar rocks in Western movies.

"Aye, nuggets, the lot of 'em, solid gold. The Welsh mines produce the best gold in the world."

Kol reached over to the taller boy and dropped a few nuggets into his pocket. Shocked, Brodie tried to return the nuggets, but Kol refused. "Call it a birthday prezzy," he said.

"But it's not my birthday."

"Okay, your un-birthday, then," the goblin said, smiling, and then he began to whistle again.

Llyr turned to look at Brodie. "He probably stole those. You might want to get rid of those before the owners find their belongings with you," he said jokingly, but Kol ignored him.

A moment later, Kol was humming a tune, then began to sing. "Brodie bum, stop listening to nonsense, my little chum. You look like a goat and smell like a loo. Your breath smells bad. It smells like poo."

They continued to follow the path; the lake was now in sight. Llyr and Grub continued to converse, leaving the boy to chuckle at the cheeky rhymes. Kol, who found Brodie's laughter to be flattering, puffed out his chest a little.

This was definitely how his gumpy acted, and the thick Welsh accent also reminded the child of the old man.

Kol, who was thoroughly impressed with himself, continued.

> *"A little man at half past nine went to town to*
> *buy some wine*
> *The little man at half past four went to town*
> *to buy some more—"*

His rhyme was interrupted.

"Very mature," said Llyr, who found the singing, whistling, and the very presence of the goblin disturbing.

Kol looked over to Brodie; the small boy was very amused. This time, the goblin was a lot louder, making sure everybody around could hear him.

> *"Llyr, Llyr, he's my number one.*
> *He scratched his bum and had to run.*
> *He forgot to wipe, and that is why*
> *As he runs, you can hear him cry*
> *Tralalalalala."*

Llyr turned to glare at the smiling goblin.

"Just made that up. Want to hear another one?" Kol asked.

The weasel now glared at Brodie, who giggled hard but tried to contain his snorts of laughter.

"Enough now," Grub said, sounding fed up.

"Where do you come up with rhymes like that? My mum makes up songs, too, but it usually takes her a while."

"If you liked that one, you'll love this one." He cleared his voice. "Ahem.

"There was a young pixie from bewdley.
When on the bevy practically fuedly
when half in the sack and not on her back
she'd be up 'n' down town in the nudeley."

"Enough!" belted the two angry voices from in front.

"That's highly inappropriate for the child," Grub said sternly.

"What? It's a rhyme, no harm," Kol said. *Apparently, they had heard this one before,* Brodie thought, as he continued to laugh. Kol, still smiling, leaned in towards Brodie. "I'll tell you that one again. It's a good one, that."

They walked along the receded grasses of the lake. As they approached the lake itself, Brodie noticed a large grey rock. It looked different as they passed by—the ivy leaves were absent, the heavy wooden door was gone, and it just looked like an oversized, lonesome boulder now.

Brodie turned to the coloured hills. They had been bare as a poor man's pocket last night. He remembered his mother's impersonator and shuddered at the thought. Kol, who had noticed, placed a hand on the taller human's shoulder.

"Come on, mate, let's go," Kol said.

The path they had followed led them to a dirt road; it was cleared of the fallen leaves, exposing a muddy, hole-eaten road. Between the trunks of the trees to the left of the path, the sun sparkled across the still surface of the lake. The trees were tall and towered over, the leaves raining down. The leaves fell but drifted to the sides of the road.

"Magic," Llyr said.

Brodie did not speak as he watched the effect of the magic. A rickety old wooden fence ran along the right side of the road. It intercepted with another wooden fence that was posted horizontally. Beyond that were large golden meadows. The gate that had previously been centered across the road was missing. Leaves picked up in the wind, Brodie let out a fit of giggles. Kol removed his hat and swatted at the leaves as if they were something more than leaves.

Suddenly, the heavy sound of chains and something else could be heard in the distance, quickly approaching; he could not put his finger on the other sound. The three scattered back to the side of the road, pulling Brodie to safety. He looked behind them down the road, but he could see nothing but the muddy road and the forest that consumed it. His heart began to pound as two large black horses appeared from the trees. The horses grew closer within a matter of seconds, pulling behind them a black carriage. Brodie realized he had heard the sound of hooves from old Western movies.

The monstrous black figures appeared at first to have blazing red eyes, but as they grew close, he realized the red was in fact only embroidered eye flaps, which made up the only fragment of colour on these large approaching shadows.

Brodie turned to his friends. Their heads hung low; their stares met the ground. As he turned his head back to the horses and their carriage, he realized why. His hairs stood on end as he looked into the face of the cloaked driver. The driver was also dressed in black, revealing nothing but his face—his skeleton face. It was white as ebony with eye cavities hollowed and dark. Brodie felt like it was staring hard at him. The monster looked like the grim reaper pulling the devil's carriage.

The boy froze on the spot. He did not look away until the driver broke the stare to focus back to the road. As Brodie watched the carriage pass, he noticed the window of the passenger door; its black curtains were drawn back, revealing a pair of eyes watching him.

He watched the bizarre and demonic-looking carriage until it was a mound of black shadow in the distance. His hair still stood on end, and a cold shiver raced up his spine. He turned to the three, full of the heebie-jeebies, and asked, "What the hell was that?"

They continued to walk along the road, careful not to trip in the fresh and deep muddy wheel tracks. "You should not have looked at it," Llyr said.

"What was it?"

"Sorry, Brode's, we should have warned you to turn as it passed. It was a SOD!" answered Grub.

"That's what my mum calls me when I'm in trouble," replied Brodie in a confused tone.

"Bet she does," Kol chuckled.

"No, a SOD stands for 'servant of death.'"

"But the 's' is added at the end of it when they are being mischievous on their master's orders," Kol added.

"Masters," exclaimed Brodie.

"SODs serve the witches and wizards that resurrect them from their sleeping tombs deep in the ground. The moment they are woken up from their decaying sleep, they work as servants until their master dies," Grub said.

"What happens when their master dies? Can anybody from this realm have a servant, too?" the boy asked, completely creeped out but fascinated.

"I suppose they go back to their empty graves. You will often see them here. Not any of the sprites, goblins, fairies, or elves would dare conjuring up dark magic like that. Only the wizards and witches resurrect them. They are the ones to carry the burden of the deed," answered Grub.

"They look evil," the boy said, remembering the deathly hollowed expression of the driver.

As they approached the boot market, Brodie was warned by the three. "This is not a market you are used to. There are many different creatures that occupy its streets. Do not stare, and most of all, do not trust anybody. Keep your hands to yourself, and keep a clear mind."

Grub leaned in towards Brodie. "Keep that bag next to your body at all times, and don't think about its contents!"

"Righto," Brodie said, realizing Kol was slowly rubbing off on him.

A stone wall divided a few cottages and the fading forest from the little buildings, shops, and their busy inhabitants. From where Brodie was standing, he could see the rooftops and high buildings of the market. The rows of neighboring cottages along the road were old Celtic roundhouses. Their roofs were made of straw and grass. Some were neatly kept and very welcoming, while others were quite the opposite and eerie looking.

Triumphantly, they had reached the boot market. Brodie was in need of rest. He looked around for Kol, who had disappeared. Brodie spotted him a second later with his back turned to them, peeing along the stone wall.

"Shumai," he said, smiling and waving with his free hand to a little couple who passed on the road. The male giggled, and the female shook her head, irritated by Kol's ignorance.

Brodie couldn't help but watch the odd-looking couple. They were a little shorter than Grub and Llyr. The male was carrying a large mirror with him, and both were somewhat human looking, but at the same time not really at all. They dressed like humans in long green raincoats that hung off their bodies like large dresses with pleated lining. Both their hair was salt-and-pepper. It looked like they had lots of extra skin pulled into the center of their faces as if into a vortex, or as if they had no teeth and had gone out to town without dentures. The two were rather ugly. The longer Brodie looked at them, the more goblin-ish they appeared.

Grub, who sensed Brodie was staring, nudged the boy as they continued with their journey.

The boot market was nothing like he had expected. The muddy potholed roads had turned to wet cobbled streets leading off to busy alleys. A large water display stood in the center of the market, featuring a mermaid or some sort of water nymph—Brodie couldn't really see due to the busy streets. The shops looked ancient but not as old as the cottages that surround the market. The buildings were all white-washed and beautifully decorated, from the carvings high on the walls and under the rafters to the magnificently decorated bay windows. The buildings stood crooked and towered over the streets, posing what seemed like a great threat of toppling over and squishing the shopper's below.

On the tops of a few tall shops sat gargoyles and stone griffins peering down to the market. Brodie had never seen a stone griffin or gargoyle on top of a roof before. He had passed a church once that had a stone owl perched at the top of its steeple. His mum had told him it was to prevent pigeons and other birds from nesting. Maybe the gargoyles and griffins were there for the same reason.

The smell of baked goods wafted through the air, making Brodie extremely hungry again. In front of many shops, tented booths were set up with silks and satins. Their occupants sat behind tables peddling oddly shaped bottles, animals, spices, materials, cauldrons, flowers, and many delicious-looking treats. He spotted many carriages scattered along the sides of the streets. Many of them had cloaked skeleton drivers that stuck out like sore thumbs, and the shoppers didn't even acknowledge them. He continued to walk, staying as close as he could to Grub.

Llyr announced he was going to buy ingredients for supper. He would meet them at the Pickled Toad in forty minutes. With that, the little weasel scurried off into the crowd, tightly holding his pouch of money.

"This way, Brode's. Don't you get lost now," Grub said.

Brodie could tell he preferred his badger form. He looked as though he felt vulnerable and exposed.

"I want to pick a few things up, I do," he said, leading the boy deeper into the crowd.

Brodie tried not to, but he could not help but stare at the strangers that surrounded them. An old lady about five feet high clutched a wicker basket ever so tightly to her. Her facial features were pretty, but she had the strangest eyes, like two big amethysts. He didn't know if they were scary or amazing. It was bizarre.

He spotted four women heavily cloaked. Their skin was as green as grass. Brodie was a little afraid as he pondered whether they were witches. He saw many animals that walked on their hind legs as Llyr and Grub did. He guessed the majority of them were elves, too.

Goblins, gnomes, fairies, sprites, a few humans, along with many other oddly shaped creatures surrounded him. It was a whole different world, and it was all very surreal to him. Back in the human realm, Brodie often felt like his autism stood out, but here, he felt like he blended in—like he really belonged—for some reason. Perhaps it was the enchantment of this magical world.

Brodie kept checking his side from the moment they entered the market, afraid his bag would disappear at any given moment by pick pockets in the crowd. He felt afraid as hags and other intimidating creatures passed him. They stared deep into the eyes of the small boy, leaving him trembling as they disappeared. The majority of the shoppers wore hooded cloaks of all colours. It was brilliant. He noticed those who had more human features than the others wore more human-looking clothes. The women wore long skirts that came below their knees and grey, black, and brown blouses and matching blazers. Some wore furred coats of minx, fox, and rabbit. The men wore blazer suits. The clothes looked like they had been preserved from 1900s in this small little village, but often Brodie would spot a gentleman or two wearing a suit that looked like it was from the 1950s.

Grub tensed up whenever the Dirty Thirties-looking men were in view, thinking they were a part of Dayton's crew.

The little elf pulled Brodie into a shop, urging Kol to go and shop elsewhere and meet them back at the Pickled Toad. Grub knew damn well the goblin would give them away soon enough.

As they entered the shop, a beautiful ginger-haired lady passed them. She was holding a strange-looking bulb; its roots grew in abundance and wriggled as if it were alive.

The shop had a large sign over the door in elegant calligraphy: "Squatters and Stops." The interior of the store was dark burgundy and filled with dark wooden cabinets and tables. Sheer gold materials and silky satins hung around and draped over the sides of the large bay shelved window. The window shelf was filled with thick gold and burgundy pillows, a large iron cauldron, and crates that displayed a stack of worn, deteriorating books. The shop smelled musty. The lighting was dim at moments and brighter at other times; it was irritating, like there was a child playing with the light switch somewhere. Brodie had always been sensitive to certain lighting, but he was puzzled by why the temperamental lighting had no effect on him.

Brodie looked up. Decorated chandelier lamps hung from the wooden rafters of the ceiling. He rubbed his eyes in disbelief at the fancy lamps. Fairies sat in each crystal dome; there must have been nine lamps. A small blaze of light flashed from each lamp.

"What's that?" the curious boy asked himself out loud.

"It's a game they play to occupy themselves," the shopkeeper said.

Brodie kept staring at the fairies contained behind their glass barriers and shooting sparks of light at each other in what looked similar to a game of volleyball. Often the light would crash against a lamp of the player that wasn't quick enough, causing a firework effect of brightly lit sparkling dust to shower over the heads of the shoppers below.

What a game, he thought, *and they look to be having a jolly good time, too.*

Brodie wondered for a moment how the cunning little things would do at dodging paintballs. His older brother Robert had a great eye and never missed his targets. Brodie quickly moved along as the shopkeeper coughed, giving Brodie an inquisitive glare as if he could read minds.

Brodie looked around at the merchandise. Thin, long candles ranging in all lengths and colours lay heaped on a shelf next to a mound of old books. Some of the books looked as though they were on their last legs. He picked up a navy-blue bound book. It read *Belladonnas Trilogy.* It was completely dog eared. Inside were pictures of sprites and fairies, poems, and spells. The pages were browned with age, and it smelled musty. He began to read out loud to himself,

"Whispering leaves of the lilac trees will
hold you in suspense;

Wonderers please with doubting needs hold
it to yourself.
The ancient ruins of—"

The shopkeeper interrupted, "You can't read those spells out loud, boy!"

"But it's just a poem," Brodie exclaimed innocently.

"What may look like harmless poems to you could be potential troublesome spells for me. Not from around here, are you?" the shopkeeper asked Brodie with a curious, studying stare.

"Brode's," called Grub, closing the book in his hand and placing it back onto the dusty shelf.

Brodie walked away from the shopkeeper and the shelf of books quickly, thankful to be saved from the watchful eye of the shopkeeper. He walked to the other side of the room where Grub stood.

Brodie looked at the large dark dresser in front of him. On it were glass bottles. The clear bottles caught and reflected the light from the fairies. It was beautiful, like an array of shining crystals.

"Try not to speak to anyone, and don't answer questions. We can't trust no one," Grub whispered to the amazed child.

The elf was sorting through a large selection of bottles. There were sizes and shapes and colours of all kinds with outrageous labels like swamp cider, toloache oil, vampire venom mixed with angel trumpet, fruggled frog spawn, and shrew venom. Grub reached for a large bottle with both hands. The label read, "Troll's Breath."

As he continued to search through the collection of bottles, Brodie had a peculiar feeling that he was being watched. He turned, but only the shopkeeper stood aiding a hooded figure in a sale. The clerk was an odd-looking man, short and stout and very pale. Large, thick, oval glasses sat on the end of his rounded red nose. His hair was thin and matted around his bubble of a head; his was face puffy, blotched, and as bloated as the rest of his body.

Brodie turned. His eyes continued to roam hungrily. A selection of carved wooden spoons lay on a display table. He remembered his mother had one. It was a Welsh love spoon. His Nei had given it to her the second year of Mum and Dad's relationship. He moved on, resisting the temptation to touch. He passed shelves of oddly shaped pots, salts, dried herbs, preserved animal organs, and stones. He was disgusted but amused.

As he walked down the row of a shelved aisle, he noticed a pair of greenish-yellow cat eyes scrutinizing him from the other side of the shelf. He vigilantly headed towards the end of the aisle to get a clearer view. He could not see her properly from the tops of the books. He reached the end of the aisle and looked 'round the corner. A woman stood draped in a forest-green cloak. She met his stare, then quickly turned, heading towards the door. The store had suddenly filled; he walked towards the little elf that stood at the counter.

"Ten shillings and a sickle," said the shopkeeper. Brodie was distracted by the fairies that had begun to aim the fragments of light at the clientele's heads, giggling as shards of gold dust exploded against a balding old man's head. Brodie began to giggle, too. The shopkeeper did not look impressed.

"Come on, let's go," said Grub, and they left the shop.

The streets were as crowded as ever. Grub led the way. It was all very new and very exciting for Brodie. He could not take in all the delightful sights that the magical market square had to offer. A large tortoise passed them. She quickly transformed into a hunched and dumpy old lady struggling to carry her basket of goods. She accidentally dropped a few of her belongings. Brodie lowered himself to retrieve the items for her basket. She smiled, thanked him, and then lumbered away.

As he straightened up, a figure briefly towered over him, looking down. He caught her gaze. She was a much older woman. Deep wrinkles were set in her pale ivory face. In the light, he noticed she wore a long forest-green cloak that partially covered her face. Her facial features were catlike. He shivered. Before he could say anything or realize who she was, she suddenly disappeared into the busy crowd. He had a strong hunch it had been the spying lady from Squatters and Stops, the one with the greenish yellow, freaky cat eyes. He caught up to Grub, who was marking purchased items off his crumpled piece of paper.

"A few more things, then we will head over to the Pickled Toad," he declared.

They visited a few other little shops, searching for odds and ends. It was crazy that a world like this existed. Not that Brodie thought Wales was boring or anything, but he had expected fields, hills of grass, farms, and loads of sheep. This world was full of magic. He loved it, although it was a little intimidating, but the long stares of a few passersby did not vex him anymore. He loved this place.

They passed the water feature. He watched it for a moment. It was of a mermaid perched above a large jagged rock and looking over her shoulder into the distance. Waves reaching up to her from the base of the rock appeared to be moving slightly, as did the fins of her profoundly detailed tail. He blinked a couple of times.

"Spells to create illusions," Grub answered the child's unspoken question. A bell chimed in the distance. "Oh, we're late. Let's go."

The two walked away, though Brodie continued to turn back to look at the beautifully crafted water display. It kind of reminded him of the picture at Bramp's and Gran's house, the one from their first date with the mermaid in the background.

They entered the café. His heart began to pound. The aroma was strong throughout the Pickled Toad. The small coffee pub held a sufficient number of customers. Compared to the streets, it was a calm and cozy nook. Little round tables paired with cast-iron brown chairs in the shapes of mushrooms were scattered across the café. A large stretched counter to one side of the little pub displayed creamed cakes and treats on tiered glass trays and packaged breads and cheeses on shelves above the back wall of the counter. Chocolate marble goblin heads positioned at both ends of the counter matched the interior wonderfully. The floors were tiled with chocolate-and-cream marbled squares.

He wished his mum could see this coffee pub she had fallen in love with a coffee shop from her child hood in Swansea.

A giant oak tree that had not been visible from outside grew along the interior right side of the café. The tree, along with its breathtaking surprises, immediately seized Brodie's attention.

The tree was humongous. Its split bark made Brodie question how old it really was. Its grooved ridges and deep-set cracks indicated the tree was not done growing and still slowly expanding. It had a distinctly wide opening not half a foot from the ground and hollowed. Moss-covered stones surrounded the base around the hollow of the tree like a step of a fireplace mantle. The hole itself looked so hollow within, it was as if the tree had had a severe case of termites for decades or had been completely burnt out from within. The outside remained undamaged and had kept growing, trying to rebuild itself like damaged skin cells.

The most jaw-dropping aspect was not just the tree itself but what was tucked comfortably within the deep hollow. On the ash-surfaced bed was the strangest metal design ever. It was not a fender, but a realistic Celtic knot or metal nest. Rods of iron had been welded and designed to look like branches. A few decorated iron leaves sprouted from the branches and twigs in an accurate and very detailed resemblance of a bird's nest. Contained within the nest, a roaring fire danced and flickered. Its flames consumed the hollow without damage.

Brodie gasped and rubbed his eyes profusely. It took him a couple of moments to figure out exactly what it was that mesmerized him so. Then he noticed one of the babies falling from the iron nest and onto the soft ash carpet, camouflaged by the flames. His eyes had been deceived. From afar, it looked like a typical fire. He looked closely. After a few moments, he spotted four infant birds, each ablaze, hopping around their mother and camouflaged by the roaring mystical flames of their mother's amber-and-crimson-feathered wings. The mother clacked her beak a few times and made warning squawks directed towards the child who edged closer and closer to her nest.

"Oh, my God." He rubbed his eyes and looked to Grub. "Am I—Am I dreaming?" the gobsmacked boy asked.

"No, you're not dreaming, but you do need to come away from there," Grub answered, looking into the ecstatic and oblivious face of the child.

"It's an illusion. It's just an illusion, right?" asked Brodie, resuming his full attention to the breathtaking and magical wonder before his eyes. "Phoenixes," he whispered to himself seconds before two things happened; one of which was Grub grabbing the scruff of his shirt and pulling him backwards as the mother reached her neck towards Brodie and clamped the air with her magnificent beak.

"Hey, you two, over here."

Grub looked up and spotted a weasel standing on a chair and waving to catch their attention over the heads of the other customers. Llyr sat back down as they approached.

"Well, how was your first visit to the boot market?" Llyr asked, excited to hear the boy's response.

"It's different, that's for sure!" Brodie replied with a bewildered expression across his face as an overgrown snail slowly slithered next to him, leaving a glistening, slimy trail on the ground.

Brodie stood over five-feet but upon sitting down, this snail was almost at shoulder's height to him. The overgrown snail balanced a brown tray of wooden mugs on his shell. The mugs were filled to the brim and slopping slightly onto the tray from the wobbly and slow movement of the over grown snail. What hot liquid missed the tray trickled down the deep green-and-brown spiral shell of the snail. It was clear the snails were not washed often. The spilt liquids had built up on the shell-like melted wax that runs down a candle.

Now he had seen everything!

Llyr and Kol had taken the liberty of ordering hot drinks for their absent friends shortly before they'd arrived.

"As long as it was not prepared by cockroaches, I'm sound," Brodie exclaimed before he sipped his hot drink. Everybody couldn't help but laugh.

It smelled amazing and tasted like bliss.

"What is this?" Brodie asked.

"it's a turmeric latte" answered Kol as he continued to drink from his oversized wooden cup.

Like at Squatters and Stops, fairies were contained in jars dangling from the ceiling. As the other three talked, Brodie looked around at the creatures and his surroundings. A few witches sat at a nearby table. Brodie couldn't help but feel nervous as he noticed, from time to time, they would stare and whisper.

Once finished, they collected their belongings and left. As they passed the fireplace, Brodie looked over his shoulder, taking in one last glance of the mythological creature he had only read about in books.

They stopped at a few booths on the way back to Llyr's. Kol bought two pieces of enchanted willow bark. *A bit of a rip-off,* Brodie thought. They were just broken-off branches.

Grub bought Brodie a blank book and a pencil back at Squatters and Stops. He had remembered the boy saying he liked to draw. Brodie was thankful.

The journey back to the den was a lot quicker. Brodie shot off a million questions, but not all of them were answered. The temperature had dropped. It was colder outside, and winter was rolling in—as was the night.

That night, he sat curled up by the fireplace, doodling in his book. Brodie loved the boot market. It was like entering a magical fantasy, but in the darkness of his slumber, he was visited by the strange cat-eyed woman from the market, amongst other magical creatures they encountered.

CHAPTER 13

Peeping Skeletons

Days rolled into weeks. Time did not really feel as if it was changing. Brodie felt as though he had been away from his mother for a mere couple weeks at most. He tried not to think about her. He missed her. By now, his father would have heard the news of his missing son. He tried not to think about it. The parting and absence of his family upset him too much, but there was no possible way of getting to them right now.

Grub and Llyr did not take Brodie to the market too often after his first experience, afraid to expose him to the danger that was still on the hunt. Therefore, they took turns going to market to collect supplies. Llyr bought Brodie thicker throws and a few items of clothing. The boy was in need of new clothes. Brodie did not object, although he preferred his foxy animal form. The thick red coat kept him warmer than any blanket. But he did need something warmer for his human form to protect him from the cooler climates.

It was the beginning of December. One morning, after being woken from the hag that had haunted his dreams for weeks now, Brodie left the den to help Llyr collect the cream from the cow and firewood. He spotted something in front of them. A few feet ahead, on a puddle of water around the gate, a small, pale blue star-like figure moved swiftly, causing the water to freeze beneath it.

"Ah, winter's here," replied Llyr as he shut the door behind him. The light blue star figure turned and disappeared after being spotted by the two. Everything he touched as he left, frosted over in crisp icy designs.

"Who was that? What was it doing?" asked Brodie.

"That, my friend, was who we call Jack Frost."

Brodie was fascinated and asked tons of questions while collecting wood for the fireplaces. Llyr told Brodie of the different roles of the weather fairies and how the walking icicle hated the reference of fairy and preferred "ice god." Brodie decided to draw Jack in his notebook. He laughed with the others over breakfast and thought that the creatures from this realm would make wonderful stories for when he returned to the human world—if he ever could.

As the days passed, snowflakes began to fall, lightly covering the ground like dusting of powdered sugared on a cake. It was beautiful; the trees, fence, and ground held the light dusting.

The dragonfly and the grasshopper had been relaying messages to Grub of the safety of the boys family. The news was they were all together with allies in captivity. It was days at a time before any news came. Sometimes the news was passed to other fairies to deliver, but Brodie had begun to grow worried when no news came for a length of time.

One crisp, cool morning, Llyr left the den as usual to his morning routine of collecting cream and wood. He quickly returned empty-handed. Brodie woke to the door slamming shut and noticed the weasel's arms were empty.

"You're right. They are fresh, a matter of hours, but who and why?" Llyr said in a concerned tone to Grub, who was pouring out bowls of cream.

"Thank God it snowed," Grub remarked.

Somebody or something had been peeping through the window—but who?

Days had gone by, there had been no word or sight of the fairies, and the visits from the midnight intruder had increased. Grub, Llyr, and Kol had devised a plan of rotating night shifts. Grub strongly felt they should reside at Llyr's for the time being until they knew what Dayton and his gang were up to. Once or twice, Dayton's henchmen had been spotted around the boot market. During those times, hardly anybody left the den. Brodie wanted to go home. He sometimes regretted saving Grub, but he only felt like this when he missed his family.

One night, it was dark and still outside, and the crisp snow on the ground sparkled like a million diamond shards. It was quiet. Not a noise could be heard except the crunching snow slowly approaching the den. Underneath the window and leaning against the wall, Kol sat quietly, carving his branch of willow. Every now and then, he would rise to peek out from the window. There were no twinkling fairy lights in this neck of the woods. The outside looked cold and lifeless; there was nothing but the dangers that lurked beyond the garden gate. It had been fifteen minutes or so since he had last checked. He slowly got up and peered out the window. Nothing. It was safe. He was just about to lower himself when he caught sight of a dark shadow rapidly advancing from the forest. It was making its way towards the den.

Kol panicked, seeing this danger approaching swiftly across the snow. He tried to get the others' attention without making too much noise, but they were in too deep in sleep to be disturbed.

The windows were so thin. Afraid the stranger would hear the alarm and take off, he flung the only things he had in his hands at Grub—a folded pocket knife, which, thank God, hit the ground a foot or so away from Grub, and a willow branch that nailed him on the side of the head.

Thud.

"Aww, what the…?" Grub yelled as he jumped in anger.

Kol pointed outside. Grub quickly resumed his sleeping position on the chair facing the windows and door, keeping one eye open.

The sound of heavy breathing was interrupted by the crunching of the snow outside, then a slight scraping sound against the window like branches against glass. It was there. Kol tried to raise himself ever so slightly to the side of the window, but he was unable to see anything. He tried to sneak over to the other window. Grub saw a faded white blur outside of the glass only for a moment before the white blur in the window disappeared completely.

There was no dark shadow leaving the premises and entering the forest. The stranger had completely disappeared. Grub stayed on his armchair for a moment or two, trying to figure out what was going on. The blurred white figure had lingered at the windowsill for a couple of moments. Surely, had it been one of Dayton's clan, they would have ambushed the den some time ago.

A couple of days passed, and sure enough, the shadowed figure visited the den in the earliest hours of the morning. It stood outside the window—always the same window—a couple of minutes each time. There was still no word from the fairies or any explanation of their disappearance, which, along with the frequent night visitor, began to really worry Grub. Brodie was not allowed to remove the bag from across his shoulder unless it was a day when Llyr brought out the small tin bathtub. On bath days, Grub kept the bag close to him. One night, Llyr swore that on returning from the outhouse early in the evening, he saw a figure cloaked in black walking away from the den. From then on, Llyr demanded a chaperone for who-ever needed the outhouse.

It was a cold December evening. Large fluffy snowflakes drifted slowly from the night sky like the ends of large white feathers. Llyr was at the kitchen fireside, adding the last few ingredients to the cauldron of soup. Brodie had no choice to eat but refused to eat any-thing orange. Grub, Kol, and Brodie were sitting at the table, playing with a handful of old goblin coins. Suddenly, a pounding against the door caused the four to freeze—

Thud, thud, thud.

Grub hesitated for a moment, took a deep breath, got up from the table, and walked towards the door.

"Don't open it," whispered Brodie as he lifted a hand, signalling for Grub to stop.

"It's no use. If it's them, they will eventually break in," Grub replied as he opened the door.

Llyr had quickly joined Brodie's side. The three held their breath, listening to what was next to come.

"My, my, my, come in, love. You look frozen to the bone," they heard Grub say.

"Grub, I found her not too far from my home in this horrid condition," came a soft weeping voice from behind the door. The soft voice was slightly broken and sounded like the buzzing of bees.

A grey-hooded figure entered the warm fire-lit burrow. Her back was turned to the three at the table, but they caught glimpses of little shiny spikes that pierced through the material of her cloak.

Llyr fetched the guest a cup and a bottle of elderflower wine and urged her to sit by the fire to rest. She turned and walked towards the table. Her little pointed face was covered in chestnut-brown bristles and fur. Her eyes were as black as Grub's with a warm friendly twinkle. She was a hedgehog.

In her hands, she carried a small bundle of what looked like camo clothes or shams. She placed the bundle onto the table ever so gently and pulled back a corner. Peeling back the material, Brodie could see it was the hide of a rabbit or some furry animal, but then… tucked in the furs from the cold was a little warped body covered in dark green crust and liquid. It looked terribly disfigured and wrong.

Her body was pale, barely clothed, and what clothes did cover her body were torn, shredded, and dried over with dark green crusted patches, which Brodie understood to be blood. The pale skin that was exposed looked more like spots of white across the green-and-black bruised body.

She gave a slight whimper; part of the fur had stuck to her dried blood. It was a gruesome sight. Her little body looked broken beyond repair. Grub's eyes immediately filled with tears. Kol turned his head, his hands were fists clutched so tight his knuckles looked as white as snow. Llyr walked away, a paw leaning against the side wall to prevent him from losing his balance. He began to sob.

"What happened?" Grub's tone was cold and hard. It seemed as though grief had quickly drained from his body and anger and hatred had filled its place.

"I was walking along the marsh collecting beetles when I heard a call, a shriek, a scream more like it! I quickly ran over, and there, Jenny Greenteeth Half Out of Her Bog was calling for help!"

"She did this?" asked Kol in shock.

"No, she is not fond of the fairies, but this she would never do!" The climate was warmer than outside, causing the little hedgehog's nose to dribble. She paused to wipe it. "No, afraid to touch her body, she advised me to take the one that was still barely alive for help."

"There are two?" asked Llyr in disgust.

"There were two. Jenny tried to revive the poor little thing, but there was no use. She had died, too much blood loss. She died instantly. She said she heard a loud commotion. Excited, she surfaced to see what was going on, but it was too late. I picked the injured fairy up and took her to a witch a couple of cottages over from whom I get my ointments from. Her garden fairy was able to get a word or two from the poor little thing. The fairy refused to tell the witch what had been said, but she whispered your name in my ear and advised me to find you without speaking of this to anyone else. I came straight here. I had remembered seeing you with your cousin in market a few days ago. The witch's garden fairy was furious. I had no idea what had happened or what is going on, so I came straight here."

"You weren't by any means followed, were you?" Grub asked.

"Yes, at first, by two humans. I led them back to my burrow where I took the underground passage to come here. Those two, I've seen them at the market a few times now, who are they?"

The four remained silent. Every eye watched the fairy, speechless and filled with remorse.

"Oh, my God." Brodie had just realized the small creature was dragon. "Is she alive?" he asked, wanting to cry.

Grub dampened a rag and began to dab the crusted dried blood from the motionless little creature. "Yes, but barely." As he gently turned her over, the four gasped and made sickened noises. Their chairs scraped the ground as Llyr and Kol walked away from the table. Grub smashed his fist against the table, and Brodie felt like throwing up.

Llyr quickly placed a large candle on the table along with a bowl of hot water. From the candlelight, Brodie could see where her dragonfly-shaped wings had once sprouted from her back. The area was now a crusted mound of dark green mess and open sores. Her right wing had been ripped right from her back, leaving an open wound trailing down her back like a ripped hangnail. Only a stump at the base remained of her left wing. It was clear where the wing had been torn, leaving the stump of the remaining part lopsided and jagged. She would never fly again. Who knew if she would make it through the night.

"To rip the wings off and abuse a fairy like this is cruel and a level of evil all on its own," Grub declared as he continued to clean her body of dried blood and dirt.

"Who do you think did this?" Brodie asked.

"I don't know. Someone or something evil, though!"

"The best thing we can do is wait for her to gain consciousness," Grub said, holding back tears.

Brodie sat still for a moment, trying to think of some way to help the disfigured creature. She looked to be in a lot of pain. Fresh blood filled the gashes in her skin every time Grub would gently clean them. Then an idea popped into his head. "Lily," he said out loud.

"No, it's Dragon, Brode's," Grub corrected the boy.

"Yes, I know who it is," he said sarcastically. "No, what I mean is, where is the lily Mairwen gave me?"

Grub quickly got up and ran over to the other fireplace. On the mantel sat the silvery white flower. He grabbed it, then returned to the table. "Good thinking. Hopefully it works," he said. He poured hot water into a bowl, then placed the flower into the water.

He waited a couple of minutes until the water had slightly cooled, then gently placed the fairy into the miniature bath. "If this don't work, don't know what will." He dripped droplets of the water into her mouth. It soon became contaminated with her dark green blood and the dirt that began to swirl in the water.

The flower was beautiful. It emanated a strange fragrance. Usually, flowers would go limp and the petals loose and discoloured after a couple days of being picked, but not this flower. It was magic. Hopefully, its magic would heal her broken and bruised body and end the pain the poor little thing was enduring.

Everybody watched in silence as Grub gently removed the blood and dirt from her face with the rag.

Llyr refilled the hedgehog's cup. She was in deep shock. Never in her life had she been exposed to such tragedy. She grasped tightly to the cup and poured the deep purple liquid down her throat, then held out her cup for a refill. She did not stay too long after. She snuck out into the night, leaving the four and a half behind her. She was afraid, and she constantly looked around her as she left.

⌘

The fragile fairy was monitored over the next couple of days. Her physical appearance slowly healed. She still remained wingless and badly broken.

The weather outside began to change. The wind blew aggressively, causing sleet to bleat against the windows. Night after night, they were visited by the ghostly figure. Once or twice, Grub quickly darted towards the door to approach the Peeping Tom but was never quick enough. The thing seemed to visit more after Dragon's arrival.

Grub made a seat next to the smaller fire in the kitchen. He did not leave Dragon's side. Surprisingly, she had made it through the first night. With the amount of blood she had lost and the physical abuse she had endured, she should have been dead. He made a bed of straw close to the warmth of the fire. There next to her, he was able to care for her. Every so often, he would fill the wooden bowl with hot water and submerge the flower. The flower itself was still in good condition, as if it had just been plucked—although it looked smaller in size.

The hag had entered Brodie's dreams once again. He had grown accustomed to her and was able to distinguish her from his mother right off the bat. The woman transformed into a large beast, almost wolf-like; at other times, she would just disappear, leaving an awful lingering feeling.

One night, Kol's snores saved him from the outstretched claws of the hag. He slowly opened his eyes. Kol was fast asleep on the chair beside him. Brodie reached over into his pocket, remembering where he kept the silver pocket watch. He pulled it out and opened it. It was 2:40. A noise came from behind him. He turned to see Grub sitting at the table with the wooden bowl, and he knew Dragon was inside it. He got up quietly and joined them. He silently watched her for a couple of minutes. He felt great pity for her. The cuts had healed over, leaving pale green, bumped streaks across her body.

She sat up in a fetal position. Her head rested upon her knees. Her wet hair glistened in the candlelight. What was the remaining of her poor wing looked like a large shard of glass protruding from her back. It was a sad sight indeed.

Brodie looked up to Grub from across the table. The halfling's vision was fixed on the broken little creature before him.

"She was attacked," he replied, full of remorse. "She and Hopper had been traveling back and forth by my orders to keep an eye on your family and Dayton's gang. I shoulda known better. Dayton or one of his lot caught on and had them followed. They were hoping the fairies would lead them to us. It was Hopper who first noticed they were being tracked. She led them astray, but eventually, they were caught and tortured. Dayton is keener than I thought to get a hold of the scale."

"She's awake?" Llyr asked in a whispered. Grub and Brodie's discussion had woken him. He carried to the table a large brown bottle, bit the cork out with his teeth, dipped his paw into the melted wax from the candle on the table, and then peeled the wax off making a little cup, filled it with bugbane ale. It was a disgusting sight, but the broken fairy drank the liquor quickly and then held out the waxed cup for more. Brodie could not help admiring the quick thinking and compassion of the weasel.

Brodie got up, tugging a woolen sweatshirt over his human head. He had completely mastered the shape-shifting, thanks to the dragon scale, and once or twice, he had changed without the scale. Grub found this very fascinating.

151

"Where are you going?" Grub asked, a little alarmed as Brodie threw on his shoes.

"To find a tree," the boy answered, leaving the hut with a smile.

CHAPTER 14

Deceased Visitor

It was freezing outside. The wind blew coldly against Brodie's face as he walked back to the hut from the nearest tree. Huddling into himself, he kept his head hung low. He noticed a fresh pair of tracks in the snow—the demon had come. He grew edgy as he looked up and around to see if the thing was lurking in the shadows, biding its time to catch him unexpectedly—ready to pounce and attack like a tiger.

The tracks were fresh, but the wind caught the snow in strong bursts, carrying the glittered specks across the ground in waves. A rustling noise from close by terrified Brodie. He quickly made his way to the siding of the hut. There, he quietly waited a moment or two to observe the darkness. He made his way back to the door, careful not to trip.

He was right next to the window when he momentarily paused. Another distant noise caused him to freeze on the spot. The cold had deserted him, leaving in its place an overwhelming feeling of alarm. From inside, he could hear Grub and Llyr talking. Something had caught his attention, and it wasn't the disturbance from the trees. He stood quietly listening.

Grub was standing next to the window, looking out, then turned back to Llyr. "They are after Brodie. Not only is he after the boy for the scale, but there's another reason why Dayton wants the boy," Grub said.

"Dragon came to warn us Dayton's..." Their conversation began to grow muffled.

Brodie and Kol had learned a while back that one of the circular windows could be slightly pushed in and was perfect for eavesdropping. He stretched his neck, straining to listen.

"Dayton has sent half of his gang after Brodie's family. The other half are here. It's only a matter of days until he catches the boy, and when that happens, it will be the end for all of us. He will stop at nothing, and it's entirely my fault. I have brought death to us all!" Grub whimpered.

Brodie gasped. He didn't know whether he heard correctly or whether what he had heard was a figment of his imagination. He didn't know whether to cry or storm off to find his family before Dayton did.

He paused.

Deep in thought, he looked around as he brainstormed. His eyes met the faded tracks. He had an idea. The wind twirled the snow in spirals that brushed away the tracks, but he knew the tracks led into the dark forest, and his foxy nose could detect any scent. He took a deep breath and entered the hut.

Grub perked up a little at the sight of Brodie. It was fake but comforting. Brodie sat with Llyr and Grub for a while, watching the little fairy.

The worried child was deep in thought, concerned for the well-being of his family's safety, especially his mother. He focused on nothing but his fears and often drifted into his own reality, trying to make sense of it all. Luckily, he was able to pass it off for exhaustion whenever he was questioned.

Brodie got up and towed himself over to the chair and announced he was tired. Soon he was fast asleep.

Outside, the wind had calmed to a soft whisper. The pelting snow that was carried by the harsh wind no longer thrashed against the frail windows. All was quiet. Heavy breathing, the crackling of the fire, and a distant whining of the wind from the partially cracked window were all that could be heard.

Brodie sat up. He watched the everlasting fire, plotting his actions and debating his rash decisions. It still had to be some early hour of the morning. Brodie reached deep into the straw of the chair, pulling out the tatty old bag that carried the scale. Careful as to not wake the others, he lit a small traveller's lamp before slipping a thick fur cloak over him and leaving the safety of the den.

As soon as he stepped through the door, he walked to the right side of the house. *Hopefully,* he thought, *the wind hasn't cleared the tracks away.* He looked down to the ground to find the tracks. To his dismay, a fresh set were as clear as water and fairly recent. He took a deep breath, held the lamp a little in front of him, and followed the tracks into the forest.

"I wonder when our Peeping Tom came," he asked himself. "I wonder if I am close behind him. Perhaps I should slow my pace." The small boy was absolutely terrified. He had hoped to wake the others up as he left to at least have company on this nerve-racking mission. He had no idea what danger lay ahead, but he had to try to protect his friends and family. If Dayton wanted him, he could have him in return for his friend's and family's freedom and safety.

His tracking led Brodie deep into the forest and past the lake. The lake looked as if it was lit from the weedy bed below. He glanced over, admiring its magical beauty, then continued. The ground was covered with snow. His boots had become wet through and his toes were numb and bitten from the cold. Even though he had worn layers, an icy chill still managed to crawl up his spine. He quickly turned back into a fox. His human form was quiet enough to open the door and sneaked out but this was much efficient.

Thanks to the natural instinct of the fox, not only were the foot tracks a little larger due to Brodie's shrinking size, but the tracks gave off a rather foul scent, a bit like a flowerpot that, after not being watered for weeks, finally is smelling a lot like stale mold and dirt mixed with something else—something terribly disgusting, but a smell he could not put his paw on.

Brodie had come to the end of the path and found himself in front of the snow-covered road. The little fox remembered that if he turned left, the road would lead him to the boot market. He turned right; as did the tracks. He was amazed as he looked up at the stars draped across the dark sky. Afraid the light would expose him he was glad to have left the lamp. He adjusted the bag that tugged and tore at the fur around his neck, then set off.

One side of the road was consumed with snow-dusted trees that grew out of control. On the other side of the road, silent fields and hills of purple bore slumbering cottages in the distance. Once or twice, Brodie froze as dark-cloaked and hooded figures swept across the purple snow-covered ground or through the trees. To say the boy was not scared would have been a lie.

He trotted along the winding and twisted roads in pursuit of the tracks. They continued on from the road into the dark forest. A strange noise caused his heart to race. He paused briefly as the noise approached and listened breathlessly. The forest was alive with whispers and giggles. He quickly made his way towards an opening to shelter from the approaching noise that grew louder and louder. From the brambles, he waited and watched for the approaching carriage to pass. He could not lose those tracks, not now.

A black carriage camouflaged by the darkness of the night passed by. The black horses looked as though they had galloped straight from hell. It gave him shivers. He kept low and silent. He watched as they hastily disappeared.

Suddenly, a snort came from directly behind him. A twig snapped. Brodie froze. He closed his eyes and prayed that the thing behind him was Kol playing a trick to catch him in surprise.

He was beyond fear now, and he regretted leaving the safety of the hut.

The little fox turned to look up at the stranger who towered over him. The stranger gave another horse like snort.

Brodie remembered the horse from the carriage with the burning crimson eyes. The horse's head stood tall. It looked down to him, observing the little fox, then spoke.

"Why so afraid, little one?"

Brodie gulped in shock as he stared into the creature's eyes. Like round pools of onyx, its eyes were blacker than the night. Brodie trembled with fear as the creature towered over him. It was disfigured. It didn't have a human head to match its human body, but instead it had the head of a horse or a large goat. A thick, matted, black mane surrounded its head and trailed down across his chest and arms. It was human and barely covered. Its muscle density was thicker than that of any human Brodie had ever seen.

"'Tis not safe for nature's children and kin of kind on these forsaken lands, especially during these crude and dangerous hours."

Brodie felt intimidated.

"Why doth you hide among the dangers of the wood on the eve of a full moon, little friend?"

Despite the fact that the stranger had called him *friend* and seemed to possess no sign of immediate danger, Brodie kept on guard, looking for paths to dodge past the creepy horse-goat man.

"Who?" was the only thing Brodie could mutter without choking on his words.

"My name, Phooka. One does apologize for lack of introductions."

Brodie did not answer but kept his eyes fixated on the half-horse man. The longer Brodie stared at the Phooka man, the more his head resembled a goat. Two dark twisted horns grew from the top of his head in opposite directions.

"Are you the devil?" Brodie asked the frightful figure after a courageous gulp.

Phooka laughed. His laugh was very deep but animal-like. It almost caused Brodie to piddle right there on the spot from fear.

"You are not from these lands, little one, are you? I mean you no harm, and if my memory do serve me correctly, I know of you. Dayton has returned to these lands. He has allied with witches and wizards alike. These roads are no place for you, my friend."

"How do you know me?" Brodie asked.

"The woods have whispered of a badger and a fox that are sought out by Dayton and his men."

"But I'm just a fox. You have me confused for somebody else." It was the only thing that came to mind. He had no idea if the thing was friend or foe.

Phooka laughed again. His laughs were more like bells. "My apologies. Although caution as it may be, it would be safer for you to refrain from the road. I bid you adieu, only a fox." He let out a gruff horse-like snort. "Till next time, my friend," he said as he bowed.

Brodie stared up at the monstrous sight as he passed by cautiously. Once a little distance had grown between the goat man and himself, Brodie quickly sprinted away. Without looking back, he kept as low as he could to the ground. He kept close to the road, relying on the scent of the tracks, until he was a good distance from the overgrown, deranged-looking goat-man.

The snow crunched under his paws. It was crisp and fresh. The air was cold and very invigorating. The hooves of horses and the wheels of the carriage had crossed paths with the tracks a few times, but Brodie was still able to continue forwards. The unnameable scent was still potent. The strange resonance of taunting bells echoed from a distance.

He kept on guard, keeping an eye on the shadows that danced among the forest. He would often spot fairies in the trees, weaving through the woods. He thought of Dragon and hopper as he continued on. His nerves were still on edge. His curiosity grew as the bells grew louder and closer. There was more than one. They chimed sporadically.

Once or twice, Brodie thought he had spotted Phooka striding through the trees, slouching in the shadows, but he thought it was only a figment of his imagination. More or less, he was seeing what he did not want to see.

The whispering forest frightened him; as did every noise he heard right now. As the trees thinned out, Brodie was able to see lights ahead between the trunks of the trees. The closer he advanced, the more it appeared the lights were moving, bobbing from side to side, outlining shadowed gravestones. He approached an iron fence that ran as far as he could see, dividing the road from a graveyard.

He was intrigued by the bells. He knew he should continue the hunt, but curiosity got the better of him. He quietly slipped through the fence and watched for what was causing bells to ring. He could not see any bells, though.

He sat for a moment to spectate the unnatural midnight scene. This menacing and eerie place did not feel safe. As dangerous and demonic as Phooka had appeared, Phooka had, in fact, been quite friendly. He would not be that lucky a second time, he thought.

A grave closest to Brodie, began to toll. With his accurate night vision, he was close enough to see where the ringing was coming from. In front of a headstone on the snow-covered grave, a domed, mesh metal box sat two feet high by two feet wide. The domed box appeared old and decorated; a bell protected within the box swung from side to side.

Brodie wanted to get a little closer to investigate but thought differently. Suddenly, two large hooded figures glided towards the grave from nowhere. He kept as low as he could to the ground. A third figure carrying a lamp approached. A woman spoke in a cracked voice.

"Start digging," she said. She pointed down towards the grave, then turned, leaving the other two behind. When they removed the cage from the grave, Brodie could see a rope attached to the bell that had been submerged into the grave through a hole in the cold earth. The hooded figure reached down, retrieved the rope, and wrenched it out.

Once the rope was removed, the two began to carve away at the cement-like ground. There was no sign of struggle—no heavy breathing or strained noises as they hit the pickaxe into the frozen earth. Then came the sound of gravel scraping against metal as the second figure used a shovel. They gracefully cut into the hard ground like they were slipping a knife into butter. They made it look so effortless and easy.

It was only when Brodie caught a glimpse of thin white bones exposed from the cuff of a cloaked arm that he realized the diggers where SODs. He looked across the graveyard. A couple of lamp lights were scattered across the grounds. Swift black figures drifted in front of the lamps, blocking the lights for seconds, then blending into the darkness as the bell tolls began to soften.

The little fox, terrified, backed through the fence as quietly as possible. He knew this place was a dangerous threat. He felt it deep inside.

He was after a SOD, but not these ones. He headed towards the tracks on the road. He turned briefly to see a shadowed figure standing next to the fence where he had been seconds ago, watching as Brodie trotted out of sight. He turned, hastening his pace. He ran away from that deathly graveyard as fast as his paws could take him with his bag banging against the side of his body.

The tracks led away from the road and turned on a smaller path—a driveway. The driveway continued a little further out of sight. A stone wall was built around an ancient-looking home. This house looked more like a modern cottage opposed to the Celtic roundhouses Brodie was used to seeing. Brodie's heart began to pound harder and harder. He was positive he was close to having an anxiety attack. He tried to take deep breaths as he approached the house. But the magenta smoke wafting from the chimney was not helping.

The house was not small. Its roof was made of swamp reeds. The snow that lay in patches across the rooftop glistened and reflected the bright color of the smoke that had now turned purple. A second roof branched across the driveway.

During this lonely dark hour of the night, the house was still but not asleep.

Brodie darted towards the stone hedge that was sporadically lit by the odd fairy here and there. He sat there a moment or so, panting. *Snap*—a twig snapped in the trees around him. It caught Brodie off guard. He froze. His body lowered to the ground as he listened to his surroundings.

Ease rained upon him as a gnome ran across the drive. The thing let out a stream of profanity as it followed a field mouse. Brodie smiled, shook his head, and turned his attention back to the house.

"I better change back before I go in there."

He gave a knock against the door. The door was made of thick old oak. A holly wreath hung in the center. He looked around him as he waited for someone to answer. The awning of the roof provided shelter to any visitor from the wet elements. He stood fidgeting nervously as he waited. He had just turned back when the door opened with a whine.

160

Brodie jumped in fear as he was greeted by death.

A SOD welcomed the unexpected young guest in with a waving gesture and lowered himself in a courteous bow. The SOD was clearly a servant. It wore a navy-blue suit with a white ruffled undershirt that looked as if it dated back to the seventeenth century. It also wore a white curled wig. As the SOD turned to lead the way, Brodie noticed the wig had a small black bow holding a ponytail in place. Brodie diverted his eyes away from the SOD, disgusted and frightened of its appearance. He looked around as he followed.

The exterior of the house was deceiving. It was a lot larger inside. As he was led through a hall, Brodie noticed long holly wreaths decorated along the pillars of old oak support beams on the ceiling. As he walked underneath the beams, he heard giggles. He looked up.

Two vines hung on every awning pillar with large globes of fresh dark green holly. Sitting on each globe of holly were small pixie-like creatures. They looked like Santa's elves, but miniature versions and younger. They were dressed in red, one-piece outfits with matching red hats that stood up on their heads like little pointed caps. It looked like their ears were holding up the hats. Childlike in appearance, they giggled as Brodie walked underneath them.

His mouth dropped in astonishment as he past under a pillar. It dawned on him it was Christmas time. He felt horrible. He had never been parted from his mother on the holidays.

If the pixies are used for decoration, I feel sorry for whatever is used as a tree topper, Brodie thought to himself. He imagined an elf stuck on top of a Christmas tree with an unpleasant look on its face while holding its behind. He giggled.

They came to a shut door. The SOD knocked twice and then held out its bony hand, signaling for Brodie to wait as it entered. He was making so many mistakes. His mother had taught him never to talk to strangers and never to enter a stranger's home. If she could only see him now, she would have a conniption fit. But did it count if the stranger was already dead? He wondered.

Brodie looked around as he waited. The halls were lit with candled lamps. The walls were painted burgundy and decorated with golden frames of old paintings. The floors were dark hardwood and draped with a long beige corridor rug. He spotted a familiar vase against a wall holding curvy and twisted branches. The vase had two coloured peacocks with gold trim. His mother had a similar vase, only it was smaller. She had inherited it from her aunt years ago.

The door creaked open as the servant signalled for Brodie to enter. He clutched the hidden bag under his thick woolly sweatshirt tightly, took a deep breath, and entered. He could feel sweat bead across his forehead.

The room was large. The fireplace directly in front of him emitted a cozy light. His fists were tight against his sides as he walked slowly towards the two seats facing the fireplace.

"That will be all," a cracked old voice said.

Brodie stood still as the SOD departed from the room, shutting the door behind it.

"I don't know what you want, but leave my family alone, and we can negotiate whatever it is you are after," Brodie said sternly, trying to contain his growing anger.

The old woman cackled. "You have a lot of my duchess in you, my boy."

Brodie froze. He was terrified, and witchy laugh intensified his fear.

"Come closer, Brodie Rhys," she said politely.

It felt like someone was stabbing him along his spine with pins. *How does she know my full name?* he thought. "Who are you? Please," he asked.

"I am someone who has been waiting a very, very long time to meet you, child. It's okay, I am an old woman. I won't hurt you or your family, I promise."

He edged around from behind the empty chair towards her, slowly trying to catch a glimpse of the figure that sat facing the fire. She had not turned to him as she had spoken.

A wrinkled old hand reached out to a side table. Her nails were long and chaffed. They were curvy and grew inwards, animal-like. She picked up a teacup by its saucer. It disappeared from behind the chair.

As Brodie walked around the chair, he finally saw the frail old woman.

"Please sit. Tea?" asked the old woman.

"No, thank you," Brodie said as he lowered himself into the opposite armchair nervously. He quickly jumped as a startled tabby cat sprung from the cushion of the chair where Brodie had sat.

It was her—the old catlike woman from the boot market he had crossed paths with weeks ago! The deep wrinkles made her face appear saggy and ancient. Her white hair was pinned back in a neat bun. Her catlike eyes remained watching the fire as she sipped at her tea. It looked like thin whiskers grew from her cheekbones. The ala of her nose was identical to that of a cat with the slightly puffed-out philtrum. She was wrapped in a pink silk dressing gown with a knitted shawl draped over her shoulders. Besides the creepy catlike resemblance, she looked like a harmless old lady, but it was her, all right. He could feel it in his gut.

"Who are you, and why have you been spying on us?" he asked.

She calmly sipped her tea. Thick drapes concealed the windows. The room was large and warm; area mats concealed a great portion of the hardwood floor. Plants and small trees in small basins were scattered around the cozy room. The fireplace was large, and the mantel around it was built with a thick slab of slate. Brodie looked at the smoke that rose from the fire. It had changed colour from white to lilac.

"Its lavender and sage leaves ward off evil spirits or magic," the old woman answered as if hearing the question in his head.

Brodie turned to look at the door, wanting to remark on the SOD, but he refrained as the old cat woman began to talk again.

"Where are your friends?"

"That's none of your concern," he replied.

"I apologize, my dear. I was told you had disappeared in your mother's realm. We have all been very concerned. When I saw you in the market, it startled me. It was a shock to be face-to-face with you here in this realm. It was a puzzling question how you got here in the first place."

163

She paused, taking in every detail of Brodie's features. "You look so much like to your mother and Nei. I never imagined ever meeting you. I had my servant follow you home that day from the market. I have had you checked on every night since we crossed paths," she said as she pointed to the fireplace.

He was confused at first but got up to see the large collection of picture frames she had displayed on the fireplace mantel. He turned slightly to keep her in view, afraid she would pounce.

There were pictures of a younger couple on their wedding day, a few strangers and—

Lying on her tummy on the stone slab edge of a garden pond was a little girl, four or maybe five years old, with short brown pigtails and an uneven fringe. One hand concealed a troublesome smile or a giggle, the other hand held up fishing line with an enraged half-pixie, half-fish dangling from the end of the line.

"No way," he said loudly in disbelief. He let out a burst of laughter. He knew this cheeky little face. It was his mother as a child.

He turned to the old woman. She merely nodded as she continued to sip her tea quietly, watching the child before her. He turned back to look at the pictures.

A big pair of blue eyes stared at Brodie. It was an infant picture of himself. His mother had the exact picture displayed on her nightstand and her work bench.

The next picture was of a younger version of his gumpy in a white jacket and with a striped pinny around his waist. He was bent over, his head against a wooden table. An older man stood over him in an identical white jacket and pinny, holding up a cleaving knife over his gumpy's head. Both men were smiling.

"Hey, that's Norman!" Brodie exclaimed in surprise.

"Yes, my late husband," the old woman answered.

Brodie turned to the old woman, then turned back. He continued to look at the familiar faces of his family and the not-so-familiar faces. Then he said, "But if Norman was your late husband, and you have tons of pictures of Mum and Nei, that would make you my…" He gasped and stumbled backwards. "But you d-d-died! Or, you're supposed to be… Are you a SOD, too?" the frightened boy asked.

The old woman began to laugh. Her catlike features for the first time were soft. "The picture of Norman and your gumpy was taken when gumpy first began to court your Nei, or date, as the humans now call it. We had a little shop we owned. Your gumpy worked there for a spell. It was such a humorous picture and so ironic. Your gumpy had long hair at the time, and Norman wanted it cut short. It was ever so scruffy looking. He hated it. Plus, your nei was our youngest. Naturally, a father would be protective of his little girl." She quietly laughed.

"But I was told you died," Brodie said in shock. "Gumpy and Nei still put flowers on your grave."

"I cannot live in the human realm, my darling." She had a tone of elegance as she spoke. The old woman sounded identical to his nei. "Our family are different from the humans. But we shall discuss that another day."

"Nei filled me in when they told me about fairies and magic. Nei looks like a cat, too. Well, her eyes, at least."

The old woman was a little shocked of his intelligence on the matter but smiled an admiring smile. She paused to sip the remaining tea before ringing a small golden hand bell.

A moment later, a SOD entered the room with a silver tray. He set the tray down and refilled her cup, then left once more.

"Firstly, Brodie, and most importantly, you have to know the family are safe."

"How do you know? How can you be sure? My friend sent fairies to check on them, and they were attacked and killed by Dayton."

"Yes, the sisters have said he has entered our realm once again. We have what you would call magic. I have ways to communicate with your nei as I have done for decades."

He looked up towards the mantel of the displayed stages of his life, along with his immediate family's photos. She wasn't kidding.

There was a small metal picture frame tucked and camouflaged behind two of the larger pictures. The image was a duplicate of one he had seen a few weeks ago on the fire mantel at Nei's.

"The image is hollow. Inside is a box of ground beeswaits, unicorn hair, and mermaid spit. It is a magic powder both your Nei and

I throw into the fire, sending its fiery fairy through. It enables us to communicate and send small parcels to each other."

"Nana, you mentioned your sisters. Do your family live here, too?" the boy asked, wondering if this realm was the final destination for his family before death and whether he would be able to come back here, too.

"When I spoke of my sisters, I spoke of others like myself joined by magic. We were once a coven. We feasted and celebrated the festivity of the seasons with the fairies and elves. It was a harmonious time."

"What happened?" Brodie asked.

"We were overpowered by one. She was youthful and very powerful." The old woman spoke with dislike. "And in alliance with a very dangerous dark sorcerer who had returned from the past."

"Dayton," interrupted Brodie.

"The coven grew wicked. Sacrifices and offerings were used in spells. This was not our way. So others like myself faded into the background, leaving the power hungry to their spotlight, as we called it, but we had daren't miss the coven's meetings as death would have been the penalty for many. After that, many of us broke free. We still meet in secrecy and help those around us, but it is hard to place trust in one another as there are spies lurking dangerously in the shadows."

"I know that feeling," Brodie said sarcastically.

Brodie thought about what his great-grandmother had said and understood why, when the hedgehog had saved Dragon, the garden fairy had refused to speak to the witch. It made sense now.

"Where is my mum, Gumpy, and Nei?"

"They have entered a gnome portal in your great-aunty Winifred's backyard."

"Oh, shit," Brodie said.

The old woman's catlike eyes widened from the profanity of her great-grandson.

"Um, sorry, sorry, it slipped out. It's just, well, I don't think my gumpy would be safe there amongst the gnomes. Let's just say he's a little sling shot happy."

"I am sure that boy will get his comeuppance at a more suited time. Right now, we are more concerned with trying to keep you all safe."

"What do I call you? Do I call you great-granny or great-granny nanny?"

"Nana Pat," she said with a warm catlike smile.

"Nana Pat, I overheard my friend saying Dayton is after me and the family. Why?"

"I don't know, my darling, but he's not the only one. The witches are currently looking for you, too. They are unaware you are of my relation. It's only a matter of time until the coven finds out."

"What do you mean?"

"The family will be safe with the gnomes. Until we figure out why Dayton is after you, there's nothing we can do but for you to keep low. I am going to try to get you to your mum. The witches are working with him. All that we know is that a child with an old source of magic must be captured! Over my grave will I hand you over!"

"That's just great. The first half of my life was a struggle to be normal and fit in while everyone judged me, and now I'm gonna have to struggle to stay alive. Just my luck."

❧

The two conversed for some time. It was lovely. It was hard to digest, though.

After a while, the old woman paused a moment and then continued. "The rest of us slowly change over many, many years."

The small ginger-and-white tabby that Brodie had almost sat on brushed its body with affection against his legs. He looked down into the remarkable green eyes that were so common to the women of his family.

"So is this your mother or sister?" he asked, looking at the feline.

Nana Pat got up, looking past the boy towards the curtains that were drawn closed. "No, love, I found her behind a dumpster," she said absentmindedly as she slowly shuffled across the room.

"Nana, are you okay?" He was afraid to speak too loud, trying to listen to the noise that had been absent to him a moment ago.

A hand rose then dropped as the fire grew momentarily out of control. Its flames grew black.

It happened in an instant. The old woman pounced across the room. She grabbed the boy by the sleeve of his sweatshirt and dragged him towards the hall. He clutched the bag tight as they darted across the room. She reached into her old stationary desk and grabbed something. A large grandfather clock stood against the wall. She ripped the door open, kissed him on the forehead, and pushed him through.

She placed something solid into his hand and whispered, "Find Bramble Meir. Tell him Pat sent you."

With that, she slammed the door.

It was dark inside. A muffled clinking sound was followed by a spinning feeling, sparks shooting around him. He felt dizzy as he tried to rest against the back of the grandfather clock, but nothing was there to support him. He fell backwards as if through a worm-hole in space.

A horrid gut-lifting feeling came over him as he continued to fall backwards, then he hit the ground with a hard thud.

CHAPTER 15

Inquiries

Pat resumed her seat. She tidied herself, then rang the hand bell. A couple of minutes later, an outstretched arm passed her a cup of tea, but this arm was not a bony arm belonging to her loyal servants.

"Good evening, Patricia," a charming English voice said from beside her. "Hope you don't mind we saw ourselves through."

"In the neighborhood tonight, then, are we?" Pat asked politely as she brought the cup discretely to her nose before she lowered it to her lips.

"Mmm, something like that," the tall figure said, pausing after each word as he looked around the room. He walked over to the mantel of the fireplace, leaned his right arm against the stone frame, and he picked up a picture. He was dressed in a black coat with a bright blue scarf. He unbuttoned the top button of his coat and loosened his scarf, exposing his grey business suit. His features were well-kept—face shaved and short brunette hair neatly styled.

"Well, this is a pleasant surprise," she said sarcastically. "Shall I call for tea?"

"Bet you've had your fill of those tonight," he replied.

"Tea or surprises," the old lady asked.

The ginger tabby by her ankles arched its back and hissed, showing off her pearly white fangs; little beads of saliva sprayed from her mouth.

He bent low towards the agitated cat, and a deep-seated growl escaped from his clenched teeth.

"Please, please enough of that," Pat said in complete detest. She lowered a hand to comfort the arched tabby. She looked towards the fire; the black tips of the flames swayed and danced.

"We had word you had a visitor tonight." His eyes shifted, slowly scanning the room, maybe for a trace of Brodie. He looked at the picture and placed it back. "No visits lately, then."

Pat covered her shoulders with her wrap, straightened her back, and answered ever so elegantly, "I am not one for games. Would you mind frightfully enlightening me with the true purpose of this late-hour visit!"

"Don't play coy with me, witch. You know exactly what I'm on about. You had a visit tonight from a kid, and not just any. What would your coven say if they found out you were harbouring fugitive thieves, to be exact?"

He was interrupted by a pudgier man with a darker complexion at the door. "He's not here, and his footprints continue down the road into the forest."

"Try to protect him all you want, but we'll catch up to him." The first man walked past Pat, his posture bent. "I bid you adieu. Till next time, my dear. Enjoy your tea."

Pat remained upright, very proper and very dainty, until the treacherous man had left. She listened to the doors slam behind him.

"Make sure he has gone," she said, looking down to the tabby. With that, the tabby sprinted after the intruder. The tabby paused. She let out a high-pitched howl and hissed as she stared at the concealed window.

Pat jumped. She, too, had heard a sudden noise from beyond the window. Once again, she pursued the noise.

CHAPTER 16

Follow Rebecca

There was a loud *bang*, then a *thud*. Brodie opened his eyes, then rubbed his head. The pain was piercing. He was lying on an old wooden floorboard. He coughed after breathing in loose dust and dirt from the floor.

He slowly got up and looked around. A moment ago, he was being pushed into an old clock. A second later, he was lying face down on the ground in a cold and dark room.

The clock's door was stretched wide open. He got up, trying to put his hand to the back of the clock. Nothing. It was solid. He knew he had just come from some weird portal inside the old structure. He had to think for a second. He was not used to Roman numerals, being as everything today was digital. After a moment, he figured out it was four thirty.

He studied the face for a moment, examining the profile of the tall dark clock and the painted image displayed over the top of the face.

He heard an approaching noise. He quickly transformed back into a fox and made his way under the table.

The house was bare, cold, and musty. A fireplace maintained the little warmth there was in the room. The furniture of the room consisted of a wooden cabinet, a table, and chairs, and another set of chairs in the far corner behind a staircase that looked like a rickety old ladder.

The door opened.

Brodie sat, nervously waiting.

A thick pair of wet and muddy boots came trudging into the room, trailing behind little mounds of mud. They briefly stopped in front of him. His little heart pounded deep in his chest.

What if it's Dayton? he thought. He sat still, afraid to breathe.

The heavy, dirty boots remained there for a moment or so. The owner of them let out a sarcastic chuckle. He made a noise from above the table like that of scrunching paper. A second later, a paper ball fell to the ground next to Brodie's paws. It was hard to read what was written across the half-crumpled part of the paper.

The boots turned and walked towards the other side of the room. The clinking of glasses and gulping of liquid being dispensed from a bottle was all Brodie could hear. It was followed by a satisfied, "Ah."

A second later, the man was on the move again. He now walked towards the clock.

"How did that get open then?" he said with a deep Welsh accent.

The door of the clock creaked and moaned as it shut. Brodie grew intensely worried as he spotted a dirty hand reaching for an object that lay motionless on the floorboards next to the grandfather clock.

A loud pounding noise from the door caused both the man and Brodie to jump. The man quickly turned and dashed off towards the chairs in the corner of the room, kicking his boots off and pushing them under a chair with a free foot. Brodie looked over to the object that lay on the ground, remembering his great-grandmother had forced something into his hands. He looked back. His mouth dropped as he watched the big man drop his long skirt and bonnet.

Where in the hell am I? Brodie thought.

The man pushed the bundle of clothes under the chair, then raced quietly towards the ladder as fast as the wind.

When the man was gone, Brodie quickly transformed back. He picked the object up from the ground. It was a book, and next to it lay half of an old key. He placed the key between the pages and dropped it into his bag, then opened the wooden door of the old clock, but there was no change whatsoever. The portal he had entered through was no longer there.

He looked around the room for an exit as the pounding on the door grew louder. A light passed by the nearest window. It hovered in the darkness for a moment, then disappeared. Then another appeared.

He darted for the table as heavy footsteps came down the ladder. They echoed loudly in the room. Loud voices carried from outside. Brodie crept along the boards towards the doorway.

"Cumin', cumin', holds on, holds on now, 'en," said the hysterical and terrified man.

The door opened, revealing a small crowd of men dressed in dark uniforms holding torches in their gloved hands. The brass buttons and silver handles of the cutlasses in their free hands reflected their lit torches.

"What time you calling this, 'en, I'm sleepen', mun?" Brodie could see the man in the doorway from where he was crouched.

"By the order of Her Royal Majesty, you are under arrest."

"On what charge? Snoring loud?"

"For partaking in the burning of the Llanelli toll house." The officer was clearly not from Wales; his accent was English and very snotty.

"Not I, Officer. Been in my bed, 'I ave?"

The officers seized the man of the house, who had quickly dressed into his night gear before answering the door, and dragged him away while he protested.

The door lay partially opened.

What was that about? I wonder what he has been up to. Brodie turned towards the grandfather clock to inspect it again, but it was no use. He would have to find Bramble Meir, the man his great-grandmother had told him to search for. He quickly changed back into a fox and sprinted for the partially opened door.

The morning was cool. A fog hung heavy across the ground. The snow was absent, and thick, sloppy mud had taken its place.

Brodie began to run. He had no idea where he was going or where he was. All he knew was he had to find this Bramble Meir; he had to get back to his family.

He ran through fields. The ground was wet. His paws sank in the cold mud and soggy grasses.

After a while, Brodie found a barn some distance away. It was a bit shabby and was in need of repair, but it was sufficient enough for a few hours of rest. At the very back of the barn was a mound of mildewed straw covered in pigeon poop and little smashed eggs. He nestled his body on a clear patch to rest. He was exhausted and emotionally drained.

Due to nightmares, he was permitted only a few hours of sleep. He woke to whispers of two men from the horse stall next to him. He kept still.

"We're to meet behind the barn here tonight."

"It's getting a bit out of control now, Osian," one man said to the other.

"Rebecca will outsmart the dragoons. You wait and see if she doesn't."

"But you know what will happen now and the queen's proclamation. I don't like this one bit. Found out, we'll all be…hung." the men's thick Welsh accents were slightly difficult to follow.

A rustling noise from a mouse in the loose straw quickly ended the men's conversation. Both men darted out of the barn, afraid of being overheard and tattled on.

Brodie waited until the coast was completely clear before looking for food. It didn't take long. Brodie walked on the outskirts of the small village. The stone houses and the muddy streets were quiet. *Where have the villagers gone?* he wondered.

He passed a little building that looked like a chapel. It must have been late morning; the villagers spewed from the doors in every direction.

Must be Sunday, he reminded himself. The women and young girls all wore tall circular black hats, a bit like top hats with white lace frills under the brim that edged around their faces. They wore long black dresses with aprons and thick wool red plaid shawls with white threads as edging. The men wore capri pants, tall socks, black or brown shoes or boots, button-up shirts, and long jackets.

Some chickens that were scattered along the road would have been appealing on a spit, but he was quickly shooed away by a man with a cane who called after his grandson for a gun. It was hopeless. He went back to the barn, where he broke down and began to cry. He was starving. No chicken nuggets no ketchup no hot dogs he was going to die.

A whistle from behind him caught his attention. Brodie turned.

"Kol, what are you…? How did you get here? Where are the others?" he asked in sheer delight and excitement at the sight of the goblin.

"Woke up, saw your tracks on the snow when I went for a pee. I didn't even fink to go back to get the others. When I did, I was too far from the hut. I followed you to that house. That batty old cat woman told me you had come and gone, then pushed me into the clock saying I had to bring you back."

"Well, the batty old cat woman is my great-grandmother," he said happily.

"Brodie, that explains it all. Now I know where you get it from," Kol chuckled. "The batty bit, I mean," Kol added, happy to have found his companion.

"Where are we?" Brodie asked.

"I don't know. Back in the past, by the looks of it."

"Are you saying we entered a time machine?"

"Not a time machine, more of a time portal. As if they don't have enough magic already—witches! They collect extraordinary items and power. Don't ask me why," Kol said. "She hides me in the clock when Dayton's gang ambushed her house. Her bloody cat caught me peeking in one of the windows. Bloody thing bit my leg…"

Brodie gasped.

"Yeah, there were two of them watching the house. Almost got caught if it weren't for the Phooka," Kol continued.

Brodie remembered the goat-man.

Kol pulled off his cloth-booted foot; his long, dirty, curvy toes were exposed as he scratched the sole of his foot. "Turns out, the queen of the fairies has been captured."

"How do you know?"

"Grub was told. I only just found out myself, mun."

Kol caught sent of something in the air, and without explanation, he was gone, leaving Brodie to mull over this news.

He pressed a paw to the scale, concentrating hard on his human appearance. He sat there staring into the shimmering bronze scale, then decided against the change. His clothes would not fit in with the town.

You have caused a lot of trouble for me, he thought, looking at the magnificent thing.

At this point, he wished he had never crossed paths with Grub. He would be home in Canada by now, reunited with his dad and older brother. He would have gone back to a normal life, a normal family, to a world that did not understand him and judged him, a world he had difficulties fitting into and a family based on extreme differences.

He knew it was not his mother's fault that she hadn't told him about this world. He doubted very much he would have really truly believed her. He was a boy of science and evidence, not theories. He loved her even more knowing she treated him as any other normal child when he was a child labelled with autism. His dad loved him, too, but it was his mother who would say he was a child blessed with powerful abilities beyond any other normal child. While others labelled his condition as a disability or a weakness, she referred to it as a magic he has not yet channelled.

He now understood why she did not really fit into his father's family, or the city life for that matter, and why she seemed more content in the country and in the rain. He realized she had never lied to him but more so told the truth through bedtime stories.

He returned the scale into the bag. He remembered Pat had given him something as his hand brushed against a hard object in the bag.

He pulled it out. It was a book. It was old. The red fabric was worn on the spine and the corners. The book had silver letters inscribed across the cover that read:

"Legends secrets and more."

Wedged between the pages was half of an old key. It was tarnished brass the handle was slightly decorated.

He put the key in the bag and flipped through the pages. It was amazing. There were field guides to herbs, fairies, nymphs, and other magical creatures; potions maps; and footnotes that Pat must have added herself.

Kol returned with an armful of food. "I think we should stay here till it gets dark. I have learned the villagers are not fond of goblins."

Brodie agreed and continued to read. While Kol discussed the critical situation, they ate. As he raised a chunk of bread to his mouth, he recalled once upon a time not so long ago, he had difficulty eating most prepared foods, certain foods and colours couldn't touch. But now food was scarce, and the food in this realm tasted different. Perhaps it was the absence of chemical-infused preservatives and manufactured flavours and colours. He had no idea. His new friends were very considerate of Brodie's fussiness to food, and he felt himself smile as he brought the rich bread to his mouth.

Hours had passed by. The night had swept in along with a wind that caused the leafless branches to rustle. High-pitched squeaks and rustling noises inhabited the dark shadows of the ceiling. Something splattered on the ground next to him. He looked up as he moved aside.

The windowsill was lite. Brodie scratched behind his ear as he yawned. Kol lay in a deep sleep next to him. The barn was more of an overgrown shed or stable and bitterly cold.

Brodie got up and walked to the glowing window. He quickly ducked as he caught sight of a dark figure mounted above the ground on a large black horse. It was a frightening sight.

He slowly and carefully positioned himself next to the window so as to view the scene, but was careful to avoid the crowd that surrounded the figure below.

It was a crowd of women holding pitchforks, hay cleavers, shot guns, and torches.

Wow, they must be rebelling against their husbands. Wonder what the men have done—or, for that matter, not done, Brodie thought.

As a dark shadow slid to his side, overwhelming fear caused him to jump.

"Don't sneak up on me like that, you turd." Luckily, Brodie had not screamed when Kol appeared next to him, chuckling.

Kol was suddenly silent as he caught sight of the angry mob of women who thrashed their weapons into the air.

"I have seen my mom get angry and grossed out when she vacuums behind the couches and finds my dad's collection of toenails, but I don't think she would go to this extent. Their husbands must have done something bad to deserve this. They don't look like they own any video games," the little fox said, humoring himself.

"Shhh, they are not women, Brode's," Kol said as his eyes widened with anticipation.

The figure that sat upon the saddle of the huge black horse suddenly waved a torch into the air. The crowd fell silent instantly.

A deep Welsh accent projected across the mob of an audience. The speaker and leader of this rebellious crowd was dressed just like the women of the town Brodie had seen earlier in the day. A tall top hat with white frills under the brim sat on the dark figure's head. His devilish face was concealed by a scarf. The remainder of his face was blackened by soot or boot polish. He wore a long black dress with a white pinny. A red plaid shawl with white frills along the edges draped over his huge muscular shoulders. The only things manly about this frightful figure was his voice, the heavy set of muddy boots, and his musket.

Brodie thought about the man whose living room he had ended up in after stepping out of the portal of the clock. It made sense now, and that must have been the reason he had been arrested.

"My daughters, proud am I to call myself Welsh and to have the lot of you by my side. We will put fear into the dreams of those pathetic, greedy magistrate pigs. Their pockets gain in weight as our animal's work, and suffer we do from their collections, and our families' bellies go unfed. I'm fed up. Skint we are, living in hovels—for what? Empty and broken promises. Promises to fix the roads, to rid the tolls, promises geneth [Welsh for *girl*]. Yeah, well, tonight, my cariads, the toll house of Davedd Davis, burn it to the ground, we will."

A riot of cheers, whistles, and the clanging of objects against each other was unleashed. Brodie caught glimpses of fairies and pixies and other small creatures enjoying the chaos as much as the humans.

"Now, my darling daughters, into the night you go, for Davedd Davis has collected his last shilling before this night is done. His gate and blood will fall; the toll house, burn it to the ground. And as for the dragoons, they 'ad a tip that the south gate in Aberystwyth is on Rebecca and her daughters' list tonight."

They cheered a little louder, then vanished into the darkness of the night. Brodie stood there in the darkness. He preferred his fox form in the dark for the swiftness and night vision. Kol left the barn and was running behind the bandit Rebecca and her daughters to catch up to the angry mob.

"Kol, get back here!"

"Not missing this," he said as he left the small barn. He was full of excitement.

Brodie trotted close behind. They traveled behind the large crowd. The road was lit up from the torches of the rioters.

"What are you doing, Kol?" Brodie asked, slightly irritated. "You're going to get us killed."

"I want to see what they do."

"You heard them speak of what they're going to do. Don't you have an imagination to figure out the rest?"

The goblin ran ahead, getting closer to the crowd. Brodie slowed down. He began to look around him cautiously, concentrating on the whispers that filled the darkness. He felt distant, as if he was tuning out. *What a time to space out,* he thought.

Then, suddenly, faces began to appear. He was not drifting into a bubble. He slowed down. From out of nowhere, thick white fog crept along the ground. It was heading right for him. He couldn't move; he was scared and mesmerized. His four paws were cemented to the cold, muddy ground.

A large centipede the length of a small snake crawled from the smoke towards the woods. A light darted before Brodie's eyes.

"Come, you have to follow," said a musical voice from the darkness. A firefly led him into the ferns by the roadside. A number of spectating creatures and fairies watched from the shadows of the ferns.

"Wait, I have to get Kol."

"He will be fine."

"What is that?" the little fox asked the firefly, looking towards the disappearing road.

"It's fog, and it's a dangerous kind," another brightly lit insect replied.

"We should get Kol," said the little fox as he paced back and forth. He didn't want to part from his friend again, not here, not now.

"No! Stay off the road, little fox." Her light turned from a green to an orangey red instantly. "Your friend will be safe. It's not quite a fog, but a goblin in the form of fog."

"What is it doing?" Brodie asked.

"The goblin is drawn by the angry energy of the townspeople." Answered the second fairy

"The Rebecca man and his followers," Brodie said as he stared back to the road.

"Yes. The Welsh are superstitious but respectful of our presence. We have lived among them in peace ever since they took over our land. But the rich and the English, through their greed and corruption, continue to destroy our lands within its domain. When the Beccas march, the creatures of our kind follow to watch the destruction of the law. Some follow to watch and encourage bloodshed and wickedness. Some enjoy the thrill.

"Your friend will be safe. He is undoubtedly a goblin. The stench gives it away. There are only a few that will turn against its distant relative. The fog is not one. Although if not a goblin, it is not safe to cross paths with it."

"So what would have happened if the fog hit me?" Brodie asked.

"You would feel enraged—a desire deep within to attack and cause destruction."

"Oh, a bit like anarchy."

"I'm unfamiliar with your 'an artchy,' but it is safe to follow now."

The road was clear of the fog. Many of the animals and magical creatures left the safety of the shrubs, hastening to catch up with the Beccas.

"Are you a wizard or an elf?" the firefly asked. "Or just a halfling?"

"I'm a boy," replied the fox as he trotted along to catch up with Kol.

"You posses power. I can smell it."

Brodie gulped as he stumbled into a large hole in the road. He tried to clear his mind of the scale as he nudged his body against a tree, making sure the scale was still there at his side.

Suddenly, the firefly began to dart across the sky. She was joined by another, then a third, then a fourth firefly.

"Troll," she said, loud and afraid as she looked around them.

Brodie could smell something, too, then realized it was coming from his bag. When he had brushed himself against the tree, he must have knocked the cork off the bottle of troll's breath, releasing the potent smell of the residue that remained in the bottle.

"No, it's just me, sorry."

"Relative, are you?" she asked more calmly.

"Well, my mum smells like one after fast food, but no, a bottle of troll's breath opened in my bag," Brodie said apologetically.

The torches of the Beccas had disappeared. The troll's breath was so overpowering that it crippled his tracking senses.

"Could you please help me find Kol?"

"Find him we will, little fox." She giggled.

The conditions of the roads were despicable. Large holes that ate away at the uneven muddy ground caused Brodie to trip numerous times. There were many small pools of water.

"How can people use these roads?" he said.

"They can't. That's why they are rebelling," the firefly answered.

Rebecca and his daughters had reached a fork in the road. The slumbering residents of the Llanelli toll booth slept peacefully through the night, unaware of what was to come with their stomachs full, coal burning in the fireplace, and a bag full of collected dirty money to aide their sweet dreams.

The lonely little toll house was the size of a large shed. It was positioned between a fork in the road that branched into two separate roads. There were large wooden gates outstretched from both sides of the house, blocking passage. Large studs held the thick gates into the stone wall.

When Brodie and the fireflies caught up to Kol, the goblin was amongst the crowd, full of anticipation. Light reflected from the glass windowpanes, carried by the torch of the frightful, mysterious Rebecca.

Ten feet away from the toll house, Rebecca raised his torched hand into the air. The crowd fell quiet in their places. He dismounted from the enormous black steed, walked a little, then reached for something in mid-air. He pulled on some invisible line that instantly caused a small iron bell mounted on the wall to ring. He mounted back on to the saddle of the patient horse. He looked like a demon, a shadow of darkness that had been sent by the devil into the night.

"Up you get, Mr. Davis," he yelled.

The daughters remained silent, watching, waiting. Gruesome smiles stretched over their blackened faces.

A couple of seconds passed. Nothing.

Holding the reins with one hand and a torch with another, he pulled on the strap to direct his now antsy horse to and fro. "Up you get, Mr. Davis," Rebecca called out louder and more aggressively than the first time.

He waited. They waited. Nothing.

Rebecca looked to the crowd behind him. After pulling the musket into the air, he let the pistol blow.

Bang.

Brodie jumped from shock at the startling, loud noise.

"Get out, Mr. Davis, or we burn your house down with you and your family in it."

A moment later, a greasy, pudgy little man in his night dress and night cap opened the door, huddling close to an almost pudgier little woman in her nightgown. She clutched a child younger than Brodie.

A roar of disgust came from the crowd as the huddled family came into view.

"Good evening, mochyn (Welsh for *pig*)," the deep voice of Rebecca said. The daughters burst into laughter.

"What do you want?" asked the trembling toll collector in fear.

"Come now. Think you know what we want—retribution and justice. Justice for what you and your fellow rats have done to our lands, our businesses, and our families. For every last penny that could 'ave bought a loaf of bread to feed our young, our old, and our ones with child. Families ripped apart, good Welsh men sent abroad to slavery cause they can't pay the taxes, wives left behind getting kicked out of their homes cause they too poor to pay toll taxes, can't afford way of life."

Davedd shook, afraid to look into the blackened and enraged faces of the crowd.

"For years, we were promised by your magistrates our roads would be fixed, and for years, we watched as more toll houses were built no less than miles from each other, doubling rates people can't afford."

Brodie listened intently.

"Have your money back," Davedd said, now in tears as he pushed his wife towards the door of the toll house. A moment later, she returned, carrying a leather sack of clicking metal chips. Rebecca strode over on his horse, leaned down to grab the sack, and then turned to Davedd.

"Lucky you'll be to survive this night, but you will relay a message to the greedy, rich magistrates that Rebecca and her daughters are coming to tear every single toll gate down across Wales till the land is free again. This is our land." He turned to his daughters, raised his torch into the air, and yelled out, "Burn it to the ground, my beauties!"

Two men dressed as women branched out from the advancing crowd. They bound the collector and his wife together against the closest tree. The woman screamed and lashed out. Brodie tried to stay close to Kol as the remaining daughters headed towards the toll house. The sound of their axes hacking into the wood grew. Others cheered as they smashed the windows and threw their torches through the crevices.

The woman screamed in anger as she watched her house blaze from within and the flames grow out of control. The collector sat bound silently as his young son watched with amusement at the destruction.

The young child was not the only one. Elves, goblins, and sprites all jumped for joy as they watched the humans demolish the house. Kol, for one, found it highly amusing. He picked up rocks and threw them into the crowd, as did many others.

Brodie grew nervous as he caught sight of the fog growing closer to the furious crowd and their spectators. It moved so silently, drifting across the ground, almost invisible to those who had not noticed it approaching.

"Kol, I want to leave. I don't feel good. I want to go back," the nervous little fox said.

"In a minute," Kol replied as he threw a rock towards the collector and his wife.

"We have to find Bramble Meir. He can help us get back."

"It's no use," said the firefly. "He is a goblin. They feed off mischief. It's in their nature."

Brodie suddenly had an overwhelming desire to join in. A rush of anger coursed through him. He looked down to his paws and realized he was standing in half a foot of fog. He stepped back from the scene, watching from a distance.

Ten minutes or so later, Kol was running through the crowd, calling for Brodie, afraid the little fox was in danger.

"I'm right here," Brodie barked out.

Kol ran to him. "We have to go. Let's find this Bramble Meir guy and get the hell out of here."

"What's wrong?" Brodie asked.

Not sure whether he wanted to scare the young boy, Kol pointed through the crowd to pairs of animal eyes in the darkness reflecting the light of the fire. "Wolves," he said. His fear was present and very strong in his tone.

Brodie focused on the background, blocking everybody else out—a set of greenish silver spots reflected in darkness.

"Let's go," he said, and they took one last look at the flames climbing out of the broken windows and doors. The smoke billowed towards the stars. The daughters of Rebecca stood cheering Welsh hymns as they watched the fire consume the house and remaining fragments of the gates on the ground.

Brodie turned to see Rebecca mounting his black horse; he looked scary. *Evil* was a better word, but overall brilliant.

Then he turned his head to catch a last glimpse of the young boy curled up to his bound and crying mother. One of the men had wrapped a thick shawl around the small child to keep him warm. The man's gesture made Brodie feel a bit better. At least the child was not in danger. *They're humane,* he thought.

They fled from the scene, avoiding the dangerous roads. They ran as fast as they could back towards the barn.

They were out of breath and very exhausted, but they made it.

CHAPTER 17

The Elf King

"Sorry, Brodie, I got caught up in the commotion, I did," Kol apologized as he rested against the interior wall of the barn, mopping the sweat off his brow with his sleeve.

"That's okay. I was just afraid something bad would happen," Brodie replied. He was panting, and he collapsed to the ground.

An old swill bucket had collected water from a rotten hole that ate away at the ceiling. As disgusting as it was, Brodie got up to lap a couple of mouthfuls, followed by Kol.

"Bloody epic," said Kol in amazement.

"It doesn't taste that good," replied Brodie, who resumed lying on the ground to catch his breath.

Kol looked over his shoulder in Brodie's direction, then turned back to the window that revealed a flicker of warm amber in the distance. "Do you know what just happened there, boy?"

Brodie paused. A smart remark left his mouth even though now was not the time, and he was exhausted. "Yeah, cross-dressing pyros went berserk on that house."

Kol stared, unimpressed by the ignorance of the little fox. "History," Kol said, looking back to the lite scene in the distance. "That will go down in history as the Rebecca Riots, a big part of the Welsh history. And I can honestly say I watched it." Kol rubbed his hands in delight.

Brodie had seen old books in his mother's library, one by Dylan Thomas and a couple of others that had the bolded name *Rebecca* written across the spines. He did not reply. He removed his head from the strap of his bag. It was not comfortable to wear for long periods of time. The bag was much heavier when he was in his fox form.

The ground began to vibrate ever so slightly like distant thunder in the horizon.

"Brodie, look!"

The little fox quickly threaded his head through the bag's strap and returned it to his side where he knew the bag was best protected. He trotted over to the window, where Kol had remained since their return.

How odd, he thought as swift black shadows scattered in different directions past the barn. Brodie sat for a moment observing the fleeing women.

Perhaps we should go back to the clock and retrace our steps to find this Bramble Meir."

After playfully witty remarks were tossed back and forth to each other, they headed for the house that had brought them to the past. The two walked up and down the lonely broken roads of the sleeping town in search of the house. It was no use; all Brodie could smell was the troll's breath, and Kol was no help either. The sky was beginning to lighten. The pitch-black sky was now a little softer shade mixed with a hue of purple. The village men dressed as women would now be safe in their beds, dreaming of the victories of their night's work.

Brodie gave up. He was tired and hungry, and the bag was heavy around his neck, and just for once, he would prefer to sleep in a clean, warm human bed instead of mouldy old straw one. The ticks and fleas had bitten behind his ears. From carrying the bag so close to his body, he had begun to smell like a troll himself. He sat in the mud underneath the window of a house. His beautiful red coat was brown and clumped together with dried mud.

Kol had not given up. He was pulling himself up to the windowsills to peek in through the glass.

"Fought it was this one," he said disappointedly.

Brodie's ears suddenly went up on end. He focused on the shadows of the houses around them. Something did not feel right. He whispered to Kol to follow him. they slipped around the corner of the house and hid behind the neighbor's coal shed.

"What's wrong, Brodie?" Kol asked cautiously.

"I didn't see anything! But something has been following us. I could feel it. I don't think it's friendly either."

The silence was interrupted by a stampede of horses. The two left the temporary safety behind the coal shed to investigate the sudden noise.

Kol watched the men on horseback carrying torches whilst Brodie scanned the darkness for the unseen danger that he could feel was still watching them. The men split into groups of two and departed in different directions. A moment or two later, two men returned to a corporal-looking lieutenant who had been waiting on horseback in the center of the road.

"Town's asleep, sir."

"Not a single light on, sir," said the Englishman on horseback.

"Then carry on to the next town. Those blaggarts won't slip through us again, not tonight. Keep two men here to patrol the road, just in case."

A bugle was blown. The riders returned to the road in front of Brodie and Kol.

"Quick, while there's a distraction," Brodie said to Kol as he sprinted in the opposite direction. Kol hesitated for a moment, then followed. A small green light on the road in the distance disappeared around a corner. Brodie followed his instincts and made his way towards the light. He ran as fast as he could down the street and was not surprised when he had caught up to it. It was the firefly Brodie had met earlier; he'd had a feeling it was her.

Her butt grew brighter as Brodie approached.

"I was looking for you," she said. "You had mentioned a name back at the toll house to your friend before you disappeared."

"Do you know him? I'm supposed to look for him," Brodie exclaimed.

A second later, Kol ran out from around the corner, out of breath and stumbling. "Don't do that, mun. It's hard enough to keep up with you when you're a human but bloody impossible as a fox."

"Follow me," said the firefly.

They followed the firefly for some ways. She was leading them away from the small town now. Brodie wanted to find Bramble Meir but didn't want to get lost in the past. His sense of smell was shot, and Kol was a bit hopeless tonight. He was completely caught up in the events of the past rather than their current event—getting back home.

"And why we following this fairy now, 'en?"

"She's a firefly."

"If you say so and if you think she's trustworthy." Kol stuck his nose in the air.

They followed the firefly until they came to a hilltop. The small town was nestled below, left behind in darkness by the departing lights of the dragoons who were in full throttle to catch up to Rebecca and her daughters. They climbed to the top of the hill where an isolated old oak tree stood. Its trunk was thick and wide. Its bare branches wound together in different directions. A black shadow hung from one of the closest branches to the ground. Once they had reached four feet away from the tree, the hanging shadow lit up.

Brodie gazed at the lamp that swayed in the night's breeze. His attention was diverted to the trunk of the tree as a thin, short stripe of light appeared to grow from within the tree itself. The firefly disappeared into the crack of light. Kol followed without any questions as if he had done this a thousand times. The lit opening stretched wide enough for the goblin to step through. Brodie approached the crack, not sure what he was supposed to do.

He changed back into his human form. He placed his right hand on the tree. A warm layer of fur-like moss covered the trunk. The light began to gradually open, exposing a sight that caused his jaw to drop.

He breathed in deeply and blinked hard. The sight was astonishing and enchanting sight. The interior of the hollow was enormous. What looked like an old tree on the outside was a huge open ballroom on the inside. It was the most amazing sight Brodie had ever seen. The ceiling was covered in ivy vines that trailed from the ground upward. The ivy was lit up from dozens of smaller fairies sitting on the vines, watching the magical dancers waltz on the floor. The large banquet hall was lit with a thousand lights Brodie thought to himself. The smell of sweet honey, cream, and other foods rose from the party.

The branches of the tree rubbed together, causing a slight creaking. He looked over his shoulder. The swinging lamp's light dimmed, then grew brighter.

"Cum on, get a move on," Kol said as he extended an arm, pulling Brodie through the strange lit entrance.

"There are so many portals in this realm," Brodie huffed aloud.

What a sight it was. The faces spiralling in dance were full of contentment. They looked as though they were masks. Brodie felt like he had stepped into a fancy masquerade party. Elves, nymphs, and many other beautiful, strange, and scary-looking creatures occupied the banquet hall of the enchanted oak. The orchestra played flutes, bells, chimes, pan pipes, violins, and drums in the farthest corner of the large crowd. Lit torches bound to the walls of the tree, filled the miraculous hollow.

To the right of the musicians, a little between the ceiling and ground, was a carved-out ledge in the wood where two raggedy birds sat perched on what looked like wooden thrones set on branches. The two watched the dancing, thoroughly entertained. Brodie could not help but wonder what breed they were, perhaps a cross between owls and ravens or some kind or maybe osprey.

Whatever the breed, one was a large brown-and-white bird with a soft golden chest. When the bird moved, the glow of the fairies illuminated the feathers, making them shimmer. It had to have been a male—the majestic bird radiated masculinity. He sat clenching a golden goblet between his claws, excusing himself from the gathering. He was deep in thought, concentrating in a set direction. The light casting down on him—presuming it was a *him*—from this angle made the bird look grand and very wise.

The smaller one had to have been a female. She was more of a sandy brown with a white chest, and speckles of gold kissed the tips of her wings and left traces along her longer feathers. She was a much prettier and far more delicate-looking bird than her partner. She was immensely amused with the merriment, flapping her wings and bobbing her head in delight.

Kol gave Brodie a nudge, then picked up a golden goblet from a table that was occupied by a group of rowdy and ugly dwarves. The elves, pixies, and other strange-looking creatures on the dance floor looked like they belonged to a dream. Some of the females were beautiful. Some wore gowns of sheer material made of spider silk, and some wore dresses made of natural debris and dried materials.

Bubbles floated around the dancers, which amused the fairies; their chimed giggles moved sporadically across the room.

The elfish men were uglier. Brodie remembered seeing elves from movies. They were portrayed as graceful and good-looking, with sharpish edges but a hint of female beauty. The elves in front of him were giddy with glee, uglier, and smelled very unpleasant; they had an earthiness to them. Their attire was similar to the females, but their clothes looked a lot like the silver caps' clothing, as if made from old burlap. Then there were the smaller animals like the mice, birds, and other creatures Brodie could not name.

He looked around and noticed tables displaying wooden plates of hazelnuts, walnuts, beechnuts, beans, fruits, and berries of all kinds, with wooden bowls of thick golden honey. He felt hungry. There had to have been eight or nine types of mushrooms. He could recognize the majority on the table, and closing his eyes, he could see the page of the book he had once read showing the different species of fungi. Pyramids of warm breads, round plates of golden cheeses, and cakes of all shapes and sizes decorated with wild summer berries were stacked in inviting piles. Large wooden egg cups were filled with golden creams. Their buttery rich aroma tantalized him.

He stared as an elf reached for a purple flower from the large floral centerpiece, then greedily devoured it without haste.

"That's gross," Brodie said under his breath.

"What is?" asked Kol, hearing the child's remark and looking around.

"All that food, and that creature is going for the decorations."

Kol began to laugh.

"What's so funny?" Brodie asked.

"Your ignorance," he said, chuckling again. "Magical folk don't eat meat. Their bodies are not adapted to eat such things. Instead, they get their source of protein from the plants and nuts. The flower he just ate was a *vicia sepuim*. That type of plant to us is like a stuffed roast goose to you."

"I wish there was roast goose," Brodie mumbled.

Out of nowhere, the large bird swiftly swooped from his balcony throne to the middle of the dance floor. The crowd parted, giving the increasingly vulture-like bird space. His long brown feathers draped down his back like a cape. The somewhat roundish body became thinner and leaner. His chest feathers absorbed into his body and hardened, leaving a golden metal armor.

It didn't have the face of a bird any longer. The feathers had disappeared. An old elf was left behind where the bird had once been. Eyes black as little beetles read Brodie all over. His fingers twisted into one another as he clasped his hands together in a menacing way.

The bird man said menacingly,

"'Tis the morning on the old willow.
Tell me, child, who you to be.

He had such a unique voice. It was cold and cruel but musical. It made Brodie uneasy. What had been a bird a moment ago had transformed into an elfish-looking creature. His little black eyes watched Brodie. His breathtaking chest of golden armor held Brodie's attention.

The bird man licked his chops, then repeated himself.

Brodie was absolutely flabbergasted and completely wordless.

A second later, the smaller bird was at the elfs side. She was beautiful and dressed in silver cobweb silk, leaves, and feathers. Her long brunette hair hung over her shoulder in a loose braid decorated with little flowers. Her voice was delicate and soft. She had the most beautiful, large, animated blue eyes that sparkled.

"He is only a child, my love."

"He possesses no harm, he is unlike the townspeople," the firefly was at the smaller bird's side now, whispering into her ear.

The crowd stood shorter than Brodie. He felt like a giant compared to the magical creatures that inhabited the old oak.

"Please, my love, won't you invite him to feast and dance?"

The bird man smiled and turned his focus to Brodie again, then to his bag.

"Thank you, but no, thank you," Brodie said. "I have come to seek a man called Bramble Meir."

The king placed his hand upon his chin, considering the name.

Although he was very hungry, and it all looked so delectable, Brodie could see the enchantment of the elfish food. Every time the majestic elf made a sarcastic remark or a joke, the crowd would begin to laugh. This evidence alone indicated he was the authority, or grand ruler, of these magical creatures.

The goblin's eyes constantly lowered to Brodie's bag. His tongue ran across his lower lip as he rubbed his hands together.

Brodie clenched the bag tighter.

Kol, who was close to Brodie, whispered to him, "Be careful. The king of the elves is cunning and sly. He is a trickster. They all are." Kol turned from Brodie and walked towards the food, keeping a close eye on the boy, ready to jump to his aid if needed.

Brodie wished he had refrained from changing back into a boy. He looked around at the animals scattered through the crowd, thinking the king would not have been so vile had Brodie been in his animal form.

"What is hidden within your bag, child, you hold so tight to you?" the king asked.

Unconsciously, Brodie relaxed his tight grip. "Nothing, Your Highness."

"You may do this two ways: you may show me, or I shall take it from you."

All eyes silently watched the boy. Some had menacing smiles.

Brodie met Kol's eyes. The goblin discretely nodded in a hopeless manner.

Brodie held the bag from him and opened it, watching the king with caution.

The king's eyes widened with delight. He reached into the bag, but Brodie quickly pulled it back.

The king looked furious.

"Your Highness only requested to look at what was in the bag. You did not specify you were going to touch my belongings."

The crowd paused. His queen tugged at his side, smiling a delightfully charming smile at the cheeky boy. Brodie did not smile back but watched the king.

"Answer my riddle, and you may keep your belongings and anything else I may provide you with, but answer incorrectly, and you shall remain here with me and your belongings in my possession for eternity."

Brodie turned to Kol, who shook his head disapprovingly.

"And if I don't answer?"

"Remain here with me as a prisoner rather than a guest."

"Well, I have no choice by the sounds of it," Brodie answered with a cocky tone.

"Answer me this:

Coat red, home on fire. Not animal nor human ither.

In the sky or on the ground. Creating smiles when found. What am I?"

Brodie paused. He gave the short riddle his full concentration. He seemed to be getting further and further away from his family. First visiting the moon, and then entering the fairy realm, then going back into the past, and now being stuck in a tree with an ugly little elf or whatever it was forcing him to answer silly little riddles.

Oh, he couldn't think.

"Red coat, home on fire and not a human or animal—what the hell is it!" he huffed.

He looked around the room. What a brain fart he was having.

Brodie glanced over to the bug hovering around the queen of the fairies. Its bottom was brightly lit. Brodie could not concentrate. The firefly had become very distracting. An image popped into his mind.

Wait a minute, Brodie thought. "Ladybug, ladybug, fly away home. Your house is on fire. And children alone," he whispered to himself.

"You're a ladybug!" he belted out. It was a nursery rhyme his mother had recited to him as a child.

"Incorrect." The king smiled as he reached for the bag.

Brodie clenched the bag tightly to himself. "What is it then?"

"Ladybird," answered the king.

"What! It's the same thing. It's a bloody insect," argued Brodie angrily.

"Incorrect," the elf king jeered.

"In Canada, they are called ladybugs, not birds. They don't have feathers," Brodie said agitatedly.

The queen gave a quiet giggle. She admired the fire that was within the young child and tugged at her king's side once more. "He answered correctly, my darling." She walked behind Brodie and placed a hand on his shoulder. "He is only a child, my love, and you a great ruler."

"Very well, my essence of life. Child, you may keep your belongings," the king said, waving Brodie off with his fingers. He looked utterly disappointed and defeated.

"Thank you. All I want to know, Your Highness, is where I can find a man called Bramble Meir."

"Walk with me. Talk with me, child."

The music continued, and the crowd started to dance once more.

Kol remained behind to eat and dance but insisted that Brodie converse with the king. The king escorted Brodie to a hole in the wall. The dark little tunnel led to stairs. The firefly followed, providing light for the two in the dark, tunnelled staircase.

It was only when they reached the top of the stairs and stepped out into the night air that Brodie realized he had shrunk. The king stepped out onto a bare branch that sprouted from the tree. Brodie looked down. It would be quite a distance from the ground if he were clumsy.

"What is your name, child?" the king said as he walked towards Brodie.

"Brodie Rhys, Your Highness."

"Tell me, child, where did you come across that item you possess in your bag?"

Sensing the king possessed no threat at this point, Brodie carefully walked out onto the branch and sat down close to the king. He told the king the story right from the beginning. He started from when he and his mother had hit Grub, adding in the people and problems along the way.

As beautiful and as mesmerizing as this realm's secrets were, he longed to reunite with his family more than anything and finding bramble meir would get him back he was really hoping.

The king sat in silence, watching the dawning sky approach, then said, "So Dayton is still alive."

Brodie was surprised by the king's remark. "How do—"

Before he could finish the question, the elf king stood and paced himself along the branch. "A man of great power from victims. he skipped back and forth through time, collecting power and knowledge. Greed and corruption finally got the better of him." He shook his head. "If he is after the elements and is victorious, your world as others will crumble ruled by a cold-hearted wizard who will stop at no end to gain power. You need to enter the past further to rid yourself of the scale. As for you, child, there is an aura of magic about you. The old oak would not have opened for just any human."

Brodie went on to explain about the women of his mother's family.

"We thought, or hoped, Dayton to be lost to the past, future, or some void in time or space. As I recall now, he traveled and created havoc wherever he went."

"Sir, could you please tell me what I am up against? The gnomes are hiding my family from Dayton," Brodie said, looking out into the sunrise.

"If your family is with the gnomes, they will remain safe for the time being, but you must destroy the scale before it reaches Dayton's hands. As a child, he walked among these lands. He played, laughed, and loved, but as he grew, so did the jealousy, evil, and greed in his heart—always compared to his cousin, always ridiculed."

"Merlyn," Brodie mumbled.

"Dayton was Merlyn's younger cousin. I remember them both from my earlier years of ruling. He possessed a different type of magic. He could skip back and forth through time. Really, it was the only thing he could do. After that, he became one of the most powerful and evil wizards that have ever walked our woods. He disappeared for times at end, gathering magic from distant countries and eras and returning with his own band of followers. His henchmen are shape-shifters and very dangerous, with a power of their own—and, may I add, just as evil.

"Dayton declared a law that his army would be the only shape-shifters. It caused thousands to flee for their lives. Thankfully, Merlyn, the beautiful young Aanieda, his younger sister, and another wizard banished him. They bound and kept him prisoner within a tree, not to be heard of until now. I can understand Dayton's desire for the scale. He hungers for its power, I cannot deny my desire to obtain it"

What an odd sight it must have been on that branch—two small bodies no taller than little pocket dolls high in the tree top. The sun was climbing into the waking sky. Its rays coloured the clouds. The wind had tamed to nearly nothing, causing the few remaining leaves to softly rustle against one another. What a peaceful beautiful morning. But something did not feel right. Something felt cold and hollow within.

"Your friend the goblin, he is trustworthy knowing what you possess?" asked the king.

"He hasn't the foggiest, Your Majesty."

"The foggiest?" asked the king with a confused expression.

197

"He doesn't know, but he is very trustworthy, sir," answered Brodie.

The king paused, looking out into the distance. "The man you seek, how was it you came across his name?"

"When my great-grandmother's house was invaded by that gang, she pushed me through a clock that brought me here and told me to look for Bramble Meir."

"The man you seek has been imprisoned by the humans. He has been locked away in a stone-breaking cell two towns over as punishment for his crimes whilst he waits trial."

"Oh no, that's horrible. Is there any way we can rescue him, Your Highness?"

"No harm will come to our friend. He walked with me many a time when the harvest moon was at its full. I shall send one of my children to guide you to him. I say this to you, do not be misled from your path. You must destroy Dayton. But above all, trust no one. He must be destroyed."

"I can't commit murder," Brodie protested.

But it was too late; Brodie was lying on the ground of the exposed roots underneath the oak tree alone. He had resumed his normal size. He looked around. The elf king was nowhere to be seen. Brodie got up to look for the entrance in the tree. He felt the mossy trunk, but it was useless. He picked up the bag that had managed to escape his shoulder. He checked its contents and began to look around for Kol as he walked down the hill. The familiar twinkle of the firefly caught his attention. He followed it. It was crucial he find Bramble Meir to get home.

He became exhausted as he walked down the hill. He turned back into the little fox for the warmth. A large yawn indicated to the firefly that he needed to rest, so they stopped for a moment brodie concerned for Kol refused to go any further without him. Firefly suggested he rest quickly whilst she flew back to look for his friend. The overwhelmed little fox fell into a deep sleep curled around his bag on a soft bed of grass.

Giggles surrounded him as little green arms tried to pry Brodie's tail and head away to expose his belongings. Realizing what was going on as firefly quickly returned without Kol, she tried to awaken the boy from his sleep.

Feeling the tugs at his fur and seeing the firefly dart to and fro to aid Brodie from the mischievous grips, Brodie quickly rose to all fours and shook his body like a wet dog. Clumps of grass flew off him from left to right. Once freed from their clutches, he began to run away from the enticingly soft bed.

"Where is Kol and what were those things?" he asked as he ran away.

"What appeared to be a thick bed of grass was in fact a swarm of *sustantivo hierba femenino*, a pixie that derived from Spain when the Spanish king settled in Ireland, unaware these creatures existed and had hidden among the cargo of the Spanish ships as stowaways. They infested the mainland once they got there, making it their new home," the little firefly explained. "Today, they are known as crab-grass. The cunning little pixies, when resting, look like patches of grass. Some camouflage with weeds like dandelions. Their backs are covered in sprouted grass and weeds, and their bodies look like a cross between frogs and beetles—long arms and long legs with bulging little, round bellies. They take pleasure in tricking humans. As humans look for landmarks to direct them along their journeys, these little tricky creatures move around, causing changes of scenery to confuse the travellers who lost their ways, I could not find him."

"Perhaps we should just look for Bramble Meir first then look for Kol on the way back he is really good at tracking me" Brodie told the firefly, who landed on him and held on tightly to the fur on the scruff of his neck as he slowed his run to a walk.

"He may very well still be in the hall the tree seals during the day but the king will see that he exits Brodie don't be concerned" dragon fly said.

CHAPTER 18

Gnoman's Land

"This is torture. If I have to eat another bloody mushroom, I'm going to—" Rhys stopped mid-sentence, interrupted by the heartfelt sobs of his daughter.

His wife was to the left of him and his daughter to the right; he reached an arm around both of them, pulling them into a hug. Beth stood and walked to the wooden bars of what felt like a jail cell. They had been placed in a holding cell waiting to see the gnome king. The dug-out cave in the rocks was least inviting. The ceiling was narrow and made the three feel a little claustrophobic. It was damp and cold. Rhys was under the suspicion the gnomes had chosen this particular holding cell as punishment.

"It's my fault. I should have made him stay with me," Beth said as she exhaled, holding back tears.

"You can't keep going over it. We all can't. We should have taken him to Aunty Winifred's, but we didn't," Rhys said. "But we will soon get answers from the king on what's going on."

Beth reached for her daughter's hand "I know he's okay babes, trust me."

"I don't even know how long we have been down here, feels like weeks. He could be dead," Katrin exclaimed before bursting into tears in her hands.

A vole wobbled through the stony, damp passage of the empty holding cells. A podgy gnome followed close behind, dressed in a bluish-grey lengthy smock with a thick brown leather belt strapped around his expanded tummy and a worn, peaked brown cap upon his white hairy head. His hair trailed down, covering the majority of his face. In one hand, he carried a little lamp. In another was a large wooden plate with assorted cheeses, breads, and roasted toadstools.

Beth accepted the plate from the gnome, who shot a filthy glare at Rhys.

"Mmm, mushrooms, yay," Rhys said sarcastically. His one eye squinted shut, and he opened his mouth in a sarcastic rock star expression and nodded, waving his pointed index fingers in the air in mock celebration.

The gnome smiled with sarcasm. "Lovely, then, I will bring you some more," he said as he left, shutting the wooden gate behind him.

A minute later, a second gnome was jingling a set of keys in search for the right one. The gate finally opened, and the funny little gnome announced in an odd little voice, "The king would like to see you. Follow me."

The three rose from their stone bench. They followed the gnome through the dark and damp passages of the dungeons in silence, each deep in personal prayer for news of Brodie's safety. They passed through a wooden hall that led them out of the cave-like dungeon. It was warmer and lit up with candles.

"How much longer, please?" asked Beth. "I wouldn't mind stopping to use the restroom."

The gnome remained silent. Using all of his might, he pushed open a large decorated door.

They stepped through—all a little nervous as to what was to come next. Rhys straightened himself up and clutched his girls' hands, reinforcing them with strength and courage.

They walked through. The floors were polished marble, and on each side of the large room was rows of gnomes. Their heads turned as the three entered the room. The gnome led them to the back of the room where seven ancient gnomes sat.

The one in the center was slightly larger than the three on either side of him. He looked a bit like a miniature Father Christmas. His hair that hung from his face was longer and faded than the others; he appeared withered with age. A sapphire-blue silk smock made him look grand and important compared to the other gnomes.

"I do apologize for your living conditions. This past week, there had been other accommodations for you, but there was a misunderstanding." The head gnome said as he cleared this throat looking directly at the gnome closest to Rhys.

Rhys noticed gnomes seated in the nearest rows giggling into their hands. He was irritated and shook his head.

"We had to take full precaution in your concealment. Your family is wanted by a dangerous and powerful wizard. Our council was notified by the fairies. Once we had word from the garden gnomes at your relatives that you were all there, that's when we intervened for your family's protection. Your son is safe and well." He paused for a moment, giving time for his words to sink in as he looked at Katrin.

Whispers weaved across the crowd in the rows.

"Where is he?" asked Katrin anxiously.

The king did not respond.

Beth cleared her voice. She inquired why the gnomes had captured them and brought them to this place.

Rhys nudged his wife. She ignored him. There was no time for jokes or witty remarks, not when their baby was lost.

"We are all alike—the fairies, gnomes, and so forth. We are different in many ways, but deep down, we share the same concerns. Our concern is Dayton. He is—how I should say this with the utmost concern and means not to scare or upset you?"

Katrin fell to her knees. Streams of tears ran down her face, leaving clean streaks through the dirt. Kept as a prisoner in a cave-like jail with small pales of water to wash from did not leave her the cleanest, nor smelling of roses.

"My dear, please, I do not wish to upset you, but more so to inform you of your son."

Katrin raised her head. Rhys and Beth both lowered themselves to aid their daughter in rising to her feet.

The king continued. "My dear," he said with compassion for the heartbroken young mother, "your son is safe. He is with companions. Your mother has been keeping an eye on him." He looked at Beth.

She closed her eyes. For a moment, she looked at peace. A small smile warmed her face.

Everybody's eyes fell on Beth.

"What's that supposed to mean? She's dead," Rhys remarked in fury.

"No, she is well and very much alive. Brodie is not too far from her, with companions who are protecting the child, but he is in our realm," the king replied.

"Mummy didn't die, Rhys. She's still alive on the other side."

Rhys looked confused and angry. "Other side of what? Town, country, world—what?"

Katrin stared at her mother, still sobbing. "But we buried her."

Beth stepped closer to Katrin, realizing this was a big shock for her daughter. She hugged Katrin and said, "No, it was an empty casket. Your nan arranged with your aunties and I to fake her funeral to not cause suspicion to the people around us—why she was not aging, why she was growing more catlike than human, and why she would outlive her friends and the majority of her children.

"We have kept in touch through the absent years. I sent her pictures of the family—of you, your sister, and your families. That probably explains how she recognized Brodie."

"Elves, witches, and any other creatures of the realm that are sided with us will provide as much help and protection for the boy as they can," the king said. "But we must keep you here for your protection. Dayton will use you to get to him. When we retrieve Brodie, the child will be brought back here to join you. You will be shown to more suitable accommodations in the meantime.

"We don't know why the child interests Dayton so. Many of our kind are disappearing. The queen of the fairies has been taken by Dayton and his henchmen we suspect why but we shall take extra precautions."

"Thank you, Your Majesty."

"Question—how did we get here? One moment we were standing in my aunt's garden, the next thing we woke up in jail. It feels like it is punishment rather than protection," Rhys asked, slightly agitated.

"Well, Rhys, I will answer your question if you answer mine, I was not going to do this at present time" the king said sternly.

"Go on then," Rhys said as he crossed his arms, bracing himself.

"How many gnomes are in your auntie's garden?"

Rhys removed the red-and-white baseball hat from his head and ran his free hand over his hair as he thought about the question. "Dunno. Tons! A bit batty about gnomes she is, bless her."

"Do you know where they all came from?" the gnome king asked. The king sat in his chair, watching the human who towered over them all. Thankfully, the grand hall was tall enough to fit the three. Compared to the gnomes, the humans were giants.

Rhys focused his attention on the king. He was quite interested in the conversation. He had often wondered where all the gnomes had really come from. They must have been expensive at the shops, and his aunty Winifred was not one for wasting money.

"Market, I suppose, although my aunt has said they pop out of nowhere."

Whispers hissed to and fro from the seated gnomes around them.

"She is correct!"

"I can't recall the exact time, but it was not too long ago, perhaps a few decades ago, when a gnome named red beard Noa entered the human realm, feasting on brambles and elderberry wine caused his belly to bulge. His tools from his belt pinched and dug into his sides. He removed the belt to knap in the bramble bushes.

"The problem is, gnomes' tools are magical, and to remove them outside of our realm is not always wise. If lost, the gnome's magic is lost with them. Now, when red beard Noa had fallen into a deep sleep, a pixie had pinched his tool belt. The tools possessed no source of magic away from the owner. Therefore, they were discarded. Poor red beard Noa had quite the shock when he awoke from his slumbers. He searched high and low. He followed the scattered tools to town. An odd instrument or tool would be found in the most random places of all. The tricks of the pixies, you see."

The three were consumed by the story. Katrin had become quiet of her cries.

"The belt itself," continued the king, "was found in a garden of a town house. And what a garden it was. A vegetable garden and a well-maintained little pond on the other end, and in between a variety of large plants and a little glass greenhouse. Red beard Noa was not the only one to visit the enchanting little garden. Pixies and elves were frequent visitors. Reaching into his sawdust purse on his tool belt, he grabbed the remaining handful and blew it into the pond.

"It opened up a portal to our world. From then on, the gnomes visited the garden. They would often find an offering. Your aunt had seen the gnomes many times, but as harmless as she was, we could not risk the exposure. Her memory was erased each time by sprinkling the sawdust on fruits and vegetables that grew in her garden. But over time, the sawdust's magic had very little effect on her."

"So that's why she's a bit nutty about gnomes," Rhys said. "Have you heard of an expression 'the crazy cat lady?' Well, my aunt has turned out to be a bit of a crazy gnome lady." Rhys chuckled.

Both Katrin and Beth watched Rhys, feeling there was more to this story than met the eye.

"Do you know what happens to gnomes when humans are present?" asked the king.

"No!" answered the three.

"They turn to stone!"

An expression dawned over Rhys's face; his smile disappeared.

"She was kind-hearted, one of the kindest humans since the old days. We watched her with her three grandchildren. She only spoke of us to her little ones and encouraged the children, especially the little girl—"

"Jodie," Rhys interrupted.

"Yes, Jodie—to leave little gifts and cookies for my gnomes. We decided the harmless old woman loved us, so we carved replicas of ourselves and placed them around her garden. She could never tell the difference. She named each of them and counted them daily. The numbers would vary." The king's voice became sterner. "It was our little human garden of sanctuary and peace until her spotty rotten little nephew would come to call."

Rhys could feel every eye in the hall on him.

"Not all of those stone gnomes you shot rocks at or tied fire-crackers to or sank in the pond or just plain vandalised were decoys."

His daughter and wife looked overwhelmed with the thought of the miniature people suffering from the cruelty of the giant bully.

The king looked at both Beth and Katrin. "Once again, I do apologize for the previous accommodations you have had to endure. I was not aware, as I was not here." His stare fell upon Rhys. "But perhaps the gnomes felt it was retribution and revenge for the loss you had caused them."

Rhys fell silent. He looked around the room at the small faces that stared up to meet his embarrassed gaze. They were no longer giggling. Now they were shaking their heads.

For once in his life, he felt utterly ashamed. He tried to apologize, but the words choked up in his throat. He felt smaller than the gnomes. The king smiled.

"Your aunty had quite the dictionary of names for you, boy. She tried to salvage the broken pieces or fish the gnomes out, saving many lives, but they were never the same again—a missing ear, prominent scars, and so forth. Only two were damaged beyond repair. Guy Fawkes's bonfire night, you decided to drill a hole into the gnomes and use them as firework holders."

"Oh, Rhys," exclaimed Beth as she shook her head in disgust.

Rhys could not find it in himself to look at the king nor his wife.

"When told of your arrival, my subjects begged for a chance to stone you as you did to us with that contraption you call 'sling shot.' I can be merciful. You and your family have endured enough with the disappearance of your kin."

With that, the king called for a chaperone to their residing quarters. "I will have hot baths poured and hot meals brought to your rooms."

Rhys apologized, and the three thanked the king and left the great hall behind as they followed the servant down a long, stretched hall. It was huge. How was it that such small creatures occupied such a large space, they couldn't fathom. The walls were made of stone; the floors were marble. Large containers held plants and iron rods. The ends of the rods spiralled into holders for torches. They were beautiful, like lit bouquets.

Often, an animal of some sort would scurry by. Whether it was mice, toads, or small foxes, it caused the three to jump. The halls seemed to go on forever. The three and a half continued to walk.

A small little fox with the thickest, reddest coat passed Katrin. She paused momentarily. She watched the little animal. For some peculiar reason, she thought of her son. The little fox stopped and looked into her eyes, which were like little mirrors reflecting her. He paused for a moment, and then was gone again.

Her mother tugged at Katrin's arm as she watched the little fox disappear into the shadows. A tear escaped from the corner of her eyes.

The three followed the little dwarf man until they came to a series of doors. They passed an open passage that looked into the kitchen. The smell of food filled the hallways.

Pots bubbled over fireplaces as they peered in the room. Hammocks hanging from the ceiling held breads, cheeses, nuts, vegetables, and dried plants. The enormous wooden table was surrounded by little white-bearded men giggling and singing as they prepared the meals.

"Should I ask them to prepare you a plate of roasted mushrooms?" Katrin asked her father. She sensed his regret.

"Shut up." He glared at her as he playfully clipped the back of her head.

"Follow me. Almost there," said the small man in front of Rhys.

After climbing two separate staircases and walking down a long corridor, they finally reached their rooms. Rhys and Beth entered their room. Rhys still looked upset from the news of his childhood play he had received.

Embarrassed, he disappeared behind the large door.

Katrin was led to the room directly next to her parents. She opened the door, thanked the gnome, and entered the massive room. As the gnome departed, he lit a frayed torch that was mounted on the wall beside the door. He did not struggle in reach for the torch. When Katrin spotted what it was he wanted, she reached for it, but it disappeared. It then reappeared in his hand. He lit it, smiled, passed her the torch, and then disappeared out the door.

It was so quiet and eerie. The room itself was large and spacious. A large bed with white hand embroidered linen had a nightgown draped over its side. The dark rustic wooden floors was covered by an area rug laid flat beneath the bed.

In the farthest corner of the room, the area was elevated by steps. Two small evening chairs nestled in front of the empty cavity in the wall. A draft in the room caused the torch flame to dance and her skin to crawl with goosebumps. Katrin held herself tightly, preventing the draft from entering any crevice of the loose shirt she wore. She paced around for a moment or two, lighting any other candle or torch she could find. A small desk close to the fireplace held old parchment ink bottles and a stack of old, dusty books. She wiped the thick layers of dust from the old covers.

Suddenly, a fire ignited within the empty cavity in the wall. It made her jump. She peered back down to the books. *Collaborated Works, Dragon Anatomy, Beasts of the Sea*. She ran her fingers along the spines, then pulled *Beasts of the Sea* closer to her. She resisted the temptation to open the old book and pushed it away from her.

She became distracted by the window, curious as to where the chilly draft was coming from. It was a large bay window that opened up from the center. Its shelf bench was covered with large silk pillows.

She sat putting a hand up feeling for the cold draft. The draft was not coming from the window, but once the window was opened, its cold, fresh air contributed to the chill.

She sat there for quite some time, looking out from the hills. The gigantic mansion of a castle had been built on a large hill that overlooked a lake. She looked out into the rainy night sky and prayed for her baby's safe return. She was comforted by the news of her little boy but was still devastated. It was bad enough her lack of parenting had contributed to her son's disappearance, but what if he had a seizure or something horrible happened to him? It was one thing for any child to be lost, but a child with special needs… She began to weep again. She placed a small candle on the windowsill and straightened herself up, fighting the urge to throw herself from the window. How would that possibly do Brodie any good if he was found? She sighed.

A beautiful, small fairy flew past and landed on the window ledge. She paused for a moment and then disappeared.

After the fairy disappeared into the darkness, Katrin got up, closed the window, and looked around the room once more. She could still feel the icy cool draft, and it was definitely not coming from the window. Katrin grabbed a throw from the large bed, wrapped it around herself, and listened quietly to the whispering howls of the air flow.

On the opposite side of the room, a large embroidered rug hung as decoration on the wall. She reached for a candle as she noticed the corner swaying. The rug had an image of a large human woman—or, at least, she looked human. She wore a white dress trimmed with gold. Her face was beautiful. Her golden hair hung long to one side of her body. She looked down to where Katrin stood.

Katrin stared hard at her face. The lady looked like a Celtic princess. For a moment, the lady looked to have been shaking her head.

The curious young mother pulled back the wall hanging, exposing a large crack in the stone wall. She put her hand to the opening to feel the air. The draft was coming from within. She softly pushed against the wall, then jumped as the stones concaved toppling backwards, creating a doorway into the chilly darkness.

Katrin put the candle inside the entrance and peered around the walls of the tunnel within. The flame flickered vigorously. It was dark, dusty, and filled with cobwebs. She got up from her crouched position and crawled through the entrance. She was not concerned with the gnomes or that her parents might check on her after hearing the noise of the falling stones.

She released the corner of the rug. It fell behind her, concealing the larger gap in the wall once more.

CHAPTER 19

Gaol Break

Brodie had no recollection of time. What a funny thing time was. It didn't seem to stop. As frustrated as he was jumping in and out of time and portals, and although he did not really know how far back in time he really was or even where he was, he found this new adventure fascinating. He was amazed how in-tune he was to the new world around him. He felt stronger, really believing deep down he truly belonged here in this other realm—but with his parents.

They continued on cutting through a farm, forest, and small shire until they came to a small town. Though it was day, it was grey from the heavy cloud that blanketed the sky. Its rain caused the roads to become muddy. The deep holes and cracks in the road collected the water, creating dangerously muddy pits, which the townspeople tried to avoid creating groves on the outer part of the road.

Brodie was underneath a broken-down cart, trying to keep dry from the sudden downpour. He watched the rain bounce hard as it hit large puddles in front of him. He looked down to his side to where the firefly had been a moment ago. She was gone.

He focused back on the scattering villagers who ran for shelter—baskets in hand, shawls draped over their heads and top hats to try to keep the elements off.

He wondered to himself when umbrellas had been first invented. His train of thought was interrupted, and he began to snicker, as a young farmer had tripped over landing face-first in the mud.

How different it was in this portal. He had never seen live-stock running free in the streets like this. A great deal of livestock had found shelter; all but the ducks immensely enjoyed the weather remained out.

Brodie peeked out from underneath the cart, looking up as the rain washed his muzzle. For a moment he forgot the world enjoying the moment.

The firefly returned. She darted in circular motions, trying to get Brodie's attention, then transformed into a fairy.

"He's over there," she said as she pointed towards two run-down, old cottages. He could see a partly visible, small stone building in the background between two cottages. The small fairy pulled hard at his whiskers.

He quickly got up; he was ready to dart out.

"Not yet. He is being guarded," she said. She looked different from Dragon and Hopper. They looked more like miniature human ladies, whereas she had more bug-like characteristics.

Her limbs were like the exoskeleton armour of her bug form. They were black and shiny with a metallic green-and-blue hue. Her face was unusually creepy, part bug-like but also part human. What little hair she had was pulled in a cone-like shape on her head. The only details that remained the same in both forms were her wings and the bum that shone her light.

She tugged at his whiskers again, pulling his full attention to her. "We have to wait until the storm gets worse. Bramble Meir is in a holding cell. The guards are all around the building, and once it gets worse, they will shelter, giving us a better chance to get in."

She was right. As he turned his head back towards the visible part of the building, a man dressed in a hooded cloak paused for a moment to light a pipe, then continued to walk.

They waited.

❧

The rain had been lightening up. Brodie was in the midst of conjuring up a new plan when it began to pour down harder than before. *Gotta love the Welsh weather,* he thought.

The fairy lit up and shot towards the small white building. She was back within a moment but was finding it difficult flying in the rain. "Let's go," she said.

They sneaked along the wall, looking for an entrance. Brodie didn't know what this guy looked like, but the king of the elves had stated he wouldn't be hard to recognize. There were no windows on the walls, just holes not big enough to put your head through; underneath the holes were shoots that flared out from the building. Brodie hid camouflaged behind the wheel of one of the carts that were spaced along the building.

"What is this place? How do we get in? I'm starting to feel the cold," Brodie said. This was untrue; Brodie did not like the sensation in his body when his heart rate increased, he hated the way his muscles felt, and he had hated physical activity in school for this reason. This unwelcomed feeling in his body had been making frequents visit for the past few weeks. Brodie clenched his teeth. He could feel the droplets of water run from the fur to his skin.

He waited for an answer, but there came none.

As he walked against the wall, he glanced up. A wet scraping noise had caught his attention as something quickly slid from the shoot. With a heavy, wet, splashing *thud,* it fell into the cart Brodie was standing underneath.

"In here," the beetle fairy said before disappearing into a large hole in a wooden door.

Brodie tried to squeeze through, but his bag made the tight squeeze tighter. The struggle caused the lock to rattle, but he eventually got through.

Inside smelt stale and mouldy, like decomposing hay and potent body odor. Puddles of water had collected on the ground from the holes in the thatched roof. The inside reminded him of a horse stall, except in this place, each stall from the ground up was barricaded to prevent the prisoners escaping. Narrow locked doors, were the only means of entering. Little traps located at the bottom of the doors were locked shut with sliding bolts. These were probably to feed rations to the animals—or in this case people—in captivity.

Brodie hid behind a barrel as a guard raced over, drawn by the noise the fox had made from the tight squeeze. The fairy quickly transformed back into her firefly form.

A large figure stopped as close as two feet away from Brodie. He opened the door, then quickly shut it, making sure the premises were not being invaded by the rebellious Rebecca to come to free her daughters. The coast was clear, so the man returned to his stool in the far corner where his flask waited, taking with him the only source of light.

A little yellowish-green light disappeared into each stall, weaving in and out, searching for Bramble Meir. Brodie followed close behind, careful as to not get caught by the guard.

The green light shone brighter than ever as it darted around in excitement. After the fairy unlocked the deadbolt of the trap door, Brodie cautiously pushed his head through the small gap she had provided.

It smelled horrible, like decay, mold, and urine mixed with other smells that were offensive. Amongst a large pile of broken stones in the small, dark, damp, miserable cell was a fragile figure hidden in the shadows.

Brodie kept his sight on the shadows, expecting something to pounce from the darkness.

"They will be making rounds shortly, making sure we labor till death!" an old, weak voice said.

Brodie stood in silence, hesitant to move further.

A moment or two passed. The firefly lit up the corner with the greenish yellow light.

"Bramble meir?" the little fox asked.

"'Ello," he said with a thick accent as he turned his head slightly in Brodie's direction.

"How are we going to get him out of here?" Brodie asked, looking over to the small hole in the wall, then back to the trap door. "Bramble Meir would definitely not fit in either."

"We have to think of a way," the firefly said.

"Hopefully, we can come up with a conclusion before morning. Before I am hauled out by the Court Marshal to be tried and sentenced to death, or worse, to the Americas."

"That won't do. I need you," Brodie said as he looked around the small cell. He looked for any means to get the old man out, but it was useless.

Unless…

He looked down to his side where the dirty, tattered bag hung. "I have here something that can help you escape, but you have to promise you won't try anything stupid after we help you, and you have to promise to help me get home."

The man, who was now standing, approached Brodie. He knelt to the fox's level. The firefly slowly moved around the two, her bottom blinking every few seconds.

Bramble Meir agreed.

Brodie revisited the memory where Grub had introduced him to the dragon scale. He tried to remember the way Grub had phrased it. After a few moments, he remembered.

"You have to think about an animal or insect, a small one, small enough to get through the cracks in the doors. Um, you have to see it when you close your eyes, beg your body to change into it. Have you got one in mind?"

"Yes," the old man replied excitedly.

"It has to be small. It's not a lion or anything, is it?"

"Well, naw you mention it, I wouldn't mind giving that guard a gud bite on the back side!" the old man said as he chuckled. His accent was a little hard to understand.

Brodie pulled his head through the loop of the bag, dropping it ever so gently on the wet sloppy ground. "Reach into the bag. There is a large plate-like object in there. Hold it with both hands as if it were a magic lamp."

"A what?" Bramble Meir asked, completely confused.

Brodie had forgotten they were so far back in time that certain stories like *Aladdin* probably had not been written yet.

"Um, let me rephrase that. Just grab the plate with both hands as if it were magic, then want it, beg it to change you into the animal you want."

Bramble Meir reached into the bag. His eyes opened wide as he grabbed the scale. Perhaps he was shocked by how warm it was, or maybe the old man knew what it was. He shut his eyes as he tilted his head back. He prayed the words silently.

In a split second, the scale shone in Bramble Meir's hands, then fell to the floor. It rocked in a circular motion. The little fox quietly watched the man's body mutate. Bramble Meir let out a noise of distress as he felt his body crunch and alter. Then in a moment's flash, he disappeared.

They looked around, trying spot him in the dark cell.

"Where are you?" both Brodie and the firefly called out.

A noise caught Brodie's attention. It came from the ground close to the scale, followed by another. The creature headed towards the opposite direction, then stopped. It turned again to smell the air.

Brodie's eyes fell upon a rather sickly and dirty-looking rat. Then again, anybody living in these conditions would look grotesque—animal or human!

"Okay, we' have no time to lose," said the firefly.

Brodie pawed the scale back into the bag, where it would be safe. At first, it stuck to the ground, but eventually, he managed to get it in and back around him.

He lowered his body so the rat could climb onto his back. But it didn't move. It just sat there, staring into space.

"Bramble Meir, I can't put you on my back. I have no hands. You will have to climb up!" Brodie said.

But there was no reply. The rat froze, looking dazed and confused, and then it let out a squalling sound as Brodie cornered it. "We have to go now before they realize you're missing," Brodie said irritated.

"Pick him up with your mouth, Brodie. He's in shock," said the firefly.

Brodie hesitated, looking at the spaced-out, poop-covered, mangled, flea-infested, half-decayed rat, then groaned. "You mean I have to have that thing in my mouth?" Brodie whined. "No offense, Bramble Meir," he quickly added to prevent hurting the old man's feelings.

"Yes. The sooner we get out of here, the sooner you can go home," she said.

He huffed as he wrapped his teeth around the rat, picking it up. It sounded as if it was screaming. The noise was loud and piercing and went right through Brodie.

They exited the small disgusting cell through the trap door, then ran down the hall after making sure it was safe. They quietly snuck through the hole in the door. Squeezing through caused the trapdoor to rattle again. He forced his way through and headed back towards the broken-down cart. The limp rat hung from his muzzle and screamed the whole time. Brodie didn't know what was more of an alarm: the deadbolt or the rat.

"It's okay. You will get used to it after a while. I was a bit in shock, too, at first, although I was kind of hoping you would turn into a lion, and then you could have carried me instead," Brodie said. His words were muffled from Bramble Meir hanging in his mouth. His drool ran down Bramble Meir; the smell and taste was causing his mouth to salivate. Brodie was desperately holding back bile.

Brodie tried to ignore the putrid smell, but it was difficult. Hopefully, the rain that still poured down would clean the poor guy up a bit.

They reached the cart. He spat the rat onto the puddled ground, then lapped up a bit of water to clean his mouth. A roar of laughter caught the small fox's attention. He looked over to the firefly. She had recently transformed into her fairy form again. She was curled on the ground, holding her belly as she laughed.

"What," he said, confused, missing the joke. She pointed.

Brodie saw the rat running as fast as he could into the rain. He was angry. "Where the hell is he going?" Brodie snapped. "Bramble Meir!" he barked out loud into the rain. "BRAMBLE MEIR!"

"No need for yelling, I'm right here," the old man said.

Startled, Brodie jumped at the response, knocking his head against the cart. He looked down. A little head popped itself out of the bag.

A little brown field mouse crawled up the strap of the bag, looking down at its new little paws.

"What the devil are you doing there?" Brodie asked angrily.

"Can't get over this. Fairy magic this is," Bramble Meir said, still observing his paws.

Acknowledging what had been in his mouth, Brodie began to dry heave. His back arched as he yakked, and his tongue pushed out of his mouth, trying to rid it of the rancid vermin.

The fairy laughed tremendously hard as the poor little fox lapped up water, trying to flush out his mouth again.

"Urghhhh!"

The noises that come out of the little fox are so marvellously hysterical, the fairy thought as she continued to laugh as he dry heaved.

"How long did you know, you wicked little bug?" he asked trying to keep his temper checked.

"Well, thank you for rescuing me. By morning, they would 'ave hanged me or sent me to be a slave abroad," the old man said.

"You could have spoken before now," the boy said bitterly. The fairy continued to laugh. "There's some wizard named Dayton. He is after that thing that changed you, and my great-gran hid me in a large clock that turned out to be some portal. All I was told was to look for you and tell you Pat sent me, if that means anything to you. And the thanks I get is silence while you two let me put a poop-covered rat in my mouth. At least help me get back to that realm or world or time or wherever it is I came from please," the little fox huffed. He was mentally drained and overall fed up. He sat defeated.

"Pat," Bramble Meir said and smiled, then asked where about the clock was.

"A couple of towns over," Brodie said, excited now.

"We have no time to spare. We must get you back. Did she give you anything when she hid you?" the little mouse asked.

"An old key and an old book."

"And you have them now?"

"Yes, in my bag."

"Good, we will need them."

They headed back to the little town where the portal in the clock had been. The firefly in her fairy form and Bramble Meir as a mouse both rode on Brodie's back. The roads were disgusting. For fear of drowning in the potholes, Brodie cut through the fields.

"We have to find Kol first," Brodie told the fairy. He didn't want to leave his friend behind. "The last place I saw him was at the oak tree with the king," he explained.

"Ah, shall we be retrieving your friend from the elf king and queen?" Bramble Meir asked in a rather enthusiastic and excited tone. "It has been a long time, my furry friend, since we were acquainted last."

The mouse spent the majority of the journey back to the little town talking of his visits with the king and queen.

"My first account I cannot recall, as I was an infant. The fairies tried to snatch me away, leaving behind in my place a changeling. Thankfully, my mother followed me, got me back by threatening to cut the changeling's hair with iron scissors. They don't like iron, you see."

"And the other times?" Brodie asked, thoroughly interested in the old man's story, which kept Brodie's thoughts from the rain and the rat.

"I was a young man in my early twenties. It was a warm summer's eve. The larks were singing high above. I was returning home from my travels. Back then, I worked for a neighboring farmer who had sent me to the nearest town to trade goods. Something on that dark isolated road spooked my horse, for he backed us and the cart off the road and into a tree. The horse freed himself and ran away, leaving me injured on the ground. I could feel the blood run down my brow. Hearing the sound of running water, I followed it and found a little brook. There I knelt to wash my wound.

"That's when I saw her—a true vision of beauty. A maiden sat at the edge of the brook. The light of the moon did not reach us, but she was radiant and lit as if the moon rays kissed her. She shrieked at the sight of me. I assured her I possessed no harm to her, as it was dangerous for the magical folk at that time, you see—she asked me to wait with her. I told her tales to pass the time.

"The moon had shifted across the sky three times. I continued to sit with the beautiful maiden. Suddenly, I felt the cold sharp blade of a dagger pressed upon my throat. A mere swallowing motion may have been the death of me. She shrieked as her lover stepped out from behind me. He removed his dagger before kicking me to the ground. Upon seeing I was not quite human, he refrained from pointing the blade.

"Then a noise filled the forest. In the maiden's arms was an infant wrapped in silks. Had she held the infant the entire time, I was more transfixed by her unspeakable beauty I didn't even notice the babe.

"The maiden tried to calm the fussing infant, but it leapt from her arms, transforming into a frog. The beautiful maiden told her partner I was a friend and had kept her safe in company from the darkness, declaring I was her protector in that dark forsaken forest. He thanked me and escorted me back home. He bestowed me with a golden gift from his right index finger. Thereafter, I often conversed with the beautiful maiden and the king on the eve of a new moon."

All Brodie could think about was the beautiful fairy queen who had come to Brodie's aid at the threat of her husband. "Bramble Meir, you said the king's ring as past tense. Where is it now?"

"With Dayton," the old man answered.

Brodie quickly understood. There was no need for Bramble Meir to continue. The rest of the way back, they travelled in silence with Brodie thinking of the ring and Dayton.

"Who is this Dayton guy?" the fox asked, hoping Bramble Meir would have other information about him.

But all he said was, "An evil force from the past. One to avoid."

CHAPTER 20

Winding the Future

They reached the oak. Brodie hoped to find Kol, and Bramble Meir hoped to be reunited with the king and queen once again.

There was no luck for either.

There was no trace of any magic on the hilltop. The lantern that had once hung on the twisted old branch had vanished. Brodie insisted on waiting a moment or two longer for his friend, but Kol did not show up. Brodie missed him.

They continued back down the hill towards the little village. Both mouse and fairy held tight to Brodie as he ran down the slippery wet hill, trotting slowly and carefully so as not to slip on his way down. Although Brodie's vision was blurred from the rain, he kept an eye out for the goblin.

What sounded like a sneeze from behind them caused the fox to turn quickly. He didn't think he had ever heard Kol sneeze before, but his heart raced as he spotted a tall human's figure close behind them.

Bramble Meir caught sight of the figure and let out a high-pitched squeak.

"Stop him!" the figure yelled as he quickly advanced towards the three.

Brodie broke into a dash down the wet, slippery hill. The two smaller creatures held tight to the fox's fur. Brodie's heart pounding like a drum. He was almost at the bottom when—

A blow like a torpedo against the side stopped the little fox. The hard blow flung Brodie over, causing him to roll a few times, shooting Bramble Meir and the fairy off his back like little missiles.

He rolled over from his back and shook his head from the impact. It felt like a train had hit him.

The rain bounced off the wolf-like figure that stood a short distance away. Its keen watchful eyes were on its prey, menacing and ready for the kill.

The rain was too strong for the fairy to fly through. She and Bramble Meir looked back to the fox. With what looked like a nod from Brodie, she mounted the mouse, directing Bramble Meir towards the village.

The fox lay on the ground. He felt tremendous pain and found it hard to breathe. Not once did he take his eyes off the danger in front of him. Brodie had no choice but to lie as he was. He felt broken.

The wolf let out a nasty, evil growl.

Brodie quivered with pain. He knew this would be the end of him. He looked down to his side. The partially opened bag's contents were exposed.

His heart pounded harder. He had lost the dragon scale.

He quivered once again, this time not from the watchful eye of the hound from hell but from the absence of the scale. Brodie's eyes shifted across the wet, dark grasses of the field that surrounded him. He scanned and searched for a mere glint from the scale but was unlucky.

The wolf approached ever so slowly. He was panting. The little fox could smell and feel the hot sweaty breath of the beast. Its body gave off a strange mist that swirled in the disturbance of the rain. A set of approaching, heavy, sloshing steps in the wet earth coming from behind him caused Brodie's ears to stand on end.

He lowered his head. He knew deep in his heart that he would never see his family again. He could see their faces in his mind; it would be the last time. This made him angry. The anger balled in the pit of his stomach, and he closed his eyes. All he could hear was the smug laughter of the human behind him slowly making his way down the hill, the panting of the wolf, the rain, and a strange tinkling of a faint chime.

His ears twitched as he zoned in on the strange, almost musical sound. He opened his eyes and looked towards the sound. He felt a burst of contentment as he spotted a slight shimmer wedged into the grass a short distance ahead.

His stare was broken as a loud noise distracted him. The advancing human's feet had given out beneath him, and he slipped down the wet grassy hill, yelling the entire time. The wolf, his attention broken from Brodie, began to laugh at his clumsy companion as he watched him tumble down.

It was now or never.

Without thinking of the pain, the little fox mustered his entire inner strength, shot up, and darted towards the town. His muscles burned, and the pain was unbearable, but he ran. After snatching the scale from the ground with his muzzle as he passed it, Brodie ran as he had never run in his life.

"Get him!" the man yelled as he lifted his face from the ground, watching the little fox running away.

Brodie spotted the speck of light from the rump of the firefly.

Seeing Brodie approach, the firefly grabbed Bramble Meir's tail with one hand and reached for a handful of fur from the passing fox with the other, then she swung Bramble Meir onto Brodie's back. The little mouse almost slipped off the wet fur, but the firefly held tight and climbed onto the fox's back, where once again the two rode holding tight to Brodie.

As they made their way towards the approaching village, the wolf caught up to them and ran very close to Brodie's tail. He quickly chased after the fox; even though Brodie had a head start, the wolf's paws and legs were a lot larger.

The beast growled and bit at the air in an attempt to latch his teeth deep into Brodie's tail. Once or twice, he snagged a jaw full of hair, but Brodie was smaller and darted under fences, over exposed roots of trees, and through a small creek without haste or difficulty.

The firefly ignited a small blue flame that flickered within her hand. She threw it. It missed. She threw another.

By the third attempt, it hit the beast between the eyes, causing him to stop dead in his tracks. Ferociously shaking his head, he gave a pained, high-pitched whine.

Brodie—with the scale wedged between his muzzle, the fairy and the tightly clutching Bramble Meir on his back—continued to run and soon entered the outskirts of the village.

Bramble Meir turned and congratulated the fairy for getting rid of the frightful wolf.

"It's not over," she replied as Brodie slowed his pace through the village, cautiously looking around them.

Brodie slid the scale back into the bag, afraid the monster would pounce on him again. His body was in a lot of pain. He had to get back to the portal in the clock. The fear was too overwhelming. He was afraid his body would collapse from pain and exhaustion.

"Don't like how still everything is," the mouse said, noticing a large sheep tied to a wooden fence slowly stepping backwards. The dirty, soggy thing refrained from bleating.

Rain bounced off collected puddles that had slowly consumed the muddy roads. The trees were bare. The branches were twisted and warped in all directions, looking a lot like ghostly fingers that added to the eeriness of the silent town.

Thud, thud…thud, thud.

The little fox's black-tipped ear flicked. Brodie paused.

"Don't stop. We're almost there," said a voice from his back.

Thud, thud…thud, thud.

He lowered his head, slowly directing his muzzle to the sound up ahead.

"What?" the fairy asked. "What is it?"

"Can't you hear that?" he whispered nervously.

"Hear what?" both mouse and fairy asked.

"Can't hear a thing," said Bramble Meir.

The thuds grew faster and harder. Brodie moved once more, not caring for the pain that throbbed in his ribs. He spotted the cottage and darted towards it as fast as his little paws would take him.

Suddenly, a large dark figure appeared close to where the three had stopped.

Bramble Meir squeaked. He and the fairy held tight to the fur on the back of Brodie's neck to keep themselves from being flung at Brodie's sudden halt.

Brodie could hear the sound of someone or something breathing hard. He looked to the right from the corner of his eyes. He slowly lowered his head, turning his muzzle in the direction of the heavy breathing.

The man stood drenched in a long coat that was not from this era. The rain ran from the edges of his brimmed black hat.

Brodie's heart plummeted.

The man advanced on the three slowly. Brodie turned his focus to another figure that had approached, panting hard. The wolf stood still now; its wet, muddy, black-and-brown legs were bent. Its mouth opened, revealing his white teeth as its lip curled in anger. Its head lowered; again, its watchful eyes were on Brodie, signaling it was ready to pounce. Brodie could feel the hatred emanating from it and swirling around its body.

Brodie slowly stepped backwards. The wolf stepped forward, then sideways, ready to chase the fox if he tried to pull a fast one again.

The thuds of the wolf's heart grew faster as the hound began to circle them; Brodie could hear its excitement. His growls sounded like deep, raspy, victorious laughter.

"All we want is our friend's property back. You needn't get hurt. If you cooperate, we'll make a deal with you! Come with us now without any more trouble, and he'll make sure you and your family get back safely. Boss has em now," the man replied.

Besides the odd accent, the man was slimy. It was the same man around Harry's farm, and the same slime ball down by the docked barges with the wolf when they had escaped up the river. His face was young and masculine. His futuristic dark grey business suit was visible underneath his sopping wet jacket. It was identical to the suits Dayton's gang wore.

"And if I don't?" asked Brodie, watching the wolf approaching the man's side.

The monstrous hound gave a vicious blood-curdling snarl that caused the sheep to finally bleat as it pulled from its restraint.

The two were now somewhat closer to each other, but Brodie had accidentally cornered himself against the firewood collection of one of the small cottages.

The man smiled and slowly advanced towards the three. "If you refuse, your mother will be ripped apart limb by limb, and when the boss gets what he wants from you, you'll join her fate," the man replied, letting out an evil laugh.

Brodie could not see the man's features clearly, as they were blurred. But he could feel the wicked smile across the man's face.

Brodie looked at the wolf.

"Give him what he wants, and we'll all get out of here and leave you alone," snarled the wolf.

"That won't do. He's to come with us," the other argued.

"No, I won't, and you can threaten me with my family all you want. I know you don't have them," replied Brodie through his teeth as he looked around for a way to escape. His blood began to heat from the threat. There was nowhere to run.

The wolf slowly advanced forwards. Brodie backed up. He panicked. His back was right next to the stone wall.

"We have them, you know. When we are finished with your mother, you won't be able to recognize her," sniggered the wolf as he approached.

Brodie shook with rage. His body rapidly and increasingly heating. His legs gave way beneath him. He couldn't move.

"Stand up, Brodie," the firefly shrieked into his ear.

Unaware of his actions, Brodie began to rock. His body swayed forwards and backwards. His breathing grew deeper and louder. Bramble Meir pulled his fur, trying to get the sitting fox up and moving, but it was no use. The little fox dropped his head and con-

225

tinued to rock. Everything that surrounded the boy had disappeared. He could not hear the cries from the two on his back or feel the chunks of fur being pulled everything went blank. Only the familiar blackout that he was so used to and the rage that consumed him. He could feel an electrical current scattering across and through his body, a metallic taste grew stronger in his mouth.

Thunder rippled across the sky, but the rocking fox did not hear nor care. He was completely numb.

"You have caused nothing but embarrassment and trouble. You honestly thought we wouldn't find you? Did you really think that old bird could hide you here? You may have been lucky before, brat! But you're not getting away this time even if bloodshed is necessary."

The wild beast snarled and chuckled as the man's hand reached out to grab the scruff of Brodie's neck.

Brodie caught sight of the exposed flesh between the man's sleeve and his leather glove. Brodie turned, sinking his sharp teeth into the man's arm.

The man let out a foul word as he flapped his hand, flinging blood into the air.

Once Brodie realised what he had just done the boy didn't move. He couldn't stop rocking. The fairy and Bramble Meir screamed as the large monstrosity growled and advanced towards them.

"I'm going to make a nice scarf out of you for my girlfriend," the wolf snarled. "And as for your mother, she can rot in the dingy little cell for the rest of her pathetic life." The wolf gave a deep raspy laugh as he pounced for Brodie.

Brodie glared, the rage exploded from him.

Suddenly.

Crack. A thick rope of bright light ripped through the black rainclouds. It pierced its way through an old apple tree close to them. Gold and blue specks mixed with rain showered down. The rope of lightning raced down the tree breaking loose on the ground and ripping towards the wolf, within seconds. As the enormous tree split, the tree groaned and creaked. It severed in half and collapsed, exposing the burnt and blackened center of the trunk still showering sparks from both halves. It came down quickly, pinning the limp body of the wolf who a moment ago was in mid-pounce, three paws in the air the hind paw that had just launched of the ground was snagged in a fiery rope of light that pulled the body with little effort to the ground with a painful and shocking force.

It was so quick the beast didn't even have time to howl.

In that split second, Brodie came to and darted towards the cottage. The little fox felt dizzy and confused and wanted to throw up, his body felt free, free of an invisible constriction. He had blacked out back there but felt more alive and far more awake.

Bramble Meir looked behind them, worried they were being pursued. Thankfully, the other man was trying to free the overgrown beast—

But where was the wolf?

"Help!" Brodie heard the shout from behind him.

The wolf had disappeared, the slimy man was hunched over his helpless unconscious partner wedged to the ground beneath the collapsed tree.

Another yell came from behind them but Brodie did not turn.

They reached the cottage. Brodie transformed without the aid of the scale. He heaved his body against the stiff wooden door as he opened it. He stumbled around at first in search of the grandfather clock. He was afraid their two pursuers would enter at any moment; his heart pulsed hard, and his hands were shaky and clammy, not only from the rain but from whatever that just happened.

He found the old wooden clock and opened its narrow door, hoping that climbing into the object would be enough to send him back to his great-grandmother's house.

"You need the key, boy," the mouse squeaked from his shoulder.

Brodie reached deep into the bag, feeling for the cool metal. The bag was soaked. He remembered he had tucked it between the pages of the book his grandmother had pushed into his hands.

He tilted the book, releasing the key it hit the bottom of the bag.

He glanced at it. "Now what?"

"On the face of the clock, there are three holes. You have to insert the key and wind the face of the clock."

"What?" asked Brodie, trying to comprehend the task. He still felt dizzy and a little sick.

"Turn the key clockwise in each of the holes," the little mouse said.

He inserted the old piece of metal and turned it frantically. Dayton's henchmen would soon burst through the door.

"Now what?" Brodie asked, full of fear.

"Step through and shut the door."

Brodie climbed in, but it was hard to shut the door from within. The fairy that hovered around him urged him to get in quick, sharing his fear that their pursuers would enter at any moment. Bramble Meir, on the other hand, remained on Brodie's shoulder. He wanted to return with the boy.

Suddenly, the cottage door opened. The fairy turned her head towards the gust of wind as she tried to slam the door of the clock shut.

He hit the carpet hard with a thud. The little brown mouse landed on the floor and tumbled in front of him. Brodie turned his head to see a strange light orbiting in the chamber of the clock face. He turned his head again as he scrambled to his feet. His mouth dropped.

"Nana Pat!" he shouted.

Something shoved into him from behind, causing his face to smack against the ground again.

"Gotta move, gotta move," the voice said hysterically.

Kol had landed on top of Brodie from the portal and taken out the boy's legs. Kol was on his feet before Brodie. He grabbed the boy's shoulder, trying to drag him away from the clock.

"Kol!" yelled Brodie, happy to see him but also irritated from being pushed and then dragged. He could taste the blood in his mouth from the blow to the ground.

"Move, they're coming!" Kol yelled.

Brodie quickly got to his feet. He scooped the mouse up, dropping him in his bag, and then ran out the door.

The house was completely in shambles. Everything was either out of place or broken. The house was deserted. Not a servant did they pass as they ran through the cottage.

There was no time. They had to get out of there. It was the fastest Brodie had ever seen Kol run.

"Right behind us, they are," Kol said as he led the way.

They reached the servants' exit. Brodie stopped once they were outside and quickly looked around; Kol continued to run. He looked up briefly, then called Kol back.

"What are you doing? We gotta move. Be here any second, they will," Kol panted.

"Stop, I've got an idea." Brodie headed towards the side of the house.

Kol had no idea where he was going but followed regardless. He was about to yell at the boy when he spotted Brodie's intentions—to climb the lattice to the roof. Quickly and quietly, they climbed. Once on the roof, they patiently waited. They held on tight, afraid they would fall. The hay of the thatched rooftop was slightly dusted with snow, which made it hard to hold onto because of the cold.

Brodie kept his head down and his focus on the front yard.

"Where were you? You disappeared" Brodie whispered.

"Could ask you the same. One minute I'm eating and drinking and surrounded by lovelies in the oak, next minute I'm picking grass from my gob all alone on the hill. Couldn't find you, so headed back to the cottage. Only when I got there, Dayton's clan patrolled the town looking for you! That's who we saw stalking us. I was running over to help you get away, then the lightning hit blew me and the other pratt off our feet. Then I saw you running back into the cottage. I called out to you. You went through the clock. Missed you, I did, by a second. You're bloody lucky. I would have bloody killed you had I been stuck there."

"Ssshhh." Brodie held a finger to his mouth.

The view of the front garden was clear, but two voices carried into the darkness.

"He is going to kill us. Which way do you think he went?" said one.

"We should have just killed him on that hill," replied the other.

"Well, if he wants him so bad, why doesn't he just get him himself?"

"Oh, I don't know. I think my arm's broken, and my face is still on fire."

"Can't have got too far. No, it's not."

"Yeah, right. If it weren't for that blasted tree, we would have had him. Thing almost killed me. My face hurts; I need help."

"Don't fink it was just the tree, might be why he wants him alive."

"Come on. Let's look over there, there's no point in going back without looking. Dayton will do worse to us than the lightning. Boss ain't gonna be happy when he finds out."

"You're gonna ave to tell em. I dont's wanna do it, and it's your fault he got away and your fault my face is burning."

"Oh, shut up," yelled the other man.

From the cold safety of the rooftop, Brodie watched as two now large wolves ran into the outskirts of the woods that surrounded his great-grandmother's premises. Then they completely disappeared.

"How did they get back?" asked Brodie as he watched the two figures disappear. "And where's Pat?"

"In hiding," Kol answered. "When Dayton's clan broke in, she pointed to the clock before she pushed me inside. She must have took off. I don't know."

"But how did they follow us back?" Brodie asked as he looked out to the darkness, afraid to get off the roof.

"They must have found the extra wide-wing key in the side access panel," answered Bramble Meir. "Each clock is an entrance and exit to a portal like a wormhole through time. Dayton is quite acquainted with these devices, especially the clocks, so his army would know what to look for, I expect."

"How do you know?"

"Because I created them," the mouse replied.

Brodie's head turned to his shoulder where the little brown mouse sat. Kol glanced over, too.

They remained on the rooftop for some time. As bitterly cold as they felt, they would be safe for now.

CHAPTER 21

A Gruesome Sight

In the comfort of the thirteenth-century north Wales castle, a loud knock at the door caused the legs of an armchair to scrape along the wooden floor.

The old hinges of a large wooden door creaked as it opened. From behind it, a man's head peeked into the room. He stuttered, "Boss."

The room was lit up by lamps and a large fire. "Ava Maria" played softly in the background on vinyl. The interior was decorated with mahogany. A large library occupied the walls around the room behind a large study desk. The carpets were an ugly emerald green with gold trim. The chairs were mahogany and decorated with green leather and gold metal studs. Golden lamps with emerald glass panels lit up the contents of the desk, projecting bright green light onto its surface.

"Come in and shut the door," said a haughty voice.

The man entered the room, softly closing the door behind him. He looked around the room, taking in the surroundings like it was his first visit to his boss's study.

Besides the two large windows concealed by thick, velvet, emerald curtains, the walls of the room were consumed with books. The spines looked ancient and torn. The majority of the colours were faded with age. The scent of patchouli, old paper, and ink was overpowering.

The nervous man took a seat in the empty chair in front of the desk. He looked around, wondering why these old books hadn't been thrown out years ago.

What is that god-awful smell? he thought.

His eyes widened at a sound from the lit fireplace. Misperceiving the sight at first, he had to make a double take. Above the roaring fire in the old mahogany wood and stone fireplace, a black iron cage was suspended. It moved from time to time, letting out blood-curdling squawks. The iron cage rattled.

It was only when the contained fire calmed that the man could briefly see a bird. His mouth dropped at the phenomenal sight. It was a phoenix.

"Beverage," asked the haughty voice.

"Tea, please—two milks, three sugars," the man said, his response broken, as he was still distracted by the sight of the bird.

The haughty man requested tea on the intercom. Within seconds, the door was opened once again. A blonde lady dressed in a grey pencil-skirt fitted suit entered, her hair pulled tight into a neat bun. She held a silver tray containing a silver tea pot and two china cups. She laid them down without looking at either of the men, then left the room, promptly closing the door behind her.

The haughty man's face was hidden behind an open laptop on the desk. Stacks of old books inhabited the majority of the surface along with a rather strange paperweight. Perhaps it was the maxillary lobe of a skull. It was creepy. It gave the man shivers.

The laptop closed, causing the man to shift in his seat nervously.

"Tell me a tale or whistle a tune. Tell me something to my interest. The boy."

The man swallowed. He felt anxious looking at the face of the haughty man, who now reclined in his chair and lit a thin cigar. The thick smoke seemed to fill the room, overpowering the smell of literature and patchouli.

The man waved the smoke from his face as he stretched over the desk to reach for his tea. A hand grabbed his outstretched wrist.

"The boy?" he asked, his tone now full of displeasure.

The man quickly retreated to his seat. "He got away, boss."

The haughty man released the nervous man's wrist and slammed his closed fist against the desk in anger. His face was scary, his features dark, his skin sunken around his cheeks; although slightly tanned, he still looked white and ghoulish. The music began to crackle and fade out into white noise, then resumed. The nervous man was very aware that the electronics in the room cut out every time his boss's anger intensified.

"And the others? How many men does it take to capture one insignificant little boy?"

The nervous man opened his mouth.

"Oh, don't even answer that," the haughty man said. He got up and walked to the closed windows. He pulled back the curtain and peered out briefly.

"Boss, I have ta say, he's not been the easiest. Given us the slip nonstop, he has."

The haughty man leaned in on the desk, putting his weight on his fists that were clenched and spread apart. He looked like a tiger, bloodthirsty and ready to pounce.

"Do you even have an inkling as to what this boy has in his possession?"

"No, boss. All I know is we're after some rotten kid."

"As rotten as he may be, I need him alive. Well, really, I don't."

A buzzing of the intercom interrupted the two. "Yes," the haughty man answered.

"Sir, you are requested. You have a delivery," a woman's voice announced.

"Thank you." His eyes wide were with anticipation. He straightened himself up, rubbed his hands together in excitement, and walked over to the door. He reached for a long black coat that hung on a golden hook that resembled a twisted claw.

He turned back towards the desk as he dressed himself. "Harvey."

"Henry, sir," the man corrected his boss nervously.

"Hmm, I must be excused from our little meeting for the time being—unless you'd wish to join me?"

With an overwhelming sense of importance, Henry accepted the invitation to accompany his boss. He quickly got to his feet and made towards the door. He turned and waited obediently like a dog for his master's command.

But the warmly dressed man did not walk to his side. Instead, he reached for his cane, put his hat on, and turned towards the fireplace.

Henry was confused.

"Are you coming or not?" the haughty man asked impatiently.

Henry, still confused, walked over to his boss's side. "I fought we were leaving, sir."

The haughty man waved his cane in front of the fireplace. The fireplace grew slightly, stretching out to create a walkway for the men to enter. The fire dimmed, and the cage that was suspended over it moved to the right.

The man stepped through. As he walked, he put his hand into the cage. The bird let out a large screech as the cage began to rattle vigorously.

The man looked down to his clenched hand. He opened it, revealing a handful of flames, and pocketed the contents of his hand into his coat. He then walked to the back of the fireplace, where he disappeared. The phoenix reached her beak through the bars of the cage, trying to bite as Henry passed by, but no luck. The cage merely swayed.

Henry stood frozen for a second, amazed at the sight he had just witnessed until he spotted his boss's head from behind a stone wall in the back of the fireplace; he was shouting.

"Imbecile, are you coming or not?"

Henry quickly followed.

They walked along a narrow, curved stone tunnel. Torches suddenly lit when the boss approached them. It was magical. Henry tried to initiate conversation but was unsuccessful. The man in front was intimidating. Henry really didn't know what to say. It was the first time his boss had ever invited him anywhere or even noticed he was alive. He remained quiet and followed. Besides, he had no idea where they were going. He became anxious once again.

After following a slippery set of stairs and a narrow little path between high, cobwebbed, dirty stone walls, they reached a wooden door. The castle had been fixed sometime during the 1900s. Henry wondered to himself whether the secret tunnel was as old as the original castle. It had to have been. The collected dust in the tunnel was as thick as a Welsh wool blanket.

The haughty man opened the door. It opened to a large room lit by torches and candles. Henry could see the room they had entered was full of cages that contained different creatures sitting on dirty, hay-covered ground.

The haughty man was approached by two men dressed in grey business suits. They two wore the 1930s gangster-looking hats. One had a white sling over his shoulder half of his face was blistered and oozed with open soares.

"And?" the man demanded as he walked towards the two.

"No, got away again, but brought you back something. In there," the servant said as he pointed towards another doorway.

The well-lit room revealed a black rucksack on the dirt ground. Dayton glanced at the motionless bag for a second, then he entered the room.

A large black-and-brown wolf ran in front of Dayton.

Henry turned to see where the large animal had appeared from but met the face of one of henchmen that had greeted them. The second man had disappeared.

The stone room was lit by old electrical lamps that gave off a slight yellowish hue and buzzed. On the ground, the bag lay motionless. Dayton nodded towards one of his men. The man quickly lowered himself, untied the bag, and spilled the contents onto the floor.

Henry watched silently.

A light brown ball of fur toppled to the dirt ground. He got up and looked around. He sniffed the air and spotted Dayton and his henchmen that now stood around him. He quivered with fear.

"You were spotted with the boy. Can you tell me where he is?" asked Dayton politely.

"No, I can't," answered the nervous weasel.

The wolf growled.

"I will repeat myself. You were spotted with a human boy."

"I-I don't know what you are talking about. I don't live in the human community," the weasel stuttered.

"Come, come, don't lie to me. His scent was found in your hobble of a house. What is its name?" Dayton asked as he looked at the rodent with disgust.

"Don't know, boss."

The weasel looked into the faces of the three men. His paws nervously wiped one another in anticipation.

"Llyr, is it?" Dayton asked the weasel as he tilted his head to one side with a scrutinized stare.

The weasel lowered his head and gulped.

"There were others, sir, but they couldn't be found," said one of Dayton's men.

"Do you usually harbor fugitives, Llyr?" Dayton asked in a cool, disapproving tone.

"I don't know what you're talking about. I really don't."

Dayton lowered himself to Llyr's level. His eyes were enraged. They hinted a red hue. "Don't lie," he growled through his teeth, emphasizing each syllable.

"Sir, perhaps this one could give you answers."

Dayton looked at the man who approached him. He held a box no bigger than a cookie tin. It was wrapped in old cloth tied tight with twine.

"She was helping the boy escape. When we reached the present, he had disappeared."

"How did he escape you, is what I want to know," Dayton yelled out.

"Tyrone was injured," the man said softly, unsure of his boss's reaction.

Dayton turned to look at the wolf, then back at the man. "I don't care if he's dying. You have disobeyed me, all of you." He snatched the package from the man's hand and opened it.

Inside, a half-conscious fairy laid limp, her light blinking ever so dimly. Dayton picked her up by the wings and shook her ferociously.

"Where did he go? Did he return to the present?"

She didn't answer. He shook her again, this time yelling at her. Spit flung from his mouth.

The weasel looked down. He felt sorry for the poor thing and wished he could do something to help her.

Noticing the effect, it had on the weasel, he asked once more. "My dear, I would like for you to tell me where the human child went. You may return home once the information I want is obtained. Was it to the present or another era of time? This is your very last chance." He was now calm and polite.

She raised her beetle-like head slightly and said something in another language.

In reaction to whatever she said, he talked through his teeth once more. "Are you sure that is how you feel?"

The little fairy stuck out a purple tongue in a protesting manner.

In trepidation, Llyr raised his head to a gruesome scream.

Dayton's men watched, smiling and enjoying the action.

Dayton one hand ripped the wings from the fairy's back at the same time his free hand pinched her bum, putting the firefly's light out for good.

The compressed blood splattered everywhere.

She continued to scream as he turned, tossing her over his shoulder like a rag doll.

He looked at his hands. Her purple blood ran down his right hand. He reached his left hand into his coat pocket, retrieving a cream hanky. He wiped his hands.

"Put the weasel into a cell next to the badger until he too is ready to speak, Harvey."

"Henry, sir," the man said as he spotted a ripped wing caught on Dayton's coat.

"GRUB!!!!" yelled Llyr frantically as he spotted grubs body on the ground chained to the wall.

"What have you done to him?" the weasel demanded as he was thrown into an empty cell.

Dayton collected the remains of the torn wings, wrapped them in the handkerchief, and returned the hanky to his pocket. He left the room. The wolf quickly lapped up the traces of blood from the dirt floor, then followed his partner.

Gently scooping the bleeding fairy as he passed her, Llyr cried from the horrific scene he had just witnessed. He was led to an empty cell in the next room and held the creature in his opened paws. She was barely alive.

"Dayton, you monster. Justice will prevail for these crimes," a caged woman was said as Dayton re-entered the room.

"Arrivederci, Your Highness, your time shall soon come," he said, waving his arm as he disappeared. He turned to Henry, who had resumed his side. "Find the boy, or I will put you in the cell next."

The wolf let out a laugh along with his partner, who followed close behind.

"That goes for all of you!" Dayton added. "And find his mother," Dayton demanded as he walked away.

Alone, Dayton walked to a locked door at the end of the tunnel. He unlocked the door and slipped through. A torch lit as he walked past. It was the only source of light in the room.

The room looked like a dug-out part of a cave. The ground was covered in a thick layer of coarse salt that crunched under his feet. One wall was shelved and displayed hundreds of bottles, a few old books, and caged creatures—the majority deceased and shrivelled up. The center of the room had a large open fireplace. Hanging over it and supported by thick, large rods was an enormous cauldron. It looked like it belonged to a giant.

Dayton walked to the shelf, frantically looking for a particular bottle. Once it was found, he spilled its contents into the massive pot. Flames suddenly appeared. He removed the handful of the phoenix feathers from his pockets. The flames danced in his hand. He dropped the golden-and-red flame into the cauldron. The surface of the water grew to a large flame, then calmed. Then Dayton threw the soiled hanky that contained the ripped fairy wings and blood into the overgrown pot. It created a strange smoke that billowed out of control.

"Where is he?" Dayton asked agitatedly as he turned from the cauldron. He walked around the vessel, stopped, and then retraced his steps, the salt crunching under his feet.

A green hand emerged and gripped the brim of the cauldron. It was slimy and appalling. Strands of slime hung from its fingers, and liquid dripped from its ends like runny snot.

A second later, a head slowly rose. Its dark, wet, slimy hair clung to her head, giving her the appearance of not having hair at all. She brushed it aside. Her face was human looking, heart-shaped, but slightly narrow. Her skin was a mutated green, like the skin of Jenny Green teeth, and just as mucousy.

Despite her skin, she was beautiful. Her eyelashes hung thick and long over her purple eyes. Her lips were full and puckered, and her cheekbones were high. She had the potential to be really attractive. She batted her eyes and reached for Dayton, but he pulled away.

"Your perfidious ways don't work on me, witch. Tell me where he is," he snapped.

She turned her back to him. The sloshing of the cauldron's contents grew louder as she slapped her tail against its surface in disappointment.

"I need that scale," he yelled.

"So concerned about the scale. You know where the dragons can be found. I've told you. You could always get another."

"Impossible. Don't be impertinent, you have not told me where the portal is" Dayton snapped.

Her lip pouted in dismay at Dayton's cold attitude. She looked down to her frayed fin, which she held in her hand. The greying scales of her tail were buckled and covered in a mucousy film. Her fins had been growing more transparent and sicker. She shook her head as she released her long, silky, slimy, fan-like tail and circled her finger on the water's surface.

"So concerned with the scale, yet," she said in a suddenly playful manner.

"I need its magic to strengthen my own. I have told you this."

"There is another way, a more powerful way," she said.

Dayton quickly knelt beside the cauldron, his face bewildered with excitement, both hands on the brim of the cauldron. She turned.

"The child." She slowly slid her hands towards his. Once they touched, he pulled away, wiping his hands against his pant legs. He got up. The knees of his pants were covered in the salt. He wiped them clean with a hand.

"The child," he said, full of curiosity and confusion.

She turned once again and huffed. She splashed in discontent. "The child holds more power than the dragon scale and the majority of the magical creatures combined from this realm and others. He is a descendant of the early elven kings of Wales."

Dayton grew excited and shot up; there was a spring to his step as he pranced across the dark room to the shelves. He rifled through the dusty book collection.

"the gene is dominant in this child," she said as she continued to splash about.

Once Dayton found the specific book, he returned to the cauldron. "His parents?" he asked coldly.

She paused for a moment, splashing in dismay as she thought about the question. "His mother is slightly touched as the witches of her family, his father I cannot see. The child possesses a strong magic more ancient than the ancient ruins itself. He was born with the identical DNA as Gre´nwyn the Late."

Dayton's eyes widened; his expression could hardly contain his sudden excitement. "I need that brat," Dayton said with an overexcited giggle. "The power, oh, the power I will be in possession of." He stood up; a chill of delight coursed through his veins.

"But his body has not fully developed. His power has not matured and may still be weak," she said as she quickly turned to the sound of the door slamming shut behind her. The sound of metal scraped as he turned the key in the lock.

The room was empty. The torches faded, leaving the creature in the cauldron with only the darkness as company. Small eyes watched from a crack between the stoned wall.

CHAPTER 22

Gypsy Magic

After what felt like forever, the exhausted and frozen three left the safety of Brodie's great-grandmother's rooftop. Brodie, who felt like an icicle and could shatter at any moment, transformed back to his warm fox form. Bramble Meir as a mouse could not keep up with the larger two, and his large ears and paws were frozen; therefore, he rode on Brodie's back once again.

The cold night air blew in their faces, but Brodie could only think about the ambush. Dayton's gang had almost caught him. Their intentions were far more dangerous than he had thought.

Kol was silent. The songs and revolting rhymes had abandoned the astounded goblin. How had he gotten caught up in this adventure? He only wanted his barge back from the blasted human, and now he had one of the most dangerous wizards after his new friend and possibly after him, too. Also, what had become of his beloved barge.

"What day do you think it is?" asked Brodie to whomever was listening. He was trying to refrain from thinking of his family, enemies and the cold.

"It would be the same day it was when you went through the clock. Time halts. Only add a few hours cause we've been on the roof for some time," Bramble Meir replied.

"Oh," exclaimed Brodie, confused and emotionally numb. His paws were frozen, and it hurt to walk. His ribs still hurt, and there was lack of circulation flowing through his body.

The three continued on their way. They headed back towards Llyr's, where Kol had left the badger and the weasel sound asleep in the warmth of the den.

They hid from travellers that passed along the early morning road. Once or twice, they thought they caught a glimpse of a human figure dressed in a black coat and grey attire. Not wanting to be spotted, they ran for their lives into the snow-dusted shrubs.

When they reached the hut, Brodie felt strange. He drifted off into his bubble, as his mother would always call it. Something was not right. He backed into the trees and lowered his body a safe distance from the den. Kol followed his lead in silence.

"What are you doing? Why aren't we going in there?" he asked the boy.

"It's a trap," Brodie said quietly. "Something feels terribly wrong."

Bramble Meir squeaked silently into Brodie's ear as a man came from around the other side of the old tree-stump hut.

"Not much of a bog," the man said.

It was only after another man replied that Brodie realized the area was definitely not safe to be around, that his intuition had been correct. The second man stood in the darkness of the entrance.

"Do you think they saw us coming?" whispered Kol.

Brodie did not reply but watched quietly. He hoped not.

They waited.

"Well, what if he saw us or was tipped off? What if he doesn't come back?" asked the closest man.

"Orders is orders," the other man replied.

"What if when they took the weasel, he got word out to the brat?"

"And what if he's on his way back now? Come on, let's wait inside. There's a decent bottle of wine in there. Besides, we will give ourselves away out here argued the other."

The men continued to converse as they entered the hut. They shut the door behind them, leaving Brodie and Kol watching speechless.

They quietly left, careful not to step on twigs or sound any type of alarm for the ever-waiting and ever-watching henchmen. Brodie looked at the snow-covered ground; their tracks would soon give them away. He heard Kol speak, but it grew distant and mumbled. His body hummed and felt warm; he could feel a tingling sensation through his body. It vanished when Kol grabbed his tail to direct him away. Kol's expression changed as he noticed their tracks had disappeared. They took a different route from the one they had followed.

When they were a safe distance away from the den, the three paused to break.

"Weasel? They must have taken Llyr. What do you think happened to Grub? Did you see anything different when you followed me, Kol?" Brodie asked, suspicious that perhaps Kol had accidently led Dayton's lot to his great-grandmother's.

"Can't say I did."

"How did you find me in the first place?" asked Brodie.

"I followed that SOD back to its master's cottage one night. The one been peeping on us. Thought perhaps he got you, so I checked there."

"You never told me you knew where it came from," he said, agitated.

"No, Grub told me not to. Grub and Llyr were both there when I left—think Llyr was glad to be rid of me. Poor thing. Dayton's gang must have come after I left because I saw naught."

"What do we do now? Where do we go?" Brodie began to panic.

"May I suggest a safe place for the time being?" asked the little mouse. "But it's a bit of a travel. We must go north of the boot market. I have a friend that will be able to help you if she is still there. Once we get there, I fear I will have to part from your company."

"Why?" asked the other two.

"Dayton must not find me again. If he does, he will force me to create terrible means of disaster. Centuries ago, he had heard from a traveller's ear of my abilities and magic. He sought after me and tried to persuade me to create him a device to obtain power."

"And did you?" Brodie asked, intensely interested.

"I, too, had heard from a traveller's ear that this man killed creatures for his gain of power. So no, I declined his offer of work. He tried to bargain with my life, but I was far more useful to him alive than dead."

"But he found you," Brodie asked.

"Yes, through my betrothed; he locked me away and told me he had my fiancé in captivity. He supplied quantities of material, and he forced me to build things."

"What happened to your betrolled?"

The little mouse let out a humoured chuckle at the boy's pronunciation. "He had deceived me. She was not held prisoner at all. I was gone such a long time she continued her life and wed another."

"That's sad. Did she know where you were?"

"No, she had been told I died of pneumonia. She married a human shopkeeper of some sort, wanting a simple life. When I escaped, I created my own means of entering the past to hide from Dayton and the army he was slowly creating. I only saw her once more. I couldn't live in this era without her, but I could not go without seeing her one last time. Culpable for a portion of Dayton's mayhem, I admit. I disappeared. I want him to continue to believe that I am deceased. Therefore, if he is after you, I must not be found with you."

Brodie understood, although he did not want the old man—little mouse—to desert him.

They travelled for long periods at a time, only taking short resting breaks. By now, the boy wished that he could transform into a plane to save time. He was utterly exhausted and starving.

On the second day, Bramble Meir announced they had arrived. They had entered a part of the forest where the snow was slowly disappearing. The climate was alot warmer. The more they continued forwards, the more the snow disappeared, leaving patches of budding and blossomed snow drops. Ferns grew in abundance, and birds sang merrily in the treetops.

As Brodie looked up, he noticed rusty old tins were strung from the trees and chimed to the breeze of the forest. Brodie detected a scent of something—perhaps wet fur—and something else that grew very vigilant, afraid they would once again be ambushed by Dayton's notorious clan.

"Is there a way to transform back?" Bramble Meir squeaked into the fox's ear.

Kol looked at Brodie with jaundiced eyes, then turned back, pretending he had not heard the mouse's question. Bramble Meir picked up on the look and remained silent.

Spotting something, Kol darted ahead. He crouched down. He paused. Something held his attention. Before Brodie could blink, the goblin was gone.

"Kol," the fox yelled out.

"Over here," he replied, his voice somewhat muffled.

Brodie decided to take the moment of Kol's absence to return Bramble Meir back to his human form.

"How do you do it?" Bramble Meir asked as he got down from Brodie's back.

"Hold on to the plate. In your mind and in your heart, ask it to turn you back into a human, but you have to picture your human self. Try to hurry. Kol will be back any minute."

Brodie laid the bag on the ground. A moment later, after the mouse had scurried into the bag, Bramble Meir was in his human form, crouched on the ground. One hand remained inside the bag around the scale. The bronze of the scale shimmered slightly.

Afraid, Brodie pulled the bag from him. "Bramble Meir, let go," Brodie demanded.

"What was that? Why was it so warm?" the man asked in amazement as he looked into the face of the small boy that now stood over him, clenching the tatty old bag tight within his arms.

Brodie understood what the elf king had meant by recognizing him. Besides how filthy Bramble Meir was, he looked a lot older and skinnier. His eyes were dark brown. His hair was a faded dusty gray colour. His face was round, friendly, and dirty. The characteristic that made this man so unique was his elf-like ears. They were long and pointed.

Bramble Meir pulled himself back and apologized.

Brodie called for Kol as he stared into the eyes of the dirty old man, then quickly followed Kol's voice as he placed the bag back around his human shoulder. Bramble Meir followed.

"How did you change if I was…?" Bramble Meir paused as Kol came into view.

He was in a clearing in the forest surrounded by a large hedge of ferns. In the clearing, the ground was flat, and the trees had been cleared. Wooden wagons were scattered throughout the grounds. The wagons were rounded with canvas that stretched across the tops. Some were wooden; others looked like hides sown together. A few wagons were painted in dull and worn yellows, greens, and reds; and others were plain. The majority had ladders leading to split doors. The tented carts sat on large wooden wheels.

Brodie could only see women, children, and the elderly. They were cautious, as if they sensed the three's presence and perceived them as a threat.

"Gypsies," Kol said, surprised and very loudly, as the three quietly spectated on the small campground. Kol on one side and Bramble Meir on the other turned inward to Brodie, each holding a finger to their mouths.

"That's right," said a deep, strange accent from behind the three.

The three slowly turned and looked up. Brodie realized there were no men on the campground because they were all pointing weapons at Brodie, Kol and Bramble Meir.

"What you want en?" a large man said. He was the closest to the three and the biggest of the lot. He didn't quite sound Welsh, and looked intimidating.

"Please, we come seeking refuge."

"Got papers?" the man asked as he and the others roared with laughter.

Brodie had no idea what he was talking about and refrained from any sarcastic remarks. "Papers? I don't understand," he whispered to Kol under his breath as the leader of the gypsies continued to talk to Bramble Meir.

"It's illegal for travelers to not have papers. He's being comical," answered the goblin.

"No, sir," Bramble Meir replied.

The group of men began to laugh, clearly making fun of Bramble Meir. "I'm a 'sir' now," the large man said as he waved his hands in a lady like manner in the air.

"Please, we came to see Nagna," said Bramble Meir.

"What you want with her, 'en?" the big man asked as the others continued to laugh.

"A personal matter."

A small child shoved her way through the group and tugged on the sleeve of one of the gypsy men. The man lowered himself to her level. Brodie kept watch of the small child. Her face was dirty, and her clothes were colorful. She cupped her hands over the man's ear, whispering something. Then she pointed to the three.

Brodie was a bit surprised when she looked directly towards him. Her expression was inquisitive.

The man quickly stood, barged his way through the group to the leader, and whispered something to him.

The big man's eyes opened wide, and he looked down to Brodie, then Bramble Meir. He turned and ordered Brodie, Kol, and the old man to follow.

The three were led through the campground. Brodie watched the young children playing; they were barefoot and utterly content. As the little ones ran around, he passed a few matty-looking dogs. One was scratching himself in earnest.

Kol leaned in towards Brodie. "Fleas," he said. "They all got them."

One of the gypsy men who followed close behind gave Kol a rather hard nudge with his walking stick that pushed him over.

"Shut up, goblin. You're a fine one to talk," the man said as the others laughed.

Brodie helped his companion up and glared at the ruffian.

247

There had to have been over twenty old wagon-like caravans scattered throughout the clearing in the forest. It was a spectacular sight. The only thing Brodie had seen remotely close to this were trailer parks in Canada, but nothing as spectacular.

Horses were tied to trees, grazing on hay bales. Older men sat around the scattered fires, drinking and playing fiddles, mandolins, and other instruments. Some of the men branched away from group to rejoin their drinking. They laughed and sang while a few children and women danced. Some women were washing clothes in buckets of water or sorting through gathered vegetables and berries or joining in with the drinking and song.

They came to an old green caravan. The weather had caused the paint to peel. It was decorated with handmade folk art around the door. A lantern hung from a hook of the wooden roof. An overpowering smell of lavender caused Brodie to sneeze. He had always been very sensitive to strong scents.

The narrow top half of the little door opened. A woman in her late eighties stood half concealed. Her eyes were closed. Her arms, which were spread out, suddenly joined together into a clap. Her face was old and withered with age. Her salt-and-pepper matted hair was pulled back, concealed by a silky scarf or turban tied at the back in a knot. Many of the women wore the same type of scarf on their heads. She wore excessive layers of ostentatious clothing and colourful beads around her neck and wrists, among other jewellery.

The three were on the ground looking up at her as she stood at the doorway of her domed home. She opened her hands once more, reaching out for Bramble Meir. A large smile embraced her face, exposing missing molars and decayed, yellowish brown teeth.

"It has been long time, my friend, no?" She spoke with an accent. It sounded almost Hungarian or Russian. "I saw you coming. Now here you are. What bring you to Nagna?" she asked before quickly holding her hand up to stop him from speaking. She closed her eyes, then answered her own question. "Shelter. You are in danger."

Her eyes fell upon Brodie, then Kol, then back to Bramble Meir. She had the large gypsy man escort the three to an area where they could eat and wash up. Kol, disliking humans, refused to stay on their grounds and retreated to the forest after telling Brodie he would remain close by and to call him if there was trouble.

Brodie understood. Brodie even questioned his own safety around some of these rough, and intimidating men.

"I will stay for a short period longer, then I must leave," Bramble Meir said to the boy. "Though you saved me from death, should Dayton find me, the penalty of death would be a cordial preference!"

The day slowly passed. They waited patiently to speak to Nagna once more, but she refused the meeting for the time being and encouraged food and rest. Brodie was thankful for this. He felt slightly intimidated by the old woman. Besides, his body was still in pain from the wolf's body check, and his hands shook from anxiety.

As dusk rolled in, they sat around the fire. Bramble Meir joined in with the jokes and laughter with the fellow gypsies, and Brodie sat on a log next to him, eating a bowl of soup one of the women had given him. It wasn't as bad as he had thought it would be. *Mutton cawl*—he had never eaten rabbit before. He pushed out anything orange from his bowl and tried to eat as much as he could.

It had quickly grown darker, but the cold was absent. The campsite was enchanted to keep the occupants from freezing in the colder temperature. The climate was so comfortable. He removed his thick sweater. He thought about Grub, Llyr, and his family. He could smell strong spices—cloves, frankincense, and cinnamon.

He reached deep into the bag, pulling out the book his great-grandmother had forced into his hands. It was the first time he had a chance to see it. The pages had dried together from the rain. He peeled the pages apart the best he could without ripping them. The ink had run a little, and he had accidently ripped two pages. It was a grimoire of some sort, filled with spells and maps.

Something brushed against his leg and made him jump. Brodie looked down to see a furry and matted brown-and-white cat. It reminded him of the cat in his great-grandmother's house. He lowered a hand to pet it but stopped as he heard it say "follow me," in his mind.

Surprised, he looked around the fire to see if anybody else had noticed the talking cat. They didn't seem to have, but since he had witnessed so many talking animals over the past weeks, he thought nothing of it and followed her.

She led him to Nagna's caravan, where Nagna stood behind the half-opened door.

"Come in," she said, opening the bottom half of the door for him.

He looked back to the fireplace, not sure if he should enter alone, smudging him as he entered.

"Come in." Her voice was sweet and sympathetic.

He entered the little caravan. To his amazement, it was huge inside.

"It's deceiving, no?" she asked.

"Yes," Brodie responded as he looked around the room. The wooden panelled walls were decorated with ancient scripts and colourful silks.

She pulled out a wooden stool for him at a small table and sat at the opposite side. "Sit, come sit." She gestured by flapping her hands towards the wooden chair.

The table was lit by thick candles. The built-up wax had melted and made a mess, fusing the candles to the table. The scent of lavender was overpowering but calming. The inside was very large and full of miscellaneous objects—books, bottles, and piles of clothes. Chimes and rocks hung from strings from the ceilings and made the area look even more cluttered. A small hamper bed was close by to where the brown-and-white Persian cat was grooming herself.

He sat down, still taking in his surroundings. He was excited but at the same time scared. His father had come from a family that was very religious. They were Catholic and had strong beliefs that fortune tellers did the work of the devil.

"Please, no be afraid of Nagna," she said, smiling a warm smile that exposed her remaining elongated and stained teeth.

"Is the cat your mother?" Brodie asked, looking at the watchful feline.

She gave the small boy another smile. "I read your cards, child?" she said in an accent.

Brodie had read a book about gypsies a few years ago, recalling the prophecies of fortune telling they were said to possess.

"Please, can you tell me why?"

"Shhh," she said, taking his hands as she closed her eyes.

He felt nervous. He could feel his palms become sweaty as she rubbed her thumbs into them. Her hands were warm.

She opened her eyes and let go of Brodie's hands. Her expression was intense. She dealt a set of decorated cards wrapped in silk across the table, singling out and flipping some in an extraordinarily unique manner.

"What do you see?" he asked, baffled.

"I see faces, I see fear and a gift." She continued flipping the cards, searching for something. "There is a great power about you."

She quickly got up and walked over to a pile of books and objects. She rifled through a scattered stack.

He could not help but think she was a bit of a hoarder in such a small space.

She retrieved a small black velvet pouch. She laid it on the table, then turned, collecting various objects from here and there. She returned to her seat. Her expression was curious as she laid bottles, dried plants, and a mortar and pestle in front of her on the table. She began to pour things from the bottles into the mortar.

Brodie could see the peeled and dirty dog-eared labels of each bottle as she set them aside. From them, he read *orris root, dog's wart powder, prairie smoke, adder's skin,* and *ground topaz.*

Nagna opened the velvet pouch, revealing a small golden knife. It was very handsome and very decorative.

"Brodie, I promise I won't hurt you, but I need to draw blood from your finger, just a drop. It will only prick for a second."

He looked at the knife with disgust. He wondered how contaminated the knife was with other people's blood and if it had been properly sterilized.

"No, I'm sorry, I can't. That is not very hygienic."

Brodie could see the disappointment on her face, then quickly remembered he had a deep scab on his right knee. After a second of peeling back the mound of dead skin, the small wound began to pool. He collected the blood on his finger, reached over, and wiped the blood onto the top of the bowl's contents. The ground topaz quickly absorbed the blood and sparkled like shards of rubies.

After adding a few other things to the mortar, she began to mix, pressing the pestle hard into the bowl. She pried one of the candles from the table and tilted it, spilling the melted wax into the bowl. Carefully, with the candle's flame, she set fire to the bowl. Brodie became antsy as the contents caught on fire.

Suddenly, she poured liquid from the closest bottle, one that had not been used yet. A strange aqua smoke began to rise. She leaned in, closing her eyes and inhaling the coloured smoke.

He remained silent with concentration. His body was beginning to feel weird again.

She rolled her head in a clockwise motion, then stopped. Her eyes were wide open, and she looked at Brodie with shock or bafflement.

"You, young wizard with much power, but power beyond any power I have ever…" She paused for a moment, analyzing the now frightened boy in front of her. "I see a magic as ancient as the forthcoming of the Saxons."

"The Saxons?" he asked.

She leaned across the table, grabbing his hands once more. The sudden movement made him jump. She took another deep breath of the aqua smoke as she pressed her hands into his, the way a blind man would gather knowledge from braille.

"Your family is descended from the early kings of Wales. These kings were the first wizards known to man and fairy kind they have magic beyond any power man or woman could ever possess. They were an old and magical breed, and their power has been passed down through your family's blood. There are others like you across the world, each with an old magic deep-seated within them."

He listened carefully. He wished in his heart the ranting of the old gypsy was true, but she was mistaken.

"I think you are mistaken. The only thing I was born with is a disability called autism, and you guys don't seem to understand what that is."

"Weak strains of this magic source have touched the women of your family. But you, my child—" she paused, once more intently smiling "—you have been blessed with this gift from your forefathers."

Brodie could not fathom this news. The silence crept over him as he sat speechless.

"You retain something, which causes great heaviness—the dragon scale."

His mouth opened in surprise. He looked down to his bag. *How could she have known that?* he asked himself.

"Your power has grown quite in tune to the magic of the scale. It is awakening your own magic."

Brodie thought hard about it for a moment. It did occur to him that he once had to touch the scale in order to transform into his fox form, and now he could change without it.

"You will soon realize, my child," she continued with a smile, "it is those of you with the power that can balance both our worlds. In order for that to happen, you must destroy Dayton and the scale."

"But I can't kill someone. You're advising an innocent child to commit murder. What kind of advice is that for a kid? No," Brodie said, full of anger. "If Dayton only wants the scale, isn't it easier for me to somehow destroy it and somebody else to destroy him? Not that I want people to die, but no, I refuse."

"I'm sorry, vittle vun. You are the only vun who has the power to stop him. Otherwise, he will go undefeated and continue killing." Nagna listened and pitied the child before her. She knew this was a lot for the young boy to take in, let alone act on.

Brodie felt like crying but took a deep breath, composing himself.

She poured the contents of the bowl onto the table. The contents, which had been powdered and liquid, had turned into a solid blue gem. It sparkled by candlelight and resembled a large sapphire.

"It is not just the scale Dayton hungers for now. He knows of your bloodline, your power."

"How?" Brodie asked, horrified and completely shocked.

"He has his own means; I cannot see how, his magic prevents me from seeing. but I tell you now, he will stop at nothing. Only you

253

can stop him. You must travel to the high mountain of Lyn Celyn in Gwynedd. There, on the night of a full moon, you will be directed on your path by the philosopher. Do not speak of any untruths to him, as he sees things and will punish you if you lie." She leaned over the table, placing the blue diamond into his hand. "You will know when the time comes what to do wiv this."

He rubbed his head in disbelief, not knowing what to think.

A breeze that came from nowhere caused the chimes to sing. Nagna looked up. She closed her eyes and opened them again to meet Brodie's confused gaze.

"You must go. He knows you're here! He's almost here. We can protect ourselves, but we cannot protect you here," Nagna said sympathetically.

Brodie stood up, tucking the glittering gem into his bag with the rest of its contents. He walked towards the door.

"Wait!" Nagna yelled out to the boy, holding up a hand. She reached out to him. "Your friends have been captured, be careful Dayton's henchmen and witches patrol the town in search of you. They watch for the fox," Nagna said, and her eyes closed once more.

She got up, shooing and swatting the cat from a pile of clothes on the bed. The cat hissed and moved aside, stretching out her back legs. The old woman rummaged through the pile of clothes.

"Here," she said. "Your clothes don't fit in our world. They scream human. You vill look like a vittle elf." She smiled.

He thanked her as he threw the clothes over the top of his own and left.

A moment later, the small child he had spotted earlier ran from the caravan that Brodie was sprinting away from. Brodie was surprised. He hadn't even seen her, although she could have been camouflaged. She ran towards the campfire where Bramble Meir sat.

Brodie turned to the forest, where he knew Kol waited. He didn't have to look hard. Kol, a mere shadowed figure, sat against a tree carving something. He caught sight of Brodie and hurried towards him.

Brodie turned back, facing the fire, but Bramble Meir was gone. The girl must have set the alarm, as seconds later, the gypsies were on the move, frantically picking up shop and racing in all directions.

"Brodie," called Nagna. "Travel safe, child," she yelled from a distance over the frenzied gypsies. "Go deep into your…" she paused a moment, "…bubble. Embrace your gifts, and you will defeat him."

Suddenly, a flurry of snow swirled and danced around the old woman. Brodie stopped for a moment and witnessed the flurry consume the camp, causing the caravans, the fires, the horses, and everything else to disappear.

He didn't know if he would ever meet Bramble Meir or Nagna again.

"Where are we going?" Kol asked as they walked farther from the disappearing campground.

"To Lyn Celyn or maybe save Grub and Llyr first I don't know let's get away from here," Brodie huffed, out of breath as they re-entered the dark forest, holding the bag close to him, his heart pounding with fear.

ABOUT THE AUTHOR

As my son (Brodie) thrashed about, mid- meltdown in the pediatrics office, his Dr. expressed he strongly believed that my young toddler, "was on the Autistic spectrum" Brodie would be referred to a specialist. At that moment my whole world turned upside down. Further more my heart plummeted as the Dr. explained the odds of my son not being able to talk or walk, depending on us his entire life.

I was devastated. With my parents in another country, I felt such heavy grief and isolation. I began to write; my writing became an amazing outlet to process how I was feeling. As soon as my beautiful boy was fast asleep, I dived into a magical world to escape from the difficulties the day held.

Brodie and his abilities were a great inspiration to this story.

My son has made me a better parent and person.

Remember that the difficult times you have faced during your life will shape you.

You have already made it through 100% of your worst days.

We are all truly remarkable. Each of us full of magic, so let your inner magic shine.

From Brodie and I,
Thank you.

Lightning Source UK Ltd.
Milton Keynes UK
UKHW010104090221
378429UK00002B/247